THE TROUBLE WITH MURDER

By
Kate Sweeney

THE TROUBLE WITH MURDER
© 2008 BY KATE SWEENEY

All rights reserved. No part of this book may be reproduced in printed or electronic form without permission. Please do not participate in or encourage piracy of copyrighted materials in violation of the author's rights. Purchase only authorized editions.

ISBN: 978-1-933113-85-2

First Printing: 2008

This trade paperback is published by
Intaglio Publications
Walker, LA USA
www.intagliopub.com

This is a work of fiction. Names, characters, places, and incidents are the product of the author's imagination or are used fictitiously, and any resemblance to actual persons, living or dead, businesses, companies, events, or locales is entirely coincidental.

CREDITS
Executive Editor: Tara Young
Cover design by Sheri
(Graphicartist2020@hotmail.com)

DEDICATION

Many years ago, my family and I rented a cottage on Lake Mildred, in Rhinelander, Wisconsin. It was so beautiful it became a yearly family tradition.

I had the idea for *The Trouble with Murder* sitting out on the pier on a foggy morning. So I'd like to dedicate this book to my family and all the memories we shared of those wonderful summers in my beloved Northwoods.

ACKNOWLEDGMENTS

Once again, I'd like to thank my editor, Tara Young, who does a wonderful job of hearing the voice of Kate Ryan.

To my graphic artist, Sheri, who consistently brings Kate Ryan to life.

Thanks to Denise, my main beta-gal, who sometimes knows Kate Ryan better than I do, and to betas Tena and Mercedes, who certainly make me look good.

To my publishers, Sheri Payton and Becky Arbogast, who constantly keep Intaglio moving forward. I'm grateful to tag along.

Finally, to Kathy Smith of StarCrossed Productions and the Golden Crown Literary Society, who is tireless in her effort to promote our community and lesbian fiction.

Prologue

In the dark of the night, he stood looking out of the huge picture window. Lightning flashed, thunder rolled over the lake. All was set in motion. Nothing could stop it now. Finally, she would come back to him. His heartbeat quickened at the idea.

As the lightning flashed, he saw the house. Soon she would be his again. Patience, he thought, and looked back at the empty living room. He picked up the upended chair and straightened the lamp. Then he got angry with himself. He was too impatient. He should have waited and done this later. He got too excited, too rash; he had to control himself.

He gazed around the living room. It had to be spotless for her. He nervously cleaned and straightened. "It must be clean," he said breathlessly.

Looking to the corner of the living room, he said, "You could help instead of lying there." He stared at the body lying in a heap. "Well, c'mon, time's a wastin'." With a heavy sigh, he struggled with the dead weight. "Goodness, I believe you've put on some weight. Don't lie to me. You've been sneaking the Twinkies again." He hoisted the body over his shoulder and started down the stairs to the basement.

He propped the body up against the wall and opened the large freezer. Lifting the lid, he was amazed at all the frozen items. He gave the lifeless form a scathing look. "Venison. Shame on you, killing Bambi's mother." He shook his head and cleared the freezer. His cold companion started listing and sliding to the floor.

"Whoopsi-daisey. Up you go," he said and hoisted him up again. "You must cooperate. I'm hot and sweaty, and you're beginning to annoy me!" he yelled through clenched teeth in the lifeless face. "Good grief, should it be this much *trouble*?"

He looked around and smiled as he spotted it. Propping the dead weight back in place, he picked up the crossbow. The bow twanged as the arrow found its mark, impaling the already deceased body to the wall with a quiet *thwump*.

"There now." He sighed as he walked up, straightened the dead man's shirt, and whispered, "Now you know how Bambi's mother felt."

After long minutes of rearranging the gentleman's resting place, he placed him in and closed the freezer. He put his ear to the lid and gently knocked. "Is the light on or off?" He laughed as he turned off the light and mounted the stairs.

All at once, he was exhausted and his head ached horribly. Rubbing his temples, he sat on the arm of the couch in the dark and lit a cigarette. *Soon.*

He sat alone in the darkness, silent and still. The only sign of life was the amber glow of the cigarette flashing like a small beacon, beckoning her home.

Chapter One

I sat there staring at the familiar house. It looked different in the summer. The ivy that was a vibrant orange and yellow last autumn was now a lush green, oddly reminiscent of Wrigley Field and my hapless Cubs. I took a deep breath and glanced at my companion. "What am I doing?"

Chance, my canine adviser, gave me a side-glance but kept a watchful eye on the house. I could tell she was just waiting for me to give her the okay so she could jump out like a maniac and dash up to the door.

"It's too early. Maggie's probably not even up yet," I said as we both watched the house. "Maybe we should leave, Chance. I don't want to wake her or Hannah at this hour." I looked at my watch. It was 7:30, far too early for Dr. Winfield, but I was sure Hannah would be up. I nervously chewed at my bottom lip while Chance whined pathetically. I gave her an affectionate pet. "Oh, shush."

With that, my cell phone went off and I nearly had a heart attack. I fumbled in my pocket and located it. "Hello?" I whispered and rolled my eyes. *Like Maggie can hear me.*

"Kate?" Teri's voice called out. "Why are you whispering? Where are you?"

"I—" I stopped and rubbed my forehead. I figured I'd tell her the truth. "I'm in front of Maggie's."

There was dead silence on the other end for a moment. "Why?"

I laughed at the confounded tone in my sister's voice. "Because."

Teri laughed along. "So let me understand this," she started, and I groaned helplessly. "You're sitting in your Jeep, wondering if you should go in or not. Because like a dope, you didn't call Maggie when you got home three weeks ago, as you said you would, by the way. You just took off on your assignment in South Dakota. You packed your Jeep, took your dog, and headed west."

I sat there frowning and staring at Maggie's house. Chance was itching to jump out, and Teri was laughing on the other end.

"Have you been home yet?" Teri asked.

"No," I replied.

"You drove from South Dakota to Maggie's?" Teri asked, and I heard the sentimental sap oozing. "Kate, that is *so* romantic."

"Oh," I groaned. "It is *not*. I'm on my way up to the cabin. If you recall, you're supposed to come along. I-I just thought maybe Maggie and Hannah might want to come next week, as well. It's getting to the end of the summer and they've never been. So...oh shut up, Teri."

Teri laughed heartily and I took the phone away from my ear, nearly tossing it into the woods. "Now let's change the topic. Tell me about the classes you were taking, professor."

"Very funny. They're almost over. The study group was excellent, though I'll be glad to get away. Enough parapsychology for the summer." I heard a hint of disappointment in her voice.

Teri had taken a few summer classes at a community college. She was in a study group that examined and tested one another's ability in the world of parapsychology. She also took a couple of new-age classes on astrology and tarot reading, that sort of thing. It spooks me, but Teri takes to it as I take to solving mysteries, only she's very good at it. She's a redheaded nut, but she's a psychic nut.

"What's wrong? You sound disappointed," I said. I heard a long sigh.

"No, really, it was a great class. Too many people, though, that's all. Anyway, I can't wait to get up there. Now get off this phone and go see Maggie. Tell her you're sorry you took off like a bat out of hell. You should have brought her flowers, you nut. I'll see you on Saturday. I love you."

"I love you, too. Hey, when Mac calls from Ireland, give him my love, too," I said and snapped the phone shut. *Flowers?*

I looked to the heavens for help and took a deep breath. "Okay, Chance. I—"

That's all she needed to hear. Upon the word "okay," my spastic cur leapt out of the Jeep and dashed around the front of the house, then scampered off into the woods. I jumped out, as well.

"Chance!" I yelled and winced as every bird in a three-mile radius began squawking. I felt like I was in the middle of a rain forest.

I looked up when the front door opened. It was Hannah. With her hands on her hips, she looked just like Maggie.

"Hey, Hannah." I gave her a short wave.

"Hey, yourself. What in God's name are you doing in my front yard, waking up the wildlife?"

I laughed as I walked up to the front porch. "Chance, um, took off in the woods. I think she's taking care of business."

With that, my loyal dog raced out of the woods and right up to Hannah, lavishing her with kisses and licks. Hannah looked up at me. "So answer my question."

"I, well, I was coming home from an assignment, and I-I thought I'd stop by on the way and see how you are." I shoved my hands in my pockets. I then smiled down at this adorable woman. "So how's my best girl?"

"I'm not sure, Margaret's sleeping," she countered with a sly grin. "Come in. I'll make you breakfast."

I obediently followed her in, right after Chance, of course. Hannah hurried to the kitchen. "Have a seat, Kate," she said over her shoulder.

"Hannah, I-I just came to say hey. You don't have to—"

"Aunt Hannah, what's going on? I—"

I looked up at the top of the stairs and there stood Maggie. She looked surprised to see me, I think.

"Hey," I said, keeping my hands in my pockets so she wouldn't see them shake.

Maggie ran her fingers through her thick auburn hair as she slowly walked down the stairs. She looked good. She smiled slightly. "Hello."

My mouth was bone dry and I had no idea what to say to

her.

"I just stopped by to say hey," I said. *I should have said nothing.*

"Hey," Maggie replied. She noticed Chance and her face lit up. She then bounded down the stairs. I grunted childishly. *She's more excited to see Chance.*

My loyal canine loved the fuss Maggie was making over her, and after a few pets and kisses from Dr. Winfield, which I did *not* get, she settled in front of the fireplace.

I glanced around the living room once again. "Nothing has changed much." I sat on the couch, trying to ignore the wave of contentment.

Hannah had come out of the kitchen and was standing behind the couch. She raised an eyebrow and looked from me to Maggie. "I can see that," she said dryly and gave me a stern look.

Maggie stood by the desk and leafed through her mail. *Did I notice her hands shaking?* I was rubbing my palms on my jeans and trying to swallow.

Hannah rolled her eyes and sighed dramatically. She sat next to me on the couch. "So Margaret told me all about Ireland. Now it's your turn, and don't you dare leave out one thing."

I laughed and glanced at Maggie who chuckled along. For the next hour or so, I blathered on about Peter and the treasure and Bridget and Tim. Still, as I was talking, I remembered that fishing boat offshore, waiting for Bridget and Tim and how Bridget's body was never found. I had to admit, it was nagging at me. I must have said so out loud.

"What are you thinking?" Maggie asked. It was then I realized she was sitting on the ottoman in front of me.

Shaken from my thoughts, I took a deep breath. "Oh, I don't know. The fishing boat that was offshore." I glanced at Maggie who shook her head. I could tell she didn't remember seeing it. Maybe I didn't see it, either. "It's just a nagging feeling, but anyway," I said and looked at Hannah, "that's what happened."

"Well, it sounds adventurous and I'm sorry I missed it. You have a way of getting into the oddest situations, Kate." She looked once again from Maggie to me. "But there is one situation that might not be too odd."

"Don't count on it," I said with a laugh and Maggie offered a smug grin.

Hannah laughed along and stood. "You two need to talk. Kate, you're staying for breakfast, no arguments." She bent down and kissed the top of my head. "I'm glad you're back safe and sound."

Maggie and I sat in silence as we watched Chance follow Hannah into the kitchen. "Behave yourself," I said to Chance. The mutt stopped and looked at me, then continued as if I said nothing at all.

"You look tired," Maggie said.

"Oh, I'm okay. I was on my way up to my cabin and—"

"Just happen to be in the neighborhood?" Maggie asked as she played with the ring on her finger.

"No, I actually...I was in South Dakota. I was on assignment for the last three weeks."

Maggie's head shot up and searched my face. "So that's where you were. That sounds exciting."

"The magazine wanted photos for a story on wild mustangs," I said, trying to ignore the disappointment I heard in her voice.

Maggie hid her grin. "Right up your alley."

I knew I was scowling, but I grinned at her sarcasm nonetheless. *Damn this woman.* I was about to offer a witty or a dimwitted comeback when the phone rang.

"Margaret—it's Ellen," Hannah called from the hallway.

Ellen?

"Well, maybe I should go." I started to rise.

Maggie stood in front of me and said, "Stay," and put her hand on my shoulder. "Sit," she added firmly and—I sat.

Out of the corner of my eye, I saw Chance sitting there watching, her head cocked to one side as if to say, *"So this is how it's done?"*

I looked up into Maggie's smiling blue eyes. "I'll be right back. Do not move, Kate Ryan."

She walked into the hallway past Hannah, who gave her a motherly look.

"Who's Ellen?" I whispered as Hannah sat next to me.

She leaned in and whispered, "An administrator at a hospital in Chicago. Margaret is doing volunteer work. And if you ask me, she's a bigger pest than Allison ever was."

"Really?" I looked out into the hallway. "Do they work together?"

"Well, they met about three weeks ago. Maggie was waiting for you to call her…" Hannah said with a shrug.

"Are they—?"

Hannah looked me right in the eye. "Are they what?" she asked with a raised eyebrow.

I said nothing but rubbed my forehead. I heard Hannah take a deep breath. "Kate…"

"What?" I heard the defensive tone in my voice—I was nauseated. "I shouldn't have stopped here. I should have just headed north and—"

"And what?" Hannah gently interrupted me. "Hid?"

"Oh, I don't know!" I said too loudly. "What is it with you Winfield women? You're like a tag team!"

Hannah cringed and looked down the hallway. "Keep your voice down," she whispered. "Now I don't think there's anything going on between them," she continued, and I gave her a hopeful look. "Yet," she added quickly. She then toyed with the ring on her finger; she looked amazingly like Maggie. "You know the saying…"

I instantly frowned and gave her a wary glance. "Which one?" I asked cautiously. *Oh, these Winfield women!*

"Keep your friends close and your *enemies*…closer," Hannah whispered and glanced down the hall. She must have seen the look of utter confusion on my face. "Vito Corleone," she explained as if *I* were the one who was nuts. She rolled her eyes. "*The Godfather*."

"Hannah," I started helplessly. "What are you…?" Then it dawned on me. I watched Maggie as she talked on the phone. "Hmm."

"Hmm, indeed," Hannah agreed and gave me a side-glance. "So I have other news."

I tore my gaze away from Maggie and looked at Hannah. "What news?"

"Walt's left," she said in a quiet voice.

I was shocked—Doc's gone? He was the town doctor in Cedar Lake and loved Hannah, or so I thought. "Hannah, what are you talking about, left where? Why?"

"A woman from his past came back to Cedar Lake. It seems he still has feelings for Judith Rogers. He was once involved with her—in love, I suppose," Hannah said. My heart ached at the sadness in her voice. "Now with her back, old feelings started again. That was three months ago. They left for Arizona two weeks ago. I suppose that's why he never asked me to marry him. He never quite got over her."

"Christ, Hannah, I'm so sorry," I said, not knowing what else to say.

"You know, Kate, we all have to do what's best for ourselves. This was best for Walt. I do care so much for him, but he's got to follow his heart."

We sat in silence for a moment.

"Isn't that the biggest bunch of *malarkey* you've ever heard?" she asked flatly.

I let out a healthy laugh. "Hannah Winfield, I do love you. Hey, I just had a brainstorm—"

"No headache?"

I laughed at the interruption. "You're coming up to my cabin, no arguing. Teri will pick you up on Saturday at one. Mac's in Ireland for a couple of weeks. I'll have Teri call you. You, Miss Winfield, will spend the next week having fun and nothing but fun. Maggie will come, too, won't she?" I asked in a hesitant voice.

"You'll have to ask her, which means you'll have to do more talking than grunting," Hannah said with a sly grin.

"Ask me what?" Maggie walked back into the living room.

Hannah stood and kissed my cheek. "I'll finish making breakfast."

As Hannah walked into the kitchen, Maggie sat on the couch. Before I could get next to her, Chance jumped up between us. I wasn't sure if that was good or not.

"What did you want to ask me?" Maggie asked as she petted Chance.

"I'm heading to my cabin up north. Teri is coming up on Saturday and I invited Hannah. She told me about Doc, Maggie. I can't believe it. Is she okay?"

Maggie shrugged. "She's sad and disillusioned, but she won't admit it. She's a great deal like you in that regard."

I was going to argue, but as usual, she was right. "Well, I thought maybe you'd like to come, too. You've never seen my cabin and I-I thought, you know, you would come up for the weekend or the week."

"That sounds like a good idea, though I'll have to check with Ellen, I—"

"Ellen?" I asked.

Maggie looked me in the eye. "Ellen Winters, she's a colleague. I met her at the hospital. We—"

"Fine bring her along," I said hastily. Visions of Vito flashed through my scrambled brain as I watched her with a suspicious eye. I absently scratched under my chin. "She's welcome."

Maggie glared at me. "I didn't mean I would bring her along. She's looking at property in Green Bay for a clinic. She and I—"

"Hey, Maggie. It's no big deal," I said hastily—again. What's that saying? Pride goeth before a fall? Well, right now, I was standing on the precipice. My pride was whispering in my ear—*jump, dumb-ass, jump!* "Bring her. It's fine with me."

We were glaring at each other when Hannah came into the room. "Well, breakfast is ready. How are you two doing?" she asked in a cheery voice.

"Fine!" Maggie bolted up and stormed past her into the kitchen.

Hannah winced as the swinging door to the kitchen nearly flew off the hinges. "You did more than grunt, didn't you?" Hannah asked with a sigh. She grabbed me by my collar and pulled me into the kitchen.

The three of us ate in silence. Chance was begging and Hannah was feeding her under the table. I was too upset to stop her. I glanced across at Maggie—her left eye was twitching.

"Th-this is good, Hannah," I said and realized I had eaten quite a bit.

"Thank you, dear. I love to see a healthy appetite," Hannah said and placed two more pancakes on my plate. I heard Maggie grunt sarcastically.

"Syrup, please, Dr. Winfield?" I asked and smiled slightly.

I had visions of washing Aunt Jemima out of my graying hair. However, Maggie slid the bottle toward me. I reached over and grasped her hand. She looked at me then. "Thank you," I said and looked down at our hands.

Maggie gently ran her thumb across my hand. "You're welcome," she replied in kind.

We finished breakfast without killing each other, which I thought was a plus. Afterward, I decided to drive to my cabin instead of going back to Chicago. Hannah wanted me to stay, but I really wanted to be up north. I was itching for my cabin, and to be honest, Maggie was making me nervous or I was making myself nervous and all Hannah's talk about enemies and Vito Corleone… either way, I needed to scram.

Hannah assured me that she would talk to Teri and drive up with her on Saturday. Maggie was going to do whatever with this Ellen woman. She said very little as she walked me to my car.

"I hope you can come up, Maggie. It's beautiful up there. I know you'll enjoy it," I said.

Chance jumped into her seat. Maggie playfully ruffled her ears and kissed her snout. "I'm sure I'll make it up there, with or without Ellen," she said and stepped back. She folded her arms across her chest and absently kicked at the pebbled driveway.

I jammed my hands in my pockets and watched her. *God help me!* I was floundering. I had no idea what to say next. "Don't forget your swimsuit," I blurted out, then shook my head.

Maggie laughed and I joined her. "I have no idea what I'm saying," I said with a nervous chuckle.

To my surprise and delight, she leaned over and kissed my cheek. "I know, and if I didn't think you'd have an anxiety attack, I'd tell you, you look adorable," she said with a small grin.

Adorable? Now what? "Uh, um…"

Maggie rolled her eyes. "Drive safe, Kate. We'll see you in a few days," she said and stepped back.

"I will. Thanks, Maggie."

I was about to slip in behind the wheel when I saw my savior. I picked a dandelion and quickly handed it her.

Maggie was slightly stunned but took the little offering and grinned. Her blue eyes sparkled and the dimples started. I knew I was grinning like an idiot. "See ya."

As I pulled away, I let out a happy sigh and looked in the rearview mirror to see Maggie twirling the yellow…weed.

I groaned loudly and glanced at Chance. "I just gave her a *weed*," I said with disgust, as I stared at the tree-lined road ahead of me. Chance paid no attention, as usual. She happily had her head out the window. "You could have said something."

This should be an interesting week.

Chapter Two

As I drove farther north, my cell phone rang. "Crap," I grumbled and flipped it open. "What?"

"Kate Ryan, you nature freak, how long for the last photos?" Connie's voice bellowed.

"Oh, hold your water," I complained. "I just sent them. Good grief, Connie, I've been in the muck and mud for over a month getting them. I think you can wait two days!" I bellowed back. "And don't set me up with anything for at least two weeks. I mean it."

I heard my maniacal editor laughing. "Okay, okay. You did well. The proofs you sent earlier look perfect. Did you really follow those stupid mustangs for a month? Wouldn't be surprised if there was a big bonus in your check, but don't be surprised if there's not. I think your free roaming days are over, Ryan. You need to stay put for a while. Sorry the weather was rotten. Take it easy, you deserve it. Hey, how're the women out West? Did you have a gay ole time?" She laughed heartily.

My editor, Constance Branigan was a short little pain in the ass but a magnificent editor. I remembered the first time I walked into her office.

"So, Miss Ryan, you've been away from photography for quite a while. Why the sudden interest in getting back?" she asked and put the portfolio on the desk.

I shifted uncomfortably in my seat for a moment. "I owned a business for nine years. I'm no longer in that line of work. Since then, I decided to go back to photography. I've been getting things in order—"

Constance raised an eyebrow. "Doing nothing for a year?

You must have a great deal to get in order," she said with a trace of smugness. *I'm sure she noticed the indignant look that flashed across my face.*

"As I said, I've been getting a few things in order," I repeated with a curt bite, and Constance just nodded as she concentrated on my file.

I watched her curiously. This short, gruff little woman was the best editor in Chicago for her type of photography. I figured I'd spent enough time in my private hell and decided to take a chance. Now I wondered what in the hell I was doing. I was about to let my pride get the better of me and snatch my portfolio away from this cigarette-puffing...

"Well, I have to tell you, what you see through a camera lens is remarkable. You're very good. I'm impressed, truly. And I am not easily impressed." She looked at me and smiled. "You're feisty. I like that, but I sense you're hiding something and I'm not sure I like that." She took another drag of her cigarette. "But my gut tells me I'm about to make the best decision I've made in years. Either that or I've got an ulcer."

We regarded each other warily. This could be a battle of wills, I thought.

"Okay, I tell you what. You take some assignments for a month, if I like what I see—you work for me," she challenged and gave me a smug grin.

My temper bristled. "That's fine, a month. That will give me enough time to see if I want to work for you."

For an instant, I saw the irritation flash across my would-be editor's face.

"You're a little on the insolent side. I like that," she said evenly, then laughed out loud. "Deal." She stuck out her hand.

I smiled slightly and took it.

It was the beginning of a wonderful relationship.

I smiled at the vivid memory of nearly three years before. "You really get a kick out of yourself, don't you?" I asked flatly and hung up as she roared with laughter.

It was almost three in the afternoon when I pulled onto the

access road to my cabin. Deer Lake is relatively new and the back roads are still rough. We've only had three houses built on the lake, which is fine by me. There was peace and quiet with nothing but loons and woods.

My old Jeep found every hole in the dirt road. I finally pulled into my entrance, filled with childlike anticipation as the lake came into view. Chance was sniffing the air and let out a bark. "I know. I feel the same, Chance. I love it up here."

I quickly unpacked the Jeep and tossed everything by the back door as Chance ran down to the lake.

As I pulled out my key, I noticed a rip in the screen door. There was a slice in the bottom corner about four inches long. "How the hell did that happen?" I put the key in and noticed scratch marks on my back door around the lock. "Damn," I whispered angrily.

I turned back, looked out at the woods for some reason, then walked around to the front of the cabin. The front door was fine, locked and bolted. I continued around the other side and noticed firewood piled up by the bedroom window. Absently, I scratched my head. *What gives?*

I put the logs back behind the cabin with the rest of my firewood. Now I was apprehensive as I unlocked the back door. I walked into the kitchen and nothing looked disturbed. Although I hadn't been up here in over four months, everything looked as I had left it. I checked both spare rooms, then checked mine. Seeing nothing out of order, I pulled down the staircase leading to the loft.

Cautiously, I climbed to the loft and poked my head in. There had better not be any bats or squirrels up here. I wish I had my faithful mutt with me. Chance would get them for me. I laughed out loud. No, she'd be protecting my flank, the coward.

Nothing looked out of place, but it was unbelievably hot and humid. I opened the windows to air it out, but there wasn't much relief. I stood at the balcony and looked down from the loft. My little log cabin was intact, and I breathed a sigh of relief.

In my room, I unpacked my gear and noticed the picture of Maggie, Hannah, and me. I smiled as I looked at the picture. I remembered a few short months before, when Maggie was with me in Ireland. I remembered how my heart ached when she left. *Why did I let her go? Why didn't I ask her to stay?*

Old fears, that was it. I was still haunted by the images of Liz Eddington. Just the thought of it made my stomach lurch once again. I closed my eyes and held the picture close.

Then I thought of this Ellen Winters. She was an administrator of University Hospital in Chicago. Maggie met her while volunteering at one of the hospital's satellite clinics, Hannah said. She was a pest, Hannah said. Hmm, were they *that* serious that she had to ask for permission? *Whoa, Ryan, it's none of your business, remember?*

How did I manage this? I wanted Maggie to come up here to… *To what, Ryan?*

"Hell, I don't know," I answered the pesky inner voice.

Well, she's coming but not alone, idiot.

"Oh, shut up," I grumbled. "Fine…now I'm talking to myself."

Ignoring my inner voice, I looked around my little log cabin and groaned. I have five people coming up on the weekend. "Hell, I need to get organized."

I went to my room to do the obligatory "first things first"—I put on my suit and ran down to the lake.

The cool lake water was invigorating. I climbed up on the raft and lay in the sun. I took the time to take inventory of my lake. On the west side, a new house had gone up. I shielded my eyes against the sun to see it. From what I could see, it looked like a quaint house.

My cabin faced southwest. I planned it that way when I bought the little spot of heaven four years earlier. I built the cabin two years before, and I still have plenty of work to do on it. The contractors cut down enough trees to keep a normal person in firewood for at least a couple of seasons. The way I use my fireplace, I'll be surprised if it lasts the winter.

I hadn't been up here since April, and I didn't notice any construction going on then. Great, I thought, now all the building starts. It'd been peaceful in my little section of heaven in the north woods of Wisconsin. I had hoped that it would stay that way. However, my curiosity was piqued. Perhaps later I'd take the boat and have a look at my new neighbor.

Grudgingly, I had to admit I was spoiled. When I moved up here, my log cabin and one other home were the only ones on Deer Lake. Now there were five. I lay on my back and closed my eyes. "Oh, well, things change, Kate, and you have to change with them," I said.

In the words of Hannah Winfield, "That's the biggest bunch of malarkey." I smiled openly. I lay back on the raft and closed my eyes. A week of sun, fun, fishing, and swimming.

After baking in the sun, I was ravenous. I picked a nice thick steak to grill and tossed a salad. I sat on my deck and watched the western sky turn those magnificent colors that only an artist can capture—that flaming red against the clouds that faded to a soft pink as the sun hung low just above the tree line. I was lost in the beauty when I heard a low voice, "Anybody home?"

I recognized the voice and smiled while Chance, who was sprawled out on the deck, jumped up.

"No, go away," I said quickly.

Ben Harper's smiling face appeared around the corner. "Hey, Kate, I thought that was your banged-up Jeep. Why don't you get a new car?" As he smiled, his blue eyes sparkled dangerously. What a lady-killer he must have been when he was younger, I thought.

He was in his mid-sixties, I'd say. Tall and had the air of an athlete about him. His hair was thick, mostly white, and when he smiled, you couldn't help but smile back. He owned the house next to mine. We were close but not right on top of each other.

"What's cookin'?" He peered at the grill, while petting Chance.

I gave him a smug grin. "Hungry, Ben?"

He patted his stomach. "Do I look like I don't eat?" Of course, he was exaggerating. He was very fit. He gave me a sheepish grin. "I'm starving."

I laughed and got another steak, threw it on the grill, and handed him a beer.

"Thanks, Ryan. You should get married. You're a good catch. You can cook and take care of a home." He looked at me sideways as he drank his beer.

I glared at him. "I can even sew a button or two."

He laughed heartily and I joined him. When he laughed, you couldn't help it. "So, you're always up here alone, Kate. No lady friends?"

"You're a good man, Ben, and no, no lady friends. Plenty of others, though," I said sincerely and busied myself with the steaks.

"Yeah, but they don't keep you warm at night."

"That's what blankets are for."

"You're a tough Irishwoman."

He changed the topic as he looked around the lake. "New houses are going up, Kate. Remember when it was just you and me?" he asked sadly, and I nodded in kind.

"That one went up fast." I motioned to the newest one across the lake.

"Yep, two months and it was done. I've only seen the owner once. A young flighty brunette woman." He grinned and wriggled his eyebrows.

"Did you give her your pitch? Retired Navy captain, widowed, no children. Do you honestly get women with your war stories?"

He laughed aloud. "Sometimes. You wanna borrow a few stories? It couldn't hurt."

"Drink your beer, Captain," I said, glaring at him.

"No, Kate. She's too young. Besides, she laughs like a hyena. Very annoying," he said and drank his beer. "However, Saturday night, I'm having a barbecue for all Deer Lake dwellers. I've invited everyone, you have to come. Bring your family, I insist."

We had a pleasant dinner on my deck. The sun was setting, but it was still hot and humid.

"Ben, have you had any trouble with prowlers?" I asked as we ate.

He looked up with his fork halfway to his mouth and frowned. "No, why?" He looked around my cabin. "Have you?"

I shrugged. "When I got here, there was a pile of firewood

under one bedroom window. The screen on the back door was sliced, and I noticed scratches around the locks." I saw the worried look on his face and continued. "The entire cabin was fine, nothing missing, nothing disturbed. I guess I overreacted."

"I've been up here all summer. I haven't noticed any prowlers," he said. "However, there's been a lot of activity on the lake this summer. They've found us. That boat launch has been busy. I hope you're right and you overreacted. If you're not, humanity has invaded Deer Lake."

We both looked at each other knowing what the other was thinking. "We'll continue to watch out for each other," he said seriously and finished dinner in silence.

"Thanks, Kate. You really know how to cook a steak. Don't forget about Saturday. All the Ryans and whoevers are welcome." He bent down and kissed my cheek. "You're a doll, Kate." He winked and walked off the porch.

"Bet you say that to all the girls," I called after him as I rocked in my chair. His contagious laughter rang out as he walked down the path to his house.

I was in heaven. It was quiet, and as the stars came out, I sat, rocked in my favorite chair, and watched the show. The night was wonderfully silent and the lake was smooth as glass. I watched as the moon rose over the tree line. In a few days, it would be full and illuminate the lake. Now, though, it was a crescent shape and hung low in the late summer sky.

My mind wandered, as it does more often lately. Maybe this week will be a good time to make a conscious effort to stop running from the past and start living in the present. I laughed openly. Those were the exact words of the hospital psychiatrist.

After the nightmare with Liz Eddington, I was in the hospital for nearly two months. I used to remember exactly how long—to the hour. Now, I don't even want to remember that time—flat on my stomach, stapled, and stitched. I was bitter and angry and took it out on every nurse on the floor. I'm surprised they didn't just push me off into a corner somewhere.

I was flat on my stomach for two weeks. Tired of hearing me complain, they pushed me closer to the window so at least I could look out and hopefully, I'm sure—shut up.

"Great, a parking lot, how scenic," I grumbled and the nurse sighed deeply as she rearranged my sheets. "You could at least put me on the other side by the park."

"Well, that's the children's ward. How tall are you?" the nurse asked.

I was taken aback at the abrupt comment. "Why?" I asked warily.

"I'll have you fitted for a crib," she suggested with a smirk and walked out.

After a moment of grumbling, I laughed heartily. Sarcasm at its best. I had to admit, I deserved that one.

I rocked in my favorite chair and smiled. I gave those nurses such a hard time, but they stood by me every day and helped me with the painful, tedious task of physical rehab. I do recall one nurse, however, whom I caught with a dumbbell raised dangerously over her head with a maniacal look in her eyes. Dr. Tillman, my psychiatrist, came in just in time.

"Nurse, please don't kill her. She's come so far," Dr. Tillman said, holding her clipboard.

I looked up at the smiling nurse who placed the dumbbell back on the rack.

"So, Kate, how are we doing today?" Dr. Tillman asked kindly as she took off her glasses.

"We *are* fine. We *want* to go home," I said childishly as I lifted the weights and grimaced as the pain shot through my neck and back.

"You're lifting too much again, Kate," the physical therapist said lightly and adjusted the machine.

I cursed under my breath and lay there waiting. I could feel the eyes of scrutiny upon me. I glanced over to see Dr. Tillman watching me. "This is hard, Kate, I know. You want to be finished and done with it. I don't blame you, but you know the extent of your injuries. Every muscle fiber in your body is screaming for activity, but you must go slowly."

I stared at the ceiling. "I'm tired of people telling me what I have to do. What do you know? Did you have your head almost *severed from your body? Did you have to watch your partner as his leg was nearly blown off? Or watch a woman who you thought you loved do all this? Did you? No. I did. So don't tell me how I feel or—"*

I saw Dr. Tillman motion to the physical therapist. He made a hasty retreat. "Take the dumbbells with you," I barked in his direction. I looked over and watched Dr. Tillman pull up a chair and sit next to me.

"You remind me of my husband," she said and smiled. She opened her mouth to continue, then quickly closed it. "No, we'll talk of that later."

She tossed me a towel as I laughed quietly. "I'm sorry," I said as I wiped the sweat from my face.

"Don't be. I understand. I've come to realize something in our few weeks together. Kate, patience is an attribute that you horribly lack, hence the comparison to my husband. You must remember your body was not the only part of you that was injured."

I immediately tensed, which I'm sure she saw. I couldn't help it. The nausea started and my body temperature instantly dropped. I was sweaty and now ice cold. My hands shook and I felt like someone was sitting on my chest. "I know, I know. Can we talk about this later, Dr. Tillman? I feel like I'm gonna yak," I said seriously. The bile was rising in the back of my throat.

"Sure, Kate. Come by at your regular time this afternoon," she said softly and patted my shoulder.

I sat there, trying desperately not to see the vision of Liz lying next to me in a pool of blood. Bob had shot her twice and she fell right there, her lifeless eyes staring at me. The pain in my back and neck was paralyzing. I could only lie there and stare back into the dark eyes that I loved.

I realized I had stopped rocking in my chair and was just staring out into the dark starry night. The panic started, but just as quickly, it stopped. I closed my eyes and thought of Maggie and how she helped me last spring in Ireland. Telling her was better than any therapy. Dr. Maggie Winfield was kind, sweet, and understanding laced with just enough sarcasm to keep me on an even keel. I realized how much I missed her, and I just saw her earlier that day.

I had been traveling all over on photo shoots, running from the memory of Liz, and now, running from Maggie. I practically pushed her into Ellen's arms.

Okay, calm down, Ryan. You've got Maggie practically in a relationship with this woman, and Maggie said she was just a colleague. However, Hannah words still lingered—keep your enemies close.

"I'm going to bed before I hurt myself," I said with a yawn. Chance yawned in empathy and followed me.

I lay there staring at the ceiling, my mind wandering back to Maggie. What was I going to do about this? I shifted under the sheet, which sent Chance to growling as she lay at the foot of the bed. My heart started pounding, and I began to perspire. As I drifted off, Maggie's smiling face stayed with me.

I opened my eyes to see her looming over me. Her long auburn hair framing her smiling face. I felt the weight of her small body and I instinctively parted my legs, feeling her slip in between them. Her hair tickled my shoulders as she lowered her head. Her lips were so warm as she kissed me. I felt my arms wrap around her waist. She kissed my chin, my neck, and the top of my breast. I closed my eyes and sighed deeply as I felt her light kisses travel down my chest. Her body moved into mine, her hips grinding into me. I groaned and thrust my hips upward.

"Maggie," I whispered. "Please." My hands flew to her shoulders as I pushed her downward. I heard her whispering against my chest as she moved down my body. I was on fire; my heart was racing as she kept moving lower. I spread my legs; I was throbbing, waiting for her touch. She was almost there. I felt her tongue against my stomach, lower, lower.

My body jumped as I sat up. I frantically looked around in the darkness. "What in the hell?" My voice was ragged and full of sleep. I was alone and sweating and the sheets were all over the bed. *Good grief...*I looked to see Chance lying at the foot of the bed, her head cocked to one side. She slowly jumped off the bed and walked out of the bedroom, giving me a backward glance.

"Hey, I didn't do anything! It was a dream." I flounced back down and pulled the sheet over my nakedness. "But, Good Lord, Maggie, what a dream."

Chapter Three

It was hot and sunny, the tourists were all but gone, and there was peace on Deer Lake. I was tempted to take my camera out but almost kicked myself. I had enough of that for a while. I loved my job, but three weeks is a long assignment.

As I made breakfast, I took inventory of my cabin. It wasn't overly huge. A cathedral ceiling and a loft, and though I hadn't completely finished it, it was furnished in a dormitory effect. Two twin beds and one double bed each sectioned off for privacy. Later, I'd have walls put up to make at least two rooms. One master bedroom with a private bath, which of course was mine, two smaller bedrooms and a full bath at the end of the hall occupied the first floor.

My favorite part of the cabin was the fireplace. Situated in the middle of the living room, the stone chimney was huge, separating the kitchen from the living room and was almost the length of the wall. It had a wrap-around effect as the fireplace was in the living room and the kitchen. When lit, the fire warmed both rooms. The kitchen was large, light, and airy with a table in front of the fireplace. It was nothing too extravagant, just cozy and comfortable. It was a dream I was grateful to be living. Overall, I liked it.

The rest of the morning, I busied myself with cleaning and preparations for the invasion. As I opened my front door, I heard a man crying out, echoing on the lake. I ran down to my pier and looked in all directions. Then I saw Ben.

He was skinny-dipping again. "You'll get arrested!" I called over to him, and he laughed and swam my way.

I was horrified. "Hey, put some clothes on, you crazy..." I

exclaimed as the only part of his body that was not tanned was flexing out of the water as he swam.

"Oh, God," I moaned and looked away. "Ben, I'm not kidding." I looked into the woods. He stopped and stood in waist-deep water, his laugh echoing throughout the lake.

"Don't try and fool me, Kate Ryan. I know I saw you last year at night. So don't be a prude, you're too young."

Too young? Good grief, I'm forty-three. I laughed at him. "You're a dirty old man, Captain Harper. I've decided not to introduce you to Hannah."

He stopped and gave me a serious look. "Who's Hannah?"

I explained and he smiled wickedly. "Well, she sounds delightful. Now I have to meet her. Bring her Saturday." He waved and swam back to his pier.

"This could be interesting," I said, pleased with myself.

The town of Deer Lake is small and quaint. Made up of only a few streets, the population is about two thousand, the way I like it. As I drove down the main street, I passed Sutter's Pub on my way to the grocery store and smiled. Since I bought my cabin, I've spent a few times there getting to know the locals. One time came to mind: the toilet incident.

I stormed into the restaurant and sat at the bar. Fran quickly ran over to me. "What the hell happened to you?" She reached over and took the bloody towel away from my forehead. "What did you try to fix?" she asked as she retrieved the first-aid kit.

"Nothing!" I said angrily as she washed the small cut. I pulled back and winced.

I then heard the snicker from the end of the bar. I glanced over to see Ed Samson drinking his beer and laughing. "Shut up, Ed."

"What were you trying to fix, Kate?" he asked as he ate from the peanut bowl.

"My fricking toilet," I grumbled and ate a peanut. He was making me hungry.

"Tell Ed all about it," he said with sympathy. "Your stories are more fun than watching reruns of 'Home Improvement.'"

I glared at him. Fran laughed as she put the Band-Aid over my brow. "He's right, Kate. We've all been watching you build that little cabin for the last few months. And I gotta tell you, whenever we see you coming down the street, we all place our bets."

Ed took out a five-dollar bill and handed it to Fran, who took the wager with a gleeful grin. I watched the exchange as I drank my beer.

Ed sighed. "I thought for sure it was the front porch you're working on."

"No, funny man. My toilet, well, it, I took a wrench and it slipped." *I winced as Ed roared with laughter.*

"And you smacked your head?" *he asked while laughing.*

Fran bit at her lip, then slapped him on the arm.

I just ate my peanuts.

Ah, good friends, I thought happily.

After wandering up and down the aisles of the small grocery store, I had a carload of food that took me forever to unload. As I did, I heard something in the woods behind me. I turned in hopeful anticipation—maybe it was a deer. I stood still and saw the dense brush rustling, but nothing or no one made an appearance. Nature, I laughed to myself, and continued with my groceries.

It was hot and humid, so I took an afternoon swim. Then I decided to go to town for dinner. Ben was sitting on his pier fishing and I called over to him. "Sutter's?"

He looked over at me, shook his head, and pointed to the lake. "Big fish," he said hopefully.

Sutter's Pub is a local bar and restaurant. Its nautical motif only added to its charm. I sat at the bar waiting for a table. Wednesday night was more crowded than I remembered.

"Kate! You're back."

I looked up at the bartender's smiling face. "Hey, Fran, long time," I said and slipped onto the barstool.

"I saw you at the IGA earlier. Are you planning on staying awhile?" she asked as she placed the bottle of beer in front of me.

"Two weeks," I said and raised the bottle. "Boy, it's crowded. I think I'll eat at the bar instead of waiting for a table."

As I ate my shrimp, I noticed a man sitting at the end of the bar. He was about forty with sandy-colored hair and cool blue eyes. His eyes caught mine and he smiled and nodded to me.

"Have you tried the shrimp? It's a specialty," I said, making conversation.

"No, thanks, I haven't."

Fran stood between us. "Kate here owns the cute log cabin on Deer Lake. Say, aren't you renting on that lake?"

"Sure am. What a beautiful lake. I was lucky, got the call and drove all the way. Haven't even been in it yet." He smiled broadly.

"Well, I hope the weather holds up for you." I smiled, too.

He raised his glass. "Me too."

He was a very affable fellow, tall and tanned. The three of us talked absently. I stuck out my hand. "Sorry, I'm Kate Ryan."

He smiled and took it. "Lucas Thorn."

"So, Kate, you up here all alone again?" Fran asked.

"Nope. Teri will be here tomorrow along with a couple of friends of mine. So I'll have a house full of people by five o'clock."

"Well, Luke—" Fran started, and he gently interrupted her.

"Lucas, if you wouldn't mind." He smiled.

"Lucas, ready for another?"

"No, I'd better be going." He smiled and shook my hand again. "Nice to meet you, Kate. I'm sure we'll see each other again."

I noticed Fran watching Mr. Thorn as he left. She hardly heard any of her other patrons as they talked to her. Finally shaking her head, she threw her towel over her shoulder and made her way back to my end of the bar. "What a good-looking piece of manhood." Fran sighed as she watched the door.

"Fran, I'm eating and you're drooling on the bar," I gently reminded her and ate my dinner.

The cabin was as clean as it was going to get. Chance was absolutely no help as she barked and chased the vacuum cleaner. Of course, did I stop and shoo her outside? No, I just aimed the vacuum cleaner in her direction. It's a game we play.

The rooms were ready and the fridge stocked. I sighed happily and decided to get the boats ready. I put on my swimsuit and walked down to the lake, which wasn't much of a walk, only a hundred feet or so. My beach was close. I stood in waist-deep water while I washed my rowboat and made sure the small trolling motor worked. This was my fishing boat, which I hoped was going to get a good deal of use that week.

I made sure the small motor was ready in case I needed a little more power on the rowboat than the trolling motor. It was an old Mercury motor, rebuilt and was in no way a match for the twenty-five-horsepower on my speedboat. However, it got me around the lake quicker than the nonexistent horsepower of the trolling motor.

I looked up at the cloudless sky, smiling to myself as the sun warmed my skin. I took a swim, and as I sat on the beach, I realized it was getting late and I should clean the speedboat. Ugh, I was too comfortable lying on the beach.

However, I walked down the pier and got in the boat to check it out. By now, it was nearly two o'clock and everyone would be here in an hour.

I quickly cleaned up the boat and made sure all was in order. I knelt on the pier and started tossing the life jackets back in the boat. I dusted off my hands. "There, all set."

As I walked back to my cabin, I thought I caught a glimpse of something moving in the woods. *That's the second time*, I thought. I peered closer and saw nothing, but the hair on the back of my neck bristled. I stopped at the small storage shed next to my cottage to get all the beach toys ready. As I walked in, I realized how unorganized it was. The spare oars and life jackets were all over.

"I'm a slob." I sighed and started the bothersome task.

It was then I heard the noise behind me. As I turned, I got a glimpse of something whisking through the air, right at my head. As I ducked, the last thing I remembered was the pain that ripped through my neck. *Crap.*

Chapter Four

I heard somebody calling my name. It sounded like my mother—it must be Teri. I groaned painfully and opened my eyes. Yep. Teri was kneeling next to me.

"Kate? Geezus, what happened?" Teri asked frantically.

I was lying on the floor of the shed trying to get my bearings. "Hey," I mumbled as I sat up. It was then I noticed Hannah looking anxious and worried. "Auntie Em? There's no place like home."

Hannah chuckled as she held Chance. "And Toto, too. What happened?"

They both helped me to my feet. "I have no idea. I came in here to—"

With that, Ben Harper barged in. "What's all the commotion? I saw a van pull up and heard some screaming."

I looked at Teri. "You were screaming?"

My redheaded sister blushed horribly. "Well, you were lying there with blood on you."

Hannah, as if not wanting to be left out, chimed in, "I screamed, as well, Kate."

Ben laughed. "It sounded like there were loons loose in your storage shed."

I laughed along and winced. "I appreciate you coming to my aid."

"What happened?" Ben asked.

I leaned against the small table. "Like I was saying, I came in here to—"

"Where is everybody?" Maggie's voice called out.

I groaned helplessly. "I'll never get this story out," I said. "We're in here, Maggie!" I called back and winced.

Maggie poked her head inside. "What's going on?" Right behind her was another woman—another attractive woman.

We now had six people crammed in the small shed. "Okay, we're a fire hazard. Let's exit quietly." I shooed everybody out the door.

He watched from the woods perfectly still, irritated at yet another interruption. It was close, too close. Standing there hidden by the dense woods, he watched as they carried her into the cabin. "Patience," he whispered as the sweat poured down his back. He stood still; his arm began to itch. He looked down to see a huge spider on his forearm. He smiled and still did not move as it started to crawl up his arm. He looked away and watched the cabin. "Patience," he repeated as he flicked the spider off his arm, then turned and faded into the woods.

Teri came out of the kitchen with a cold cloth. Maggie took it from her and put it on the back of my neck. "Sit still," she ordered.

"I'm fine," I insisted. I looked up at the woman standing behind Maggie.

"Oh, sorry. Ellen Winters, this is Kate Ryan," Maggie said absently as she held the cloth to my neck.

I glanced at Hannah who nodded slowly and looked back and forth between the two women. I looked at this woman. "Nice to meet you, Ellen. Sorry for the odd welcome."

She smiled slightly. "Don't worry, Kate. Maggie told me you get into odd predicaments."

I glanced at Maggie who grinned and shrugged. She took the cloth away. "Well, you're still in one piece. How do you feel?"

"Fine, just a headache." I looked at Ben, who was smirking.

"You want to tell us what happened?" he asked.

I took a deep breath. "I was in the shed to clean it up. I heard a noise and caught a glimpse of something coming at my head. Then—lights out." I winced and felt the small lump on the back of my neck.

Teri gave me a worried look. "You think someone hit you?"

I thought about how the cabin looked when I first arrived. Ben explained how much traffic there had been on the lake that summer.

"Maybe we've got a prowler. I'm calling Dan and getting him over here," Ben said definitively. "I'll be back."

I noticed Hannah watching Ben as he walked out. "He owns the house next door," I said absently to Hannah. "Ben's a good guy."

"He seems to be," she agreed with a smile.

"Sorry, guys. I don't know what's happening," I said. "Maybe it was a prowler."

We all checked the cabin; nothing ordinary was missing. "If someone was going to steal something, I don't know what. You don't even own a TV. They must have gotten spooked and left. Nothing seems out of place," Teri said.

"Hey, I'll get a TV and a better stereo. I just haven't had the time," I said defensively.

"I called Dan. He's on his way," Ben said from the doorway.

"Thanks. So you've met everyone. I would have rather it had been under better circumstances," I said apologetically.

Hannah was in the kitchen and came out with a pitcher of lemonade and glasses. "I hope you don't mind I invaded your kitchen, Kate."

"Not at all." I turned to Maggie and Ellen. "How about I get you settled up in the loft?"

Maggie nodded and looked around the cabin. "Kate, this is so you. It's adorable."

I watched Ellen. She was looking around not saying much. I went to the hallway, pulled down the staircase from the ceiling, and showed Maggie and Ellen the loft. "It's all yours," I said and waved my hand around the loft.

Maggie nodded approvingly, looking at the knotty pine paneling and the rustic log furniture. "I like it. It's wonderfully cozy."

Ellen looked around as if she was waiting for something to crawl out from under the bed. I was a little indignant, but I figured she was used to the Ritz. "Sorry, it's nothing special. It's just a cabin," I said, suddenly feeling defensive.

Maggie looked shocked. "Don't be silly. This is wonderful." She walked to the balcony that overlooked the cabin. "It's very cozy and very comfortable and very much you."

"Thank you. I'm glad to hear you say that," I said, matching her sincerity. For a moment, we looked at each other.

"This is very nice, Kate. I appreciate the invitation," Ellen said. "Maggie and I weren't looking forward to the long drive back from Green Bay. This will be a nice little vacation, thanks."

I regarded this enemy, er woman, for a moment. I figured her to be in her mid-thirties. Her hazel eyes accentuated her short curly blond hair. She was almost as tall as I and thin, very thin…not as I. I felt like the amazing behemoth next to her. Not that I was that large, but good grief, she was skinny. *God, I hope she eats.*

"You're welcome, Ellen. Glad to have you," I said. "Well, you two get settled. It's only four, get your suits and go for a swim. Ben's having a barbecue about six. Our attendance is mandatory."

Maggie put a hand on my arm. "Do you really think someone hit you? Maybe the oar just fell on your head." I heard the sarcasm in her voice. She was grinning and waiting for an answer. "For something *really* out of the ordinary."

"Get settled in, smart-ass," I grumbled and started down the stairs.

My head was aching as I walked back out onto the porch.

"This is gorgeous, Kate. The lake is wonderful," Hannah said.

"Thanks. I enjoy it. Did you bring your suit?"

She waved her hand. "Naturally. I can't wait to get into that lake."

Ben looked at her. "Great, you're a swimmer. Maybe tomorrow morning we can meet for a swim?" he asked and I glared at him, remembering his skinny-dipping.

"That sounds fine, Mr. Harper," Hannah said, smiling, and Ben returned her smile.

Hmm, a little vacation romance is just what the doctor ordered.

Dan Jackson finally came by. We had met on several occasions since I bought my cabin. He was a likable guy, about forty with dark hair and eyes to match. Tall and slender, he in no way looked like a sheriff. He had the air of a teacher about him. He smiled, took off his hat, and put out his hand. "Hello, Kate. Long time."

I shook the offered hand. "Only four months or so," I countered affably and introduced him to everyone. As Maggie and Ellen came onto the porch, it got a little crowded. I was not used to so many people here at once. Hell, I wasn't used to any people being here.

Dan, Ben, and I walked down to my shed, and I explained what happened. He listened intently as he looked around. He noticed the oar from the rowboat lying on the floor. "Probably conked ya on the head with this."

"I thought so, too, or maybe Maggie is right. It fell and hit me in the head. This place is a mess."

I explained what I found when I first came up. Again, Dan listened while looking around. Ben made mention about all the traffic on the lake lately and Dan agreed.

"We've been having calls on all the lakes this summer. Looks like our little spot of heaven is being invaded."

"Humanity," Ben said with disgust as we walked back to the porch.

Dan asked a few questions and scribbled some notes. "Well, there's not much to do. I can have one of the deputies patrol the lake more often, other than that..." He shrugged.

I agreed. "I know there's not much you can do. I appreciate you coming over, Dan."

"It's finally nice to see you here with family and friends. You've been a hermit for the past couple of years and—"

"Yes, yes...Thank you, Sheriff Jackson, you may go now," I said and gently pushed him toward his car.

"Well, I'm going for a swim," I said and Maggie and Hannah agreed.

I dove off the pier and once again felt invigorated. Hannah

and Maggie were right behind me.

Maggie called over to me, "God, this is wonderful!"

Meanwhile, Ellen stood on the deck. She probably didn't want to get her hair wet.

"C'mon, Ellen, the water's great," I said.

"Maybe later." She sat on the pier and faced the late afternoon sun.

"She's not much of a swimmer, huh?" I asked Maggie.

"I don't know," Maggie said and swam in the other direction.

Ignoring the urge to swim after her, I decided to do my ritual of swimming between my pier and Ben's. It was something I started last year. It was good exercise and I loved to swim. Hannah swam next to me and soon we were swimming laps together.

"Good heavens, you're a strong swimmer," Hannah said breathlessly as we finished and walked out of the water. She grabbed her towel, and I noticed this adorable woman was in tremendous shape. Hannah may be on the short side, although the politically correct term would be "vertically challenged," but she had a fit figure. She toweled off her silvery hair and grabbed her short robe. The resemblance between her and Maggie was remarkable. These Winfield women came from a strong gene pool. They were both strikingly attractive women.

"So Margaret brought Ellen with her," she said absently as she slipped into her robe.

"I guess." I shrugged and glanced at them. Maggie had said something and Ellen let out a hearty laugh. "What do you know about this woman?"

"Not much," Hannah whispered. I looked down into the blue eyes narrowed with suspicion. "Just that she calls Margaret every day. I don't trust her."

"Why not?" I asked in a worried tone as we watched. We must have looked ridiculous standing on the pier whispering.

I was suddenly thirsty and took a beer out of the cooler. "Thank you, dear," Hannah whispered and took the beer.

I looked down at my empty hand. "You're welcome."

Hannah took a long drink from the icy bottle, all the while

watching Maggie and Ellen. "So what are you going to do about this?" She gave me a challenging look as she drank the beer.

"Me? What can I do?" My heart hammered in my chest as I heard Ellen laughing.

"Well, if you don't do something, you might as well just push Margaret into her arms," Hannah said evenly.

With that, Ben's voiced boomed out over the lake. "Look, you mackerel, get out of the water and get down here. The party's starting!"

Ellen was sitting on the beach with Maggie as Hannah and I approached. "You're an excellent swimmer, Kate," Ellen said. "It's good exercise. They say swimming is good for you, when you can't do other things."

I noticed the curious look she received from Maggie. Honestly amused by Twiggy, I laughed. "Is that what they say? Well, whoever they are, they're right. It's very good, and it should always be followed by several of these," I said while opening the cooler. "Care to join me?" I held up the icy beer. I gave Maggie an enticing grin.

"Thanks, I think I will," Maggie said and I handed her one. "Ellen?"

"No, but it's sweet of you to ask. Thank you."

Somehow, I didn't think her heart was in it.

Chapter Five

No one but Hannah liked my Hawaiian shirt. I was gravely disappointed in Maggie, although I suspected I'd get over it. She came downstairs looking very smart. She wore a cool sleeveless summer dress, and her hair was once again braided. I must admit even Ellen looked nice—too dressy for a barbecue, though. That was some expensive-looking silk blouse she wore.

Maggie looked at my shirt and blinked a couple of times. "My, that is…colorful," she said and looked at Teri.

"Isn't it, though?" Teri, who always looked good, was wearing a green checked shirt that complemented her red hair wonderfully and lightweight summer slacks. Of course, she was the queen of accessories and everything matched.

"Don't listen to them, I like it," Hannah said.

I looked down at myself. "I like it, too. I look tropical."

Maggie laughed, completely amused, I'm sure. "Only you could wear that and pull it off. I'm sure it'll grow on me." She patted my shoulder as she walked out the door.

"Thank you…I think." I frowned and followed them out.

Ben had a huge bonfire going. Coolers were filled with every libation and two grills were going—one with roasted corn on the cob and the other with the main course of a cow or something. The aroma was mouthwatering as we walked down the path to his house.

When he saw us, he grinned like a kid. "There you are, you fish. I thought you'd never get out of the water." He hugged me and said, "Nice shirt."

I gave them all a superior look.

"Well, there are coolers everywhere. If you can't find what you want, you let me know. I bet I have it inside."

We mingled for a minute or two, and I noticed the hyena-laughing, brunette woman talking to a young man who looked totally uninterested as he drank his beer.

Ben called over to both of them. "Sandy, Martin, this is Kate Ryan. She owns the adorable log cabin, in fact the only log cabin on the lake."

I smiled and shook their hands. "I bought the house over there." Sandy Meyers pointed to the house around the bend from Ben's cabin.

"It's nice to meet you," I said.

Sandy was about thirty, and Ben was right, she was flighty but had an incredible figure. She wore a top that was much too tight and had a pair of Capri pants that looked as though someone painted them on. However, her shoes threw me. How do women stand in those things? They were three-inch stacked, goofy-looking open-toed sandals. *I'd have broken both ankles by now.*

Fashion, I thought, and shook my head. She had her long raven hair pulled back in a scarf. Her eyes were a deep violet blue, with thick but elegantly arched eyebrows. I swear her profile looked like Elizabeth Taylor at her elegant and sexy best. She was captivating. I know I was staring. Ben nudged me and I blinked. I missed what she had said and Ben quickly recovered for me.

"Kate's been here what, two years?" He looked at me.

I nodded quickly. "Yes, yes, two years."

As I made some joke about Ben, she threw her head back and Ben was right again; she laughed like a hyena. So much for Liz Taylor elegance. My eyes flew open in amazement. Looking beyond her, I saw Maggie and Teri. Their heads shot up at the horrifying noise.

This woman could scare the loons right off the lake. I quelled the urge to put my hand over her mouth to quiet her. Ben was completely amused. Soon, we were all laughing at God knows what. Everyone but the young man named Martin.

He was staring in the direction of Maggie and Teri. "Hi," I said, and he looked at me.

"Martin Reese," he said and shook my hand.

"So which house do you own?" I asked casually, looking at the lake.

He was frowning. "I don't. I'm renting the cottage across the lake." He motioned with his head, over his shoulder.

"Oh, right. I don't know the owner of those cottages. So you're up here fishing?" I asked affably.

He nodded. "Something like that," he said and drank his beer. *Good grief, what a grump.* He was in his late twenties, very short dark hair, hazel eyes, and a perpetual scowl. "Excuse me," he said and walked away.

Maggie came up behind me. "Well, interesting neighbors, Miss Ryan," she whispered in my ear.

I shivered uncontrollably. "Don't do that," I said as I scratched at my ear and shivered again. She gave me an innocent look, which I ignored. "Only on Deer Lake can you find this array of strangeness. Although, Ben is a good guy," I said as we watched him and Hannah laughing.

"Okay, I can hear your brain rattling. Are you matchmaking?"

"Do you mind? Ben's a nice man and I hate to see Hannah sad."

"No, I don't mind at all. It's sweet of you. You're a good friend. Now tell me what's going on in that brain of yours. I can almost smell the smoke."

I opened my mouth and she put up her hand. "And look me in the eyes, Kate Ryan, so I know you're telling me the truth and not something you've concocted out of your Irish imagination."

She's in my head again. "I think we may have a prowler. I thought maybe my neighbors could shed some light. I hope so," I finished and drank my beer.

She put her hand under my chin and turned my face. "Well, you're getting a nice bruise again. Soon it'll match your shirt," she said with a smug grin.

I felt her warm hand on my cheek and thought of the countless times she'd done that gesture. I thought of last spring when we were in Ireland. The night she came to my room, terrified of the storm. How I told her about my nightmare with Liz Eddington. How we comforted each other—how I held her during the night. How I made an ass out of myself when I told her that her hair smelled like apricots. *Quit it, Ryan, you had your chance then and screwed it up nicely.*

As if she read my mind, Maggie took her hand away, but our eyes still held the questioning gaze. "You might want to put some ice on that later."

I nodded. "I'm sure you're tired of showing off your doctoring skills on me," I said, feeling like a child.

She laughed quietly. "Well, you *are* a handful, Miss Ryan." Our eyes met again.

"I guess so." I took a drink of my beer.

Maggie took a deep breath and shook her head as she turned to go. "So…" I started. She stopped and gave me a questioning glance. "Are you—?"

Maggie raised an eyebrow but said nothing. I shrugged. "I just want you to be happy, Maggie."

"And what do you think would make me happy?"

"Ryan! Get your butt over here and help me with these steaks!" Ben called out.

"I-I gotta run," I said and backed up.

Maggie gave me a sarcastic grin. "I can imagine you do. Don't trip." She turned and walked away.

As I manned the grill, I watched Martin Reese. He was studying everybody, but now I knew he was looking at Teri from time to time. Not that it was bad; Teri was a very attractive person. Her flaming red hair preceded her, and it turned many a head. That coupled with her violet eyes and adorable Irish smile. Mac had his hands full, and it was to his credit that he wasn't a jealous man. He had no reason to be. She had eyes for him and him alone.

However, Mr. Reese was staring and I watched him. I was ready to go over to him and say something when a boat pulled up to Ben's pier. A middle-aged couple got out. He was smiling. She was not.

Isn't anybody happy on this lake? Then I heard the hyena and that answered my question.

Ben walked over and shook hands with the couple. He introduced himself and took them around, introducing them to Sandy Meyers and Martin Reese. I walked over and Ben introduced them.

"Ah, Kate. This is Phil and Jackie Henderson. They own the house directly across from mine."

I shook hands with the couple. I looked around and my troop was scattered, so I said, "Well, that's my group. I own the log cabin next to Ben."

Phil nodded. "We watched you build that. Quite an undertaking, I imagine," he said and smiled. Phil Henderson was my age, forty-three I'd say, gray at the temples and brown eyes. He had the look of an accountant about him as he adjusted his glasses. He looked nervous as he spotted Sandy Meyers.

"Yes, it was. I was a wreck for two years until they were done," I said and looked at Jackie Henderson. She was the same age, maybe older. Blond hair and blue eyes that looked pensive. She was tall and shapely. They complemented each other well, I thought. Though I suspected they just had a fight.

They had that detached look about them, and when Phil asked if she wanted anything, she gave him a wifely—I'm still mad at you—look and said, "Whatever you're having is fine."

He sighed and walked to the cooler. Sandy was immediately at his side and said something. He looked into the cooler, then picked up a beer and handed it to her. He quickly picked up two more, smiled at her, and turned away.

I watched Jackie, and if looks good kill, the hyena woman would have been vaporized. Phil came back and handed Jackie the beer, looking a little shamefaced. We talked for a few minutes about buying a summer home, the cost, and upkeep of living on a small lake.

"So, Phil, what do you do for a living?" I asked.

"I'm a teacher. Jackie and I both teach, as a matter of fact." I could tell he wasn't in the mood for small talk. His wife was still avoiding him as he spoke.

"Have you been having any problems lately with prowlers?"

Phil looked a little shocked. "No, why, have you?"

I nodded and explained the past couple of days. They both looked surprised. Jackie instinctively leaned into her husband, and he put his arm around her. "That's incredible," Jackie said, shaking her head.

I agreed. "Well, keep your eyes open. I'm sure if there is anyone, once they see the patrol car more often, they'll get the idea," I said reassuringly. "Excuse me."

I made my way to Martin Reese. He was staring at the lake when I came up behind him. "So are you up here for the rest of the summer?" I asked. He jumped and turned to me. "Hell, I'm sorry."

He almost smiled. "It's all right. No, I'm not sure how long I'll be here," he said, ending that discussion.

"Mr. Reese, this may sound odd, but have you had any problems or seen anyone skulking around the lake?"

He watched me, and the crease in his brow deepened. "No, I haven't had any problems. I hope the police can patrol enough. There's been a lot of activity on the lake this summer. Ben said you haven't been up here yet. Maybe whoever thought it would be easy pickings." He shrugged as if he didn't care. Why should he, he's only renting.

"Gee, thanks for your input," I said sarcastically, and he shot me a look. I looked right back at him and he actually smiled.

"Sorry, I'm preoccupied." He finished his beer and excused himself. I watched him walk away and fish another beer out of the cooler. Then he walked down the shore away from the rest of the party. *What a solitary guy*, I thought as I watched him.

Sandy's voice rang out. "Hey, Ben, where's Lucas? Isn't he coming?" She looked disappointed. I had forgotten him.

"I talked to him yesterday. He's got a hot date, but he'll drop by later," Ben said while cooking the burgers.

"A date, huh?" Sandy asked, obviously disappointed. I noticed Jackie's smug grin. Phil turned red and drank his beer.

As I watched them, Teri and Maggie came up to me. "I know you, Kate. You've been watching these people all night. This is better than the movies. Something's going on," Maggie whispered, almost excited.

"I'm waiting for Sandy Meyers to fall out of those hideous sandals," I said and drank my beer.

Teri laughed. "This coming from the moccasin queen of the Midwest." Maggie snickered, then glancing my way, she cleared her throat.

I gave them a scathing look. "I hate it when you two get together."

They both laughed as we casually watched the show.

Ben had the corn roasting on the grill. Soon, we all were laughing, joking, and having a good time. All except the brooding Mr. Reese. He ate and drank and talked but seemed distant and detached. I mentioned it at the picnic table as we sat and ate.

"Well, maybe he's lonely. He's probably here because he broke up with his girlfriend. He's sad and disillusioned," Teri said, watching him.

"God, you watch too many movies." I ate my corn.

"You have no romance, little sister."

Maggie snorted, then cleared her throat. I looked at Ellen who said, "Don't look at me, I hardly know you."

I gaped at all of them. "Hey, I got romance, plenty of romance. Just because I don't gush over everything." I looked at Hannah for help. "Hannah, tell them. I have romance."

She looked at me and said, "Of course you do, dear."

I gave all of them a superior look. "There, Hannah said so." I got up from the picnic table. "And what do you know anyway? You don't even like my Hawaiian shirt," I said defensively and walked away.

After dinner, I watched Ellen talking with Maggie. After a few moments, Ellen yawned and patted Maggie on the shoulder and walked our way.

"It must be this country air. I'm bushed," she said. "Good night, all."

"Good night," I said and watched her walk back toward the cabin. I then glanced at Maggie, who sat alone by the fire.

"I hate to see her alone," Hannah said and put her hand on my arm. "Kate, you're her friend, go talk to her. Don't leave her sitting alone. Go to the mattress."

I gave her a blank look. "Go where?" I asked. Teri put her hand to her mouth, and I could tell she was trying not to laugh.

Hannah rolled her eyes. "Didn't you see *The Godfather*?"

"Hannah, don't start with the enemy thing again," I begged her in earnest.

"Go to the mattress," Hannah repeated.

I felt like pulling my hair out. "Stop saying that," I pleaded and looked at Teri. "Make her stop saying that."

Teri put her hand on my shoulder. "It's from *The Godfather*. It means go to war," Teri explained calmly.

Hannah nodded. "All's fair in love and war, dear. And if this is love—it *must* be war. Now go to her." She gave me a gentle nudge that nearly sent me sprawling into the cooler.

"Oh, all right, although she probably wants to be left alone. I know I would."

"Yes, but you spend too much time alone as it is, and if you want my opinion…" Teri started.

"Okay, okay, I'm going," I grumbled while my heart raced. I picked up a couple of beers from the cooler.

As I walked to my fate, my stomach was in knots and my mind raced. *Okay, Vito, mattresses, enemies, war…love. Got it.*

"Hey, Maggie," I said with a smile and handed her a beer.

She looked up and took the offering. "Thanks."

"Am I buttin' in?" I asked.

"No, actually."

I sat next to her and stared at the fire. "What are ya thinking?" I asked. I wasn't at all sure I wanted to know, but I couldn't help myself—she looked so pensive.

She sighed and looked into the fire. "I'm thinking I'd like to know why you didn't call me when you got home from Ireland and took off for South Dakota."

I winced and took a long pull from the beer bottle. "When you find out, let me know."

With that, Chance came bounding up to us. Maggie laughed and ruffled her ears. "Where have you been?" I asked.

Of course, the little cur ignored me. She was on her back now, while Maggie vigorously scratched her belly. "Hiding, more than likely. Like her mistress," Maggie said.

The silence was deafening as the crackling campfire mesmerized both of us. I heard every cricket for five miles. "Ellen seems nice," I said and glanced at her.

Maggie looked up. "She is."

That's it?

"So," I asked with a shrug, "where'd you meet?"

"At the hospital. As I said, she's an administrator there. The hospital is looking for another satellite clinic in Green Bay. That's where she's going on Monday. She asked if I wanted to join her."

Again the silence. I looked down at Chance who was now lying at Maggie's feet, sound asleep. *What a life.*

"So," I said and cleared my throat. "You gonna go with her?"

"I haven't decided," she said evenly and drank her beer.

She then turned in her chair and looked directly at me. I instinctively leaned back. "Is there any reason why I shouldn't?"

Her blue eyes held a challenging gaze as they sparkled in the fire's light. I drank my beer. "Uh" was the only thing I could think of saying.

"Do you ever wonder why you're single?" she asked and faced the fire once again.

"No." I answered that much too quickly. I heard her chuckle.

"I do. You know, with Allison." She stopped and took a deep breath. "Maybe it's me—"

Now it was my turn to face her. "Are you nuts? It's not you. You're a good woman—kind and considerate. You're worth ten of her and me."

"Thanks, but I think you overestimate my net worth."

"I don't think so, Maggie." I stared at the fire. "You need someone who understands you and gets a kick out of your feisty temper and—" I stopped and took a drink, not at all sure where I was going with this. I could feel Maggie watching me.

"Like who, for instance?" Maggie asked, now looking down at her hands.

I shifted uncomfortably in my seat. I took a very long drink.

"I-I don't know. How should I know? Somebody…I don't know," I said hastily and glanced at her.

She was grinning slightly as she sipped her beer. "What about you?"

I choked on my beer as I spilled it down my shirt. "Me? I'm… I…" I stammered like an ass as I wiped off my shirt.

"Don't hurt yourself. I mean what about you? Don't you want someone in your life?"

"Oh!" I said in amazement, as if I finally understood an algebra problem. "I think about it every now and then. I don't think I'm a good candidate for anyone…" My voice trailed off and once again, I stared at the fire.

Maggie reached over and put her hand on my knee. "I think you underestimate *your* net worth, Miss Ryan," she whispered, then leaned over, kissed my cheek, and stood. "Thanks for the beer and for listening. I'll see you in the morning."

As she turned, I reached up and held her wrist. "Don't leave with Ellen," I blurted out. I heard the small gasp and looked up into her stunned blue eyes. Swallowing was impossible.

"W-why not?" Maggie asked and stood in front of me. She looked down into my eyes, searching for the answer, I'm sure.

"Look, I know you're dating her, and I—"

"Dating who?" Maggie countered and looked completely befuddled.

Now I was confused. "E-Ellen," I said.

"Where did you get *that* idea?"

"W-well, Hannah mentioned—"

Maggie frowned deeply, and we both looked as Hannah made her way toward us. She must have seen the scowl on Maggie's face, for she stopped and made an abrupt about-face and headed in the other direction.

It was then I realized my blunder—I was a snitch.

Maggie pulled her hand away and glared at me. "In the future, Kate, you might want to talk to me first. Good night." She turned on a dime and marched down the path to the cabin.

Hannah and Teri joined me by the fire. "Margaret does not look happy. What did you say?" Hannah asked. I heard the curious tone.

I tiredly ran my hand over my face. I stood and kissed the elder Winfield on the check. "I'm in deep shit. No more talk of mattresses, okay, Vito?"

Hannah raised an eyebrow but said nothing. Suddenly, my heart was racing as the image of Maggie up in my loft, lying in bed flashed through my mind. The fact that the enemy was sleeping in the bed next to Maggie irritated me for some reason. I looked at the loft window in my cabin. When the light went out, I jammed my hands into the pockets of my shorts.

I started for the cabin, then stopped. I sensed the eyes of Vito upon me. I looked up to see Hannah standing there, arms folded across her chest; she was sporting a smug grin and looked very much like her niece.

"Decisions, decisions," she said with an evil grin and walked back to Ben's.

Teri laughed and patted my shoulder. "Good night, Kate," she said with a laugh and headed to the cabin.

The urge to follow Teri and march up to the loft was overwhelming…I headed back to the party.

Chapter Six

I stood there listening to Ben's laughter and looked up at the starry night. *What a dope. How is it that I'm constantly irritating Dr. Winfield? I'm gonna kill Hannah. Go to the mattresses...Why do I listen to her?*

The sound of a speedboat broke my inane reverie and I turned toward the lake. As it slowed down and headed for Ben's pier, I realized it was Lucas Thorn. He docked his boat and jumped onto the pier. Ben welcomed him and introduced him to everyone. He saw me and waved and I smiled back. He was a likable guy. After talking to the others, he made his way over to me.

"Kate, how are you?"

"Doing well, Mr. Thorn."

"Please, call me Lucas," he offered politely.

"So you lucked out getting Henry's house for a vacation?"

"Yes, indeed. When I found out the house was available, I jumped at it. Needed a vacation," he said emphatically.

"I know the feeling." I was going to continue, but Sandy Meyers bounced over.

"Lucas, how are you?" she beamed.

"I'm fine and you?" he asked and drank his beer.

"Fine. Wasn't this nice of Ben?"

He nodded and we all sat by the fire. I was exhausted—I ate too much.

"So I've been asking everybody, Lucas, now it's your turn. Since you've been here, have you had any problems with prowlers?" I asked and stifled a yawn.

"Hell, no, have you?" he asked amazed.

I nodded and told the story for the umpteenth time that evening as he listened intently.

Sandy of the hideous sandals, slurring her words, said, "Wow, now that you menshun it, Kate, I thought I saw someone the other day at your cabin. Though I can't really remember what they looked like." She smiled sheepishly and held up her beer. "Lemme think on it. I had a bit munch tonight," she slurred and let the hyena loose, laughing uncontrollably.

Martin Reese looked at her and scowled, which was no big deal since he'd been scowling at everybody all night. Lucas glanced at her over his beer and Phil even stole a glance or two. *What gives with this woman?*

I looked at Ben who gave me a confused look. He didn't have a clue what was going on; he was too busy wooing Hannah. I smiled inwardly, hoping he could take her mind off Doc, if only for a few days.

It was getting late and as if to read my mind, Jackie Henderson leaned over to Phil and whispered to him. He quickly finished his beer and stood, albeit wobbly. They made their good nights. Ben walked them to the pier and they motored back across the lake. We watched in cautious anticipation, hoping Phil would not run the boat up on his own pier.

We breathed a collective sigh as we heard the motor stop and a minute later the front door slam. It's amazing how noises carry over water. We unfortunately heard arguing before the door slammed.

Lucas was the next to go. "Well, I'd like to stay, however, I'm bushed." He stood and said good night to all and Ben once again walked to the pier and untied Lucas's boat as he drove off to Henry's house.

That left Martin and Sandy, who had had too much to drink. Thank God she didn't drive. She couldn't even walk back to her place, not in those shoes. Martin offered to take her home and she agreed, smiling all the way to his car.

"Well, half the residents were drunk. That friend of yours, Ellen, she didn't stay long. Good grief," Ben said in a deflated voice.

I patted him on the shoulder. "It's you, Ben. It had to be you,"

I said seriously, and he reached over and painfully pinched my nose. "Hey!" I cried out and rubbed my nose. "Okay, it was a successful party, geez," I said, making sure my nose was still attached.

Hannah laughed. "It was a very nice party, Ben."

He smiled from ear to ear. "Well, if you think so, Hannah, then my evening is complete."

"Oh, brother," I mumbled nasally.

After Ben's party, only the haunting wail of the loons could be heard over the lake. Back at my cabin, everyone had gone to bed. However, it was unbelievably hot with no air circulating at all. I took the only remaining fans and started at Hannah's door.

Hannah opened her door and gave me a scathing look. "Good evening, you stool pigeon."

I glanced up at the loft and whispered, "Me? You started this, Vito."

She narrowed her eyes, trying to think of an answer. She finally laughed and whispered, "Margaret was steaming mad."

"Your niece has a feisty temper."

"Which will be your problem one day if you play your cards right," she countered and glanced down at the fans I was holding.

"Thought you could use one," I said and offered her a fan.

"Thank you, dear. It is humid."

"No problem. I have one left. Thought I'd give it to Maggie as a peace offering," I said and kissed her cheek. "Good night."

With that, Maggie came down the stairs. She stopped abruptly, and we stood in the hallway looking at each other. I glanced at Hannah, who grinned and leaned against the doorjamb. She folded her arms across her chest and gave me a challenging smirk.

I looked at Maggie. "I-I was just coming up to give you a fan. It's beastly humid tonight."

"Thanks. I-I was just coming down to get you. You've got an exhaust fan up there, but it's not working," Maggie said as she wiped her forehead.

Hannah gently cleared her throat. "Well, I'm going to bed,"

she said and kissed Maggie on the cheek. She looked up at me. "You two go take care of the heat between you."

I know my mouth dropped. I couldn't even look at Maggie. I heard Hannah's evil laughter even after she closed her door. I reluctantly glanced at Maggie. "Let me take a look at the exhaust fan," I said and followed her up the small staircase to the loft. I was trying to ignore the fact that I was watching Maggie's shapely form as she climbed the stairs.

It was dark as pitch as we fumbled around. "Is Ellen asleep?" A loud snore answered my question. I chuckled and felt fingernails digging into my arm. "Okay, okay, sorry," I hissed and scooted out of Maggie's grasp.

I made my way to the linen closet and retrieved a flashlight I kept there for just such occasions. I flipped it on and followed the low beam to the rear window. Maggie was right behind me. "I see the problem," I whispered.

"What's wrong with it?" She peered over my shoulder.

"I don't know if I can fix it."

"Why?"

"It's unplugged," I whispered and laughed as I plugged it into the outlet. "Any other problems I can help you with?"

I shined the light upward, saw the angry glare, and laughed.

"Oh, go to bed, Kate," she hissed and spun around and walked into the small chair. She let out a grunt and grabbed her foot.

I put my hand to my mouth and snorted with laughter. Maggie was trying to be quiet while hopping around holding her foot. She hopped to one of the beds and sat down.

"Are you all right?" The noise coming from Ellen was unbelievable. "Is *Ellen* all right?"

"Damn you, Kate Ryan, get out of here," Maggie whispered. I shined the low beam on her foot as she examined it.

"Not until I know you're all right." I knelt down and gently held her foot. "Do we need a trip to the hospital?" I was still amazed that Ellen slept through this.

"N-no, I'm fine."

I could hear Maggie breathing deeply as I continued to massage her foot. "This little piggy…" I whispered with a laugh.

I was going to continue, but I didn't want to have a flashlight surgically removed from a particular part of my anatomy. I may be a dope, but I ain't stupid.

I was shocked when I felt her hand lightly running through my hair. I looked up, and in the low beam of the flashlight, I saw her blue eyes sparkling. "I'm not dating Ellen." I heard her voice catch.

"Y-you're not?" I asked and closed my eyes as her small hand cupped my face.

"No, I'm not," she said in a low voice.

She leaned forward and so did I. My heart started the now familiar hammering—the onset of my stroke. "Maggie—" I whispered coarsely.

With that, the loud snorting snore from Ellen made both of us jump.

"Does Ellen sleep this soundly all the time?"

"How the hell should I know?" Maggie hissed.

There was that tone. Last spring in Ireland, the feisty doctor had that same tone. I remembered that resolved tenor from the diminutive doctor—the one that sent a shiver up my spine. I promised myself then to put it in my memory bank and try not to be on the receiving end of it.

I grinned slightly. "Should I get off my knees or stay here and beg your forgiveness?"

For an instant, Maggie said nothing. Then she laughed quietly. "I'd tell you to stay right there, but you're probably in pain. I like the begging idea, though. Go to bed."

I groaned as I stood and placed the extra fan on the dresser. As I turned, I ran into the foot of the bed, painfully stubbing my toe.

"Shit!" I hissed and hopped around and dropped the flashlight, which rolled around and down the stairs—*plunk, plunk, plunkplunkplunk*. We were now in total darkness while Ellen, like the Energizer Bunny, still snored.

"Are you all right?"

"Yes, yes, I'm fine. Good night," I said quickly and limped down the stairs.

As I lay in bed, I could still hear Ellen's muffled snoring. I was wide awake. After giving Hannah one fan and the last one to Maggie and Ellen, I lay there sweating. Finally, I could take no more. I threw on my robe and grabbed a towel.

Once down at the lake, I took a page from Ben Harper and dove in. The cool water engulfed me and I felt invigorated once again. I loved skinny-dipping, although I did it at night and not in broad daylight like Mr. Harper.

Laughing to myself, I swam around in the moonlight. Floating on my back, I looked up at the stars. It was an unbelievable sight. I lazily swam farther out into the lake. The loons were wailing their haunting melody, echoing over the water.

As I was doing my best imitation of Flipper, I thought I saw someone walking along the shoreline about a hundred feet from my property to the right. It was all wooded and was owned by no one. I stopped swimming, and as I was treading water, I watched, trying not to make too much noise. There wasn't much moonlight, only a crescent moon. I hoped it didn't illuminate me at all. Feeling extremely vulnerable without any clothes, I fought a wave of panic as I slowly looked around in all directions. Then, back on the shore, I caught a glimpse of someone. I could hear him walking on the gravelly shore.

My heart was beating in my ears. Then I saw the same tiny light as the other night and a clicking sound. My mind raced as I narrowed my eyes, straining to see, but hoping I wouldn't be seen. I tried to swallow and realized my mouth had gone dry.

I took a quivering deep breath and thought for sure whoever it was walked out of sight. The tiny light was gone. *Who the hell was that?* I swam back toward the ladder.

As I got to it, I heard the pier creak and my heart raced again. *Great, I'll have a stinking heart attack, naked in the lake—wonderful headlines.*

I sat in the water clinging to the ladder, then for some reason, which I cannot explain, I moved under the pier. I was right, someone was on the pier. It was not my overworked Irish imagination. My view was limited as my boats were in the way. In the deafening darkness, the creaking stopped as the pier wobbled.

My heart sank as I knew whoever was standing up there was only a few feet away from me. I was trapped; I could go nowhere. Maybe if I scream, he'll run away. Maybe if I scream, he'll find me. I trod water, and my only hope was he didn't know I was under the pier. Then I shivered uncontrollably as I heard the pier creaking again. *What in the hell does he want with me?*

Okay, Ryan, control yourself. You've been in worse situations before. I tried to remember the last time I was naked in the water under a pier at midnight.

I could see the planks moving as he slowly took a couple of steps. He was almost directly above me and he stopped right by the speedboat. He stood perfectly still, and as the pier swayed, I swear he had to hear my heart beating. God, please don't let some fish come by and nibble at my feet, or another part of my anatomy, for that matter.

I watched as the pier seemed to come to life as the planks moved and the pier swayed as he walked away. Waiting for a second, I eased from under the pier. All I saw were his legs. He had shorts on, then he broke into a run, and all at once, I heard his footsteps on the gravelly shoreline, then fade away.

Never have I moved so fast in my life. I climbed that ladder as if a great white was nipping at my arse. Of course, I was going too fast, my foot slipped on the rung, and I painfully banged my forehead on the metal ladder, causing a nice little *ping* to ring out into the dark night. I grunted and saw stars for a moment.

"Damn it," I hissed angrily. I threw on my robe and made a mad dash for the house. I was petrified to look back, terrified he would change his mind and be right at my heels, reaching for me, his ugly green jagged teeth—the Irish imagination was reeling out control.

I ran in and quickly closed and locked the door. I was trembling as I stood there in the dark leaning against it. I felt a hand touch my shoulder.

"Refreshing?" A low voice came from behind me. I must have jumped ten feet, whirled, and screamed like a banshee, all in one motion. It was Teri.

With that, the light by the couch flipped on. It was Hannah, standing there in her robe, looking as white as a ghost. "Good heavens! You scared the life out of me!" she exclaimed and put her hand over her heart. She looked like she was going to faint.

"What's going on?"

We looked up to see Maggie standing in the hallway. Ellen was right behind her.

We sat in the kitchen as I told them my dilemma. I suppose, if I wasn't scared to death, it would have been funny. *Who am I kidding? It was funny.*

"How did you hit your forehead?" Teri asked.

"Well, I'm treading water, *naked*, under the pier waiting for the maniac to leave. As I started up, my foot slipped, and I banged my head on the ladder. So there I was, *naked* on the pier scrambling for my robe, exposed to everyone and anyone…" I said seriously.

I noticed Teri was biting her bottom lip and Maggie ran her hand across her mouth trying not to laugh. Ellen's lips were quivering and Hannah laughed uproariously.

"I am trying to be serious," I said, and that did it. All of them laughed uncontrollably. I sat there staring at them. "This isn't funny," I insisted, and they roared.

Teri was the first to sober and the rest followed. "Sorry, Kate," she snickered, and it started again.

"Well, you'd better get to bed. Enough excitement for one night," Hannah said.

I pinched the bridge of my nose and blinked. My head was aching, then I started laughing. "Damn it, I looked ridiculous."

Laughing once again, Maggie came into the room with several aspirins and a glass of water and handed them to me. She patted me on the head, like an errant child, and walked away.

Walking to my room, I heard Teri. "Good night, Lady Godiva." She and Maggie laughed all over again.

I waved at them and never looked back. I took off my robe and threw myself facedown on the bed.

"What next?" I mumbled, grabbing the sheet.

Chapter Seven

I woke at five in the morning, turned on the radio, and got the weather. A storm was coming; I could smell the rain in the air. Same hot, humid, and thunderstorms, then a cool front. I thought now perhaps I could have my fireplace going.

Everyone would be up soon, so I dressed quickly and put on the coffee. I loved this time of the day—the world was still asleep, and all you could hear were my beloved loons calling their eerie melody over the still lake.

Remembering I only had that small stack of firewood, I grabbed the ax from the shed and went to work. God, it was humid. I had on shorts and a tank top and I was still sticky—I hate humidity. As I whacked away, I thought about the night before. It's funny in the light of day the things that terrified you in the dark aren't so bad.

"Malarkey," I said as I glanced around the woods before I chopped the firewood. It still unnerved me. However, it did seem almost surreal as if it was a dream. I still couldn't figure out what he wanted. Maybe he dropped something and came back to look for it. I shook my head and grunted as I split the wood.

After an hour or so, I had quite a bit done, and I was completely soaked with perspiration. Pleased with myself, I made a few trips and brought the wood to the back door.

She is a strong woman, he thought as he watched the wood chips fly. He thought she would have been unconscious longer than she was. Then suddenly, she looked up and scanned the woods. He stood perfectly still, as he had all along and just watched. "She's looking right at me," he said, chuckling to himself. "She doesn't even know what to look for. Soon," he said as she shrugged and continued splitting the wood. *"So very soon,"* he hissed a whisper, and walking backward, he faded into the woods.

The sweat was dripping as I walked down the hall to my room. I looked up to see Maggie climbing down the stairs. "Good morning," I said tentatively.

"Good morning." She then chuckled, as if remembering the previous night and I felt infinitely better. "How's your foot?"

"Fine and yours?"

"Just fine, thank you," she said with a grin. She looked at my sweaty appearance. "Your morning exercise?"

"There's a cool front coming. I was out of firewood."

We stood there in the hallway for a moment. "I was just going to take a shower," I said and pulled at my sweaty tank top.

"So was I," Maggie said. She chuckled nervously and I joined her. I thought better of my joke about conserving water. "Well, you go ahead."

We both tried to get out of each other's way and bumped into each other. Trying it again, we did the same thing.

"Shall we dance?" Maggie asked with that contagious laugh of hers.

I laughed along, and out of the blue, I pulled her into my arms and waltzed her around the hallway.

She laughed heartily. "You are in bad need of a shower. However, you dance divinely, Miss Ryan."

"You should see me mambo."

While doing my imitation of Fred Astaire, neither Ginger nor I saw Ellen standing by the staircase until I twirled Maggie around in that direction. Maggie stopped abruptly, and we bumped into each other.

"Am I interrupting?" Ellen asked.

I smiled happily. "Yes, but I was just on my way to the shower. Good morning, Ellen." I walked into the bathroom.

I love the aroma of bacon sizzling in a pan. Standing by the stove, I prepared breakfast, knowing full well the minute everyone smelled freshly brewed coffee and bacon they'd be scurrying to the table. I know I would be.

I was shocked to see Ellen come into the kitchen first. "Good morning again. Sorry it's so hot up in the loft. How'd you sleep?"

"Fine, thanks." There was a moment of silence. "Can I ask you something?" she questioned and drank her coffee.

Please, no. "Sure, go ahead," I said over my shoulder.

"Margaret talks about you quite often. I understand you've shared a great deal in the short time you've known each other. Is there anything between you?"

Now what, Ryan? Mattresses... I took the pan of bacon off the stove and turned to her. "Maggie and I are very good friends. Anything more than that is between Maggie and me. Why do you ask?" I watched the enemy and she watched me.

Finally, Ellen shrugged. "Just curious. I—"

Just then, Hannah came down the hall. "Well, good morning." She smiled happily. Ellen smiled but said nothing.

"Hey, how'd ya sleep?" I asked and kissed her cheek.

"Wonderfully. Thanks for that fan. It saved my life," she said as she sat.

I looked at Ellen; the discussion was over. I hoped she didn't feel the need to pursue it any further.

"Good heavens, Kate, this is good. It must be this country air. I'm ravenous," Hannah exclaimed as she lavished jam on her toast. "Is this homemade?"

"Kate? Homemade?" Maggie asked and drank her coffee.

"Hey, it could be homemade," I countered playfully and munched on my bacon, "but it ain't."

Ellen ate like a bird—coffee, one piece of toast, lightly buttered with a hint of jam. I noticed Teri watching with raised eyebrows. The rest of us felt quite gluttonous.

"So, Kate, I saw you with your ax. Expecting snow?" Ellen asked.

I laughed quietly. "No. It's going to get chilly and we'll need it. On your next visit, you can bring a chain saw. I'm aching in muscles I didn't know I had," I said and flexed my shoulders.

"I noticed a scar on your neck during your dance with Maggie," Ellen said. "Were you clawed by a grizzly?" she asked and laughed.

There was silence around the table. Maggie gave me an apologetic look, which I assured her with a wink, was unnecessary.

"No, not a grizzly, Ellen. I had an accident a few years ago," I said and drank my coffee.

It came—that wave of nausea that follows whenever I'm reminded of how I nearly died at the hands of Liz Eddington. However, as I glanced at Maggie, it passed quickly, leaving in its wake only a shiver that ran down my spine.

With the morning being cloudy and cool, there wasn't much to do but wait for the storm and sit around the fire. Hannah, Maggie, and Ellen were playing cards. Teri was reading by the fire.

I decided to take a walk. Getting a cup of coffee, I walked out to the pier and looked at my lake. There was a small boat motoring away from me. I didn't recognize it, probably some fisherman using our boat launch. There was another anchored in the cove between Henry's and the three little cottages where Martin Reese was staying.

I looked up at the cloudy sky and decided that fishing was the order of the morning.

"I'm going fishing," I said as I walked into the cabin. "Who wants to join me?" I looked at the girls. Ellen smiled as if I were nuts and graciously declined, as did Maggie. Although I sensed she wanted to join me. *You wish, Ryan.*

I walked out onto the porch and looked down at Ben's. He was nowhere around. I looked at the new house that was built in my absence. I thought I saw someone outside, and it being too far, I went back to get my binoculars so I could have a look, just in case the ugly rumor was true—there are no fish in Deer Lake.

"What are you doing?" Teri asked as I walked out the door.

"Being totally like Mom—snooping."

She sprang off the couch. "Now you're talkin'. This is better than fishing, count me in."

Hannah tossed down her cards and jumped up. "Wait for me!"

I steered the boat away from the two fishermen and went toward the cove by Henry's house. The boat had vacated the cove.

"If memory serves me correctly, I almost got a huge bass here in the spring," I said confidently.

Teri grunted. "Another fish story."

While I was coaxing the fish out of the lake, we talked about the party the night before.

"What do you think, Kate?" Teri asked absently.

I scratched my head. "Honestly, Ter, I don't know. Sandy Meyers said she actually saw someone the other day before I got here. Logically, I figure whoever scoped out my cabin saw I'm not there often and tried to break in. Maybe he got spooked and took off.

"Then on Saturday, he came back and saw me, knocked me out, and he must have gotten spotted or something because nothing is missing from my house. The door was wide open. If it was him last night, maybe he dropped something, I don't know. He didn't know I was under the pier, though, I'm sure of it." I shook my head. "Too many loopholes, but it's all I can come up with."

Figuring I could multitask, I cast my line out, then picked up the binoculars. I could feel Hannah watching me.

"What are you doing?" she asked cautiously.

"What? I'm fishing and snooping."

I adjusted the glasses and focused on Sandy's house. I was shocked to see a young man walking around the back of the house.

"I think I see someone at Sandy's," I said.

I didn't recognize him. The trees were blocking me, and I couldn't get a good look at him. "Damn." I sighed and scanned around the lake. There was some guy fishing across the lake; he caught a huge bass.

"Hey, that's where we should be," I said.

"Where?" Hannah asked. "At Sandy's?"

"No, where that fisherman is. He just caught a bass."

"Kate, are we snooping or fishing?" Hannah asked.

I looked at her over the glasses. "Both."

"See anything?" Teri asked. She is much more like our mother than I am. I keep telling myself that.

"Yes," I said absently as I watched. "He's using spinner bait. Nuts, I don't have any."

"Kate, I thought there was someone at Sandy's—"

"You have a fish!" Hannah exclaimed.

I looked up to see the end of my rod bent nearly into the water. I quickly put the strap from the field glasses around my neck and dove for my rod that was quickly being pulled from the boat. As I grabbed the rod, I started to follow it out of the boat. I heard Hannah scream and Teri laugh.

It was then I felt my neck being pulled and let out a strangling grunt. Hannah had the field glasses as she pulled me back in the boat. "H-Hannah," I groaned as I was choked. "L-let g-go."

Teri was still laughing as she pulled the back of my shorts. "Hannah, you're strangling her." This would have had more impact if she were not laughing.

Hannah let go of the field glasses before I was decapitated. "Well, reel it in!" she said and slapped my back.

"It's a big one!" I exclaimed happily, as I pulled and reeled in the line.

"Don't lose it!"

With that, the line snapped and I fell back against Hannah. I sat there for a moment looking at the broken line.

"Drat," Hannah said from behind me. She lifted the field glasses, which still hung around my neck. "Shall we snoop?"

Teri was still laughing. "Check out Sandy's again."

Completely deflated, I focused on the shore and Sandy's cottage and I saw him—Martin Reese as he got out of his car. "Good morning, Martin," I whispered.

"What's he doing?" Teri strained her eyes.

"Will you two stop?" Hannah scolded in motherly fashion. "What's he doing now?"

I laughed at Hannah's sudden interest. "Not sure. Wasn't he

a surly thing last night? Good grief," I said as I watched through the field glasses.

"He was watching Teri all nigh..." I stopped abruptly and looked at Teri. I leaned to her and whispered, "Did you tell Hannah?"

"Tell me what?" Hannah asked quickly.

Teri shrugged. "Nothing really. There was just this guy in the class I took this summer. He gave me the creeps."

"Why, dear?" Hannah asked as she watched Teri.

"I don't know really. When I think about it, Ray didn't do anything, he was just creepy, ya know?" Teri looked at us.

"I know what you mean, dear," Hannah said. "When I was younger, there was a young man who followed me everywhere, from school, into town. It was annoying."

Teri and I exchanged glances. I was thinking of last fall when we first met Hannah. Her story of her neighbor's son wearing his mother's hats flashed through my mind. From Teri's grin, I knew she was thinking the same thing.

"What happened?" I asked and couldn't help but smile.

Hannah shrugged. "He followed me into the ice cream shop. I made him buy me a root beer float—never saw him again." She cocked her head to one side. "I think it was the second scoop of ice cream."

"Maybe you should have let that guy buy you a root beer float, Ter," I suggested absently as we laughed. I scanned the lake and saw Martin talking to Sandy and she grabbed his arm.

"What's this?" I asked as I watched.

"What's what?" Teri asked. "We need to get another pair. Kate, ask Ben. I bet he has binoculars."

As I watched, Martin wrenched his arm free and pointed a warning finger at her. "God, I hope that doesn't go off," I said jokingly, amused with myself.

"Kate, no more playing," Hannah scolded, but I saw her looking in Martin's direction.

"Hello..." I said as Martin Reese gently shoved Sandy Meyers. She stumbled backward, then ran out of my focal point.

As I scanned, I noticed she had gone to her car. I quickly

scanned back to Martin. He of course had a scowl on his face as he looked around the lake. He looked my way.

"Yep, I'm watching."

"Kate, will you stop? Or at least hide yourself," Hannah said.

"Good idea," Teri said and pushed me down in the seat.

"We do need another pair," Hannah said.

I crouched down. "Nope, this is too uncomfortable." I groaned and sat back on the chair. By the time I looked back, they were gone. "Fine, I lost him."

Scanning the lake, I looked at Henry's house. "Lucas Thorn is nowhere in sight," I said. "He had a big date last night. He's probably pooped. Is it my imagination or did all the men last night, save for Ben, have eyes for Sandy Meyers?" I watched the house.

"Well, I know Phil and Jackie, and I think by now we can call them Phil and Jackie," Teri laughed and continued, "I think there was some tension between them. Jackie threw a few daggers Sandy's way."

"Something was definitely going on last night. I had the oddest feeling…" Hannah started and stopped.

"What, tell me?" Teri asked.

"Well, I just had a mental picture of Sandy Meyers being Deer Lake's...let's say flirt."

"To put it mildly," I said. "Oops, Martin has binoculars. Busted, he's looking right at me." I waved at him and he waved back, both of us looking at each other through the binoculars.

"Kate," Hannah groaned. "I told you..."

"I know, I know. Well, we have to go over there. He's seen me, so let me handle it."

"Let you handle it? We'll be in jail inside an hour," Teri said.

As we approached, I noticed Martin walking down to his pier. I cut the engine, drifted toward him, and threw him the line, which he caught and pulled us to the pier.

Shamefaced, I decided to speak first. "Good morning, you caught me. I was scanning the lake and I noticed you. Sorry."

"Well, I was doin' it, too. Sorry."

He looked at me and I knew he must have been wondering what I saw. "So how's the fishing?" he asked absently.

"What fish? There are no fish in this lake," Teri grunted.

Martin smiled. I couldn't help myself. "Oh, my God, Teri. Did you see that? Mr. Reese actually smiled. That is a smile, is it not?" I looked at him and he blushed horribly.

"Don't mind the Ryan sisters, Martin," Hannah said kindly.

Once again, Martin looked at Teri. He quickly scanned her face and hair and said, "Well, I've got a few things to do. Have a nice day." He grunted an exit and walked away.

"Good grief, he's odd," I said and started back for my pier.

Maggie was waiting for us as we pulled up, so I tossed her the line and cut my engine. As she started to tie off the boat, I jumped off.

"Do you know what you're doing?" I asked stupidly.

She glared at me and I turned red for the second time in ten minutes. *Gotta be a record.*

Teri noticed it, too. "Boy, you're racking up points right and left," she said, giving me a superior grin.

Maggie was completely enthralled. "What did she do now?"

Hannah and Teri laughed as they retold my binocular blunder.

Maggie shook her head. "Are we going to have to take away your toys?"

I busied myself with the boat. "It could happen to anyone," I called to them as they walked off the pier.

But why does it always happen to me?

Chapter Eight

The remainder of the day was lazy for all concerned. It was late in the afternoon when I decided to take the boat out again—alone. I grabbed my fishing gear and the binoculars. I dropped anchor in the same spot where the lucky guy caught the big one and lazily fished for the elusive bass.

I absently glanced around my lake and the houses. I was close to the three little cabins, one of which Martin Reese occupied, but I noticed his car was gone. Then I saw Jackie Henderson come out on her pier and sit, watching the lake. She looked around and saw me. I waved and she waved back. I remembered how we could hear them arguing the previous night as they left Ben's party. I hoped it was nothing too serious. They seemed like a nice couple. I yawned lazily and continued fishing.

Phil came out onto the pier and I heard him mumbling in a low voice. Jackie shook her head, not looking at him. I tried not to stare, only stealing a glance every now and then as I cast out my line.

Then she looked up at him and said loudly, "How many times, Phil?" She stood and walked past him and up the pier. She stopped and turned back to him. "Do you think I'm blind?"

He stood there looking at her as she stormed off the pier. Then his shoulders sagged and he slowly walked to their house.

"No more," I heard her say as the screen door slammed.

"Oops. Trouble in paradise," I said. "I hope she didn't scare the fish."

Completely bored, I picked up the field glasses once again and scanned the lake. I stopped at Henry's and watched. Nothing at all. Where was Mr. Thorn?

Then I saw movement. The front door opened and he stepped out onto the porch. He stared across the lake directly at Sandy Meyers's house. He was smiling as he lit a cigarette and snapped the lighter closed. He stood there smoking and tossing the lighter in one hand.

As I watched him, he suddenly stood straight and cocked his head. Then slowly, he looked my way and looked directly at me. I was frozen. I don't know why I didn't take the glasses away. He leaned forward, narrowed his eyes, then smiled and waved. He then beckoned me over.

"Damn," I cursed. "Busted twice in one day. I'm out of practice."

I waved and quickly headed to his pier. Feeling foolish yet again, I took the same tack as I had that morning with Martin Reese.

I decided to speak first. "Good morning. I must apologize, I got these as a gift and I'm testing them out. You caught me." I laughed and so did he.

"Don't apologize. It's nice to be noticed by a curious pretty woman. But remember, Kate, curiosity killed the cat."

"Yes, but a cat has nine lives." I smiled as I challenged him. His smile faded a bit.

"Yes, but being the mere mortal, you've only got one, Miss Ryan," he countered and watched me. Mr. Thorn laughed heartily. "Kate, you should see your face."

"Okay, okay. I'm an old Irish snoop like my mother before me." I knew my face was red.

"You turn a pretty shade of red. Now I'd invite you in for coffee, but I'm on my way out. So be a little inconspicuous with those things or you'll pay the consequences, my dear." He laughed, wagged his finger at me, threw me the line, and pushed the boat away. "I'll see you later." He waved as he watched me pull away.

Six walleye later, I happily motored myself home. The ladies were all sitting by the pier waiting for me.

"Where have you been?" Teri asked anxiously.

"Fishing," I said triumphantly and held up my bounty. "Fish

fry for dinner," I said, and Ellen looked horrified. "They're dead," I reassured her, albeit sarcastically.

I noticed Maggie giving me the Winfield look as I walked past them to the shed. She was right on my heels.

"Do you have to be so sarcastic?" she asked helplessly.

"No, but sometimes I feel it's necessary," I said as I sharpened my filet knife.

"Damn it, Kate—"

"Talk about sarcastic!" I said, suddenly angry. "Swimming is good when you can't do other things," I said, mimicking Ellen.

"Why are you getting so upset?"

"I'm not upset," I countered, getting upset.

"I just don't see why you need to be sarcastic all the time."

"Me? You should talk." Now I felt like I was ten years old. "You, Dr. Winfield, are the queen of sarcasm." I tossed the filet knife on the table and turned to her. I was angry and I didn't know why.

"She wants you, ya know," I blurted out.

Maggie wasn't expecting that from me, I'm sure. *I* wasn't expecting that from me.

"What did you say?"

"You heard me. And you don't care about her?"

The accusatory tone made her left eye twitch. She said very calmly, which scared me, "You haven't explained why you were home for three weeks and never called me, and now you expect me to just answer any questions you have about my life?"

"Well, when you put it *that* way," I said and turned back to the table. "You're right. It's none of my business."

Maggie let out a very exasperated breath. "God, you're annoying when you get this attitude. And maybe Ellen does like me. She's open and honest. You know what that is, don't you? Being open with your feelings? You might try it sometime."

A little brick here, a little cement there. "There's a lot to be said for being reticent, Doctor."

"I can see why you're single. You are such a child!"

"Oh, yeah? Well, it takes one—" I started as she turned and stormed out of the shed, banging the screen door. "—to know one," I finished lamely and concentrated on dinner.

I invited Ben for dinner. He also had a catch of the day, so between the two of us, we had enough fish for an army. Of course, Ellen didn't like fried fish, so I prepared her fish the way she liked it. *Maybe that'll get Maggie smiling again.* I was spending most of the time dodging the daggers she was flinging my way.

At least Ellen ate all of it; that was something. She even complimented me, which I took gracefully with no sarcasm.

The storm still hadn't come, but the clouds were certainly settling in. We sat in the living room around the fire, trading stories about our childhood. As Ben told about his exploits in the Navy, he looked at me. "Hey I've got a pair of night vision binoculars if you ever want to borrow them." He laughed and everyone joined in.

"I will never live this down, will I?" I asked, hanging my head.

However, Teri raised her eyebrows, "Night vision?"

We laughed and joked for a while, then someone brought up pictures. So I went into my closet and pulled out the huge box of photos. The top was gone, and I couldn't remember where it was.

I brought the box out and Hannah laughed with delight. "I want to see Kate when she was a little girl," she exclaimed.

We all took turns looking at pictures, laughing and passing them around.

Ben said to me, "What were you like as a kid, Kate?"

Teri chimed in first. "Shorter. Nothing else has changed," she said affectionately and looked at Maggie. "She was as accident-prone then as she is now."

Looking through the pictures, I couldn't find the one Hannah asked for. "Teri, are you sure I have it? I can't find it."

She frowned. "I'm sure you took those after Dad died, didn't you?" Now she was uncertain.

"Damn, that's a good picture of you and me. You must have it if it's not here," I said, and Teri shrugged and agreed.

Soon, the thunder rolled in the distance and the lightning

flashed.

"Well, here's the storm," I said, still leafing through the photos.

"I think I'll head home before it hits," Ben said and stretched as he stood. "Kate, this was a marvelous time. Thank you." He kissed my cheek and whispered, "And thank you for introducing me to Hannah. She's enchanting."

He walked over to Hannah and took her hand. "Hannah Winfield, it was a pleasure. If this weather clears, you and I are going boating and swimming before you leave. No arguing." He was charming and I found myself grinning like an idiot.

"That's sounds like fun, Ben Harper. Thank you." He actually kissed her hand before he left.

"You'll never wash that hand again?" I asked with a grin.

Hannah raised an eyebrow. "Yes, I suppose I will," she said wistfully. "But what a charmer."

I was sitting by the fire when Teri came out of her bedroom, scratching her head.

"What's the matter, lose something?"

"I'm going crazy. I thought for sure I brought that yellow nightgown Mac gave me for my birthday, but I can't seem to find it. I must have forgotten it. Oh, well, I'm going to call Mac. See you in the morning, Kate."

Everyone had gone to bed as I sat on the porch in the dark, rocking in my chair, listening to Teri laugh as she talked with Mac on the phone. The night was cooler as the half moon appeared over the tree line. Its reflection beamed across the lake. I looked down and Chance was sound asleep at my feet.

It was then I heard the screen door open. Maggie stepped out onto the porch. She didn't see me at first. Half hidden by the moonlight and with her arms folded across her chest, she stared out at the lake. It struck me what a beautiful profile she had and how I never realized it before. If I were honest, I always noticed; I just never let it sink in. However, in the darkness, she looked pensive.

"Penny for your thoughts," I said, which startled her.

"I didn't see you. I thought everyone was sleeping."

Then we heard Teri chuckling. "Almost everyone. She's on the phone with Mac."

"Thank God, I was hoping she wasn't talking to herself," Maggie said, then laughed, and I joined her.

"Maggie, if there's one thing we do better than arguing, it's laughing," I said with a grin as I rocked back and forth.

She looked out at the lake. "I'm sorry for this afternoon. I shouldn't have made that crack about you being single."

"Forget it. I deserved it."

"I can see why you like it up here, although you spend too much time here alone. It's a beautiful lake, smooth as glass tonight."

"Would you like to take the canoe out? It's a calm night and the stars are amazing from the lake. C'mon, I don't know when we'll get the chance again. It really is beautiful," I enticed her.

For a moment, we looked at each other in the darkness. "Okay, but just for a little while and none of your childish pranks. Sometimes I don't entirely trust you, Kate Ryan."

"Great, let's go!" I sprang from my chair and grabbed her hand. Maggie giggled along as we ran down to the shore.

I paddled the canoe away from the pier and stopped. "Don't want to get too far out, I don't have any night lights."

Maggie swiveled around to face me, then looked up at the starry night. "This is heaven." She sighed and I followed her gaze and agreed.

"I love it up here. I feel sa—" I stopped myself and felt Maggie watching me.

"Safe?" she whispered, and I just nodded. "I don't blame you. After what you've been through, anyone would need a place like this."

I looked out into the darkness in silence. Once again, the diminutive doctor was in my head and it unnerved me, yet it comforted me at the same time.

"I wasn't always so hidden," I found myself whispering. I took a deep breath and looked up at the moon. "You've helped me so much, Maggie. I thank God for the day I knocked you off your horse," I said with a grin and looked at her.

She laughed and the dimples started. "Well, I could think of a less painful way for us to meet, but I agree with you. I wouldn't change a thing."

"Neither would I." I looked up into the sky. "Plenty of stars tonight."

Maggie looked up, as well. "There are so many, you can't tell which constellation is which."

"Sure ya can," I said and pointed to Orion. "See right there that's Orion the Hunter. See those three stars? That's his belt."

Maggie turned and followed my instructions. "No. I can't see it," she said, her voice full of disappointment.

"Wait," I said and scooted forward. I knelt behind her in the canoe, careful not to tip us over. I put my hand on her shoulder, ignoring the scent of her perfume, and pointed again. "There," I whispered. "Can you see it now?"

Maggie leaned her body back against mine and looked up. "Almost."

My heart was hammering in my chest as I felt her warm body against mine. I shivered in the humid night air. "Well, see those stars make up the archer's bow and..." I whispered and stopped.

"I see it now. It's beautiful," she whispered and looked at me.

Our faces were inches apart. "Yes, that's the right word," I said in a shaky voice as I looked into her eyes.

For a moment, we said nothing. Then we heard the water splash lightly by the canoe. I looked over and saw two loons lazily swimming by the canoe. "Maggie, look," I whispered.

"I'm looking," she replied in kind, still watching me.

I grinned and nudged her. "The loons."

Maggie laughed and followed my gaze. The two loons quickly dove under the surface and were gone.

"They'll probably come up for air in Canada," I said and Maggie laughed again.

"Why don't you sit? You've got to be uncomfortable."

So I clumsily switched positions and sat back. I saw her frowning glance as she turned around once again to face me.

"That's not exactly what I had in mind," she said dryly.

God, Ryan, you're an idiot. "Oh, I—"

The soft wail of the loons echoed over the lake, interrupting my sterling comeback. We both looked in the direction and listened.

"It's haunting but beautiful," she whispered.

"Some mate for life, ya know," I blurted out, and I could feel the doctor grinning.

"Really? That's interesting. Why only some?" she asked and leaned forward.

"W-well, mostly they're more faithful to the nesting area than the mate. If they don't come back after the winter, then they'll find another…"

"And if the mate comes back?" she asked in that damnable soft voice.

I looked at her then. "Then I guess she's one lucky loon and realizes what a gift she's been given and never lets her go." *We're talking about loons, right?*

Maggie leaned forward, reached out, and touched my knee. The electric feeling shot right to my…

"Ya gotta love the lucky loon," she said dryly, and I laughed aloud. Maggie joined me and soon we were laughing and rocking the canoe.

"Am I interrupting something?"

We both stopped immediately and looked back at the pier. There stood Ellen with a small flashlight, shining it right on us.

"That's twice now, and as a matter of fact—" I started seriously.

"We were talking about loons," Maggie said.

Ellen looked from me to Maggie, who said nothing, but I could feel her watching me.

I made no move to paddle back to the pier. I remembered Hannah's words…and Vito's. I watched Ellen as she smiled slightly. "I was just worried when I woke and—"

"She's fine. She's with me," I said evenly as I continued to watch her.

"Well then, I'll leave you to talk about the common loon," she said and looked at Maggie. "Good night."

"Good night, Ellen," Maggie called after her. She then turned her attention to me.

"What?" I asked as I paddled back to shore.

"She's fine? She's with me?" Maggie repeated.

I hid my impish grin. "You *are* fine, and you *are* with me."

"Am I really?" she asked with a grin.

I didn't answer, but I believed I grunted something inane as I paddled to shore. Maggie hopped out. I followed and pulled the canoe up on the beach. I felt her standing close; she was looking up at the sky.

"Thanks for the loon lesson," she said, then closed her eyes.

"You're welcome," I replied. "What are you doing?"

She held her hand up as if to silence me, which it did. I waited for a moment until she grinned and opened her eyes. "Making a wish like Mary Hatch, hoping George Bailey understands," she said. Her blue eyes searched my face.

I grinned and looked up at the moon. "Using my love of old movies against me, Dr. Winfield?"

I heard the soft laughter. "I'll use any and all means, Miss Ryan."

I looked down into her eyes. Maggie reached up and gently caressed my cheek. I swallowed so hard she had to hear the gulp that stuck in my throat.

"Good night," she whispered. She looked at my lips, then lightly ran her thumb across them.

My heart was pounding and I shivered once again. When I could finally find my voice, I whispered, "Good night, Maggie."

For a moment, we looked at each other. Then Maggie grinned wildly. "What a horrible waste of moonlight." She patted my cheek and headed up the beach. I watched her as she walked into the cabin.

What a fool, Ryan. Maggie was right; you wasted a perfect opportunity. I ran my fingers through my hair. The loons started their wailing again.

"Oh, shut up," I grumbled and secured the canoe.

Chapter Nine

It was an uneventful Monday afternoon. I knew Ellen was leaving, and I felt a pang of emptiness at the thought of Maggie going with her. When Maggie walked downstairs with her luggage, my heart sank.

I avoided Hannah's challenging glance. Maggie walked up to her and kissed her cheek. "Have a nice week, Aunt Hannah."

"I will, dear," Hannah replied. "Ellen, it was nice seeing you again. Take care of my niece."

I immediately frowned when I heard the familiarity in Hannah's voice for the enemy and shoved my hands into my pockets. I carefully watched Ellen.

She put her hand on Maggie's shoulder. "Oh, I will, Hannah."

"I'll bet," I mumbled under my breath and leaned against the stone fireplace.

Teri stood there and watched the entire mess with a slight grin. She then kissed Maggie and gave her a hug. "Take care. Call me when you get home."

"I will," Maggie said with a grin and picked up her bag. She looked at me. "Thanks, Kate. I had a great time. Tell the loons I said goodbye."

"You speak their language?" Ellen asked me over her shoulder as she walked out.

Everyone laughed at the *hysterical* joke. *She missed her calling; she should be on stage.* I said nothing as I followed them out to Ellen's car and helped put their luggage in the trunk.

Ellen was in the car. "Sorry, Maggie, but we have to get going," she called out.

I glared in her direction. Maggie turned to me. "Well, I guess I should go."

"You don't have to," I said and kicked at the tire.

With that, Ellen started the car, the engine groaned and died. I raised an eyebrow and grinned childishly.

"What's wrong?" Maggie asked and avoided my grin.

"Do I *look* like a mechanic?" Ellen replied, and I heard the aggravation in her voice. She pumped the gas pedal and tried it again. The engine groaned again, as if begging her to stop.

I glanced at the angry look Ellen got from Dr. Winfield and bit my lip. Ellen angrily put her foot to the gas pedal.

I cleared my throat. "Um, Ellen, I think if you keep doing that you'll—"

Ellen ignored me and pumped her foot as she tried the engine again. It groaned and wheezed until it quietly died. Nothing, just the click, click of the dead battery.

"—kill the battery," I whispered to myself.

You could cut the tension with a hacksaw. I felt better—childish, I know, but better.

"Well, *I'm* no mechanic," Maggie started. The sarcasm seemed to ooze from her very soul, "but I think the battery's dead."

I heard the terse tone in her voice and quickly scooted out of her way, as she whirled around. "I'll be inside, Mr. Goodwrench," she said over her shoulder and stormed inside.

I winced as the screen door slammed. Ellen sighed and slowly got out of the car. "Do you know of a mechanic in Deer Lake?" She wiped the sweat from her brow.

"I'll get the phone book." I suddenly felt bad for her. "C'mon, you need a beer."

As Ellen leafed through the small phone book, I set the icy bottle of beer in front of her. Ellen looked up. "Thanks," she said with an exasperated sigh.

I didn't want to stand there and watch the poor woman, so I wandered out to the living room and saw Maggie sitting on the porch with Hannah and Teri.

The late afternoon was humid once again, so I took the time to try to piece together the weekend's events. I still couldn't imagine why someone wanted to break into my cabin. No one else on the lake was having problems. Trying not to be paranoid, I fought the feeling that this was definitely personal. I remembered Sandy Meyers telling me that she had seen someone at my cabin.

I grabbed my keys. I hoped that she'd be home and I could ask her a few questions. Maybe she had some inkling, something I could go on. As I headed out, Maggie walked in, nearly knocking me over. "Wanna try a Texas two step this time?" I asked with a grin.

Maggie chuckled. "Where are you going?"

"To Sandy Meyers's. She said she saw someone by my cabin. I thought I'd just ask her a few questions."

"Want some company?" she asked and didn't wait for my reply as she headed outside.

"Sure," I called after her.

The drive around the lake was a short one as I turned down Sandy's entrance road. We were in luck; her car was there. Maggie and I walked up to the back porch and knocked on the old screened door. When no one answered, I gave the door a firmer knock. I waited an appropriate amount of time, which for me was a nanosecond, then decided to walk around to the front.

"Maybe she's gone home," Maggie suggested.

"Her car is still here," I said as I knocked.

Still no one came to the door. I casually walked around her property. "She's probably out for the afternoon and evening with someone," I said with a shrug.

As Maggie and I started back to my Jeep, I glanced in the window and was surprised to see a chair overturned in the living room.

Maggie looked, as well. "That doesn't look good," she said, and I had to agree.

With my curiosity piqued, we walked onto the porch. I gently tried the door. It was locked, as was the back. *Curious,* I thought, and looked around the woods.

"Wouldn't you think if she knocked over a chair, she'd pick it up?" I asked.

Maggie nodded. "What are you thinking?"

"I'm thinking I don't like this," I said as we walked back to the car. "I don't like this at all."

"Goddamn it, she's nosy," he said as he watched her pull away. Sighing, he stooped and picked up his heavy bundle. "Christ, should it be this much trouble?" Then he faded once again into the woods. He would have to be more careful.

However, time was on his side. Soon nothing would matter; she'd come back once again.

Ellen apparently found a mechanic who had replaced the battery. He was just finishing up when Maggie and I returned.

"We can leave now, Maggie," Ellen said.

Maggie glanced at Hannah. "Ellen, there's something going on here. I don't like leaving Aunt Hannah."

Ellen avoided me completely. "Can we talk about this privately?"

Teri and Hannah quickly started for the kitchen. Hannah grabbed the back of my shirt and pulled me along. It was pointless; we could still hear their conversation.

"I made this appointment, Maggie, and I have to keep it," Ellen said calmly. I heard the irritation in her voice.

"I understand," Maggie replied.

"I need to get going. We planned on the weekend, and that's all. Are you coming with me?"

There was silence and I glanced at Teri and Hannah. I handed Teri a bottle of beer and poured a glass of lemonade for Hannah, who took the beer out of Teri's hand and took a healthy drink. Teri looked at me, chuckled, and took the lemonade.

I heard the calm resolution in Maggie's voice. "As I said, I have a bad feeling here, Ellen. I think I should stay with Aunt Hannah."

"All right. Why don't you call me when you get back?" Ellen said.

I looked up to see Ellen standing in the doorway. "*I* am going to be leaving, Kate. Thanks for the weekend. It was nice to meet you, Teri. Hannah, I hope to see you again soon."

She turned and walked away as we all opened our mouths to reply. I glanced at Hannah, who grinned childishly.

Ben invited Hannah over for dinner. She happily accepted, which left Teri, Maggie, and me to go to Sutter's for dinner.

Sutter's was packed, and as we walked in, I immediately shivered. Maggie laughed. "Did someone walk over your grave?"

"No, you morbid thing. I just had a feeling. I dunno," I said and looked at Teri who was watching me. "What, Teri?"

This time, Maggie saw Teri's gaze. "What's wrong?" Maggie asked.

Teri shook her head in confusion. "I don't know, something odd," she said and gazed around the crowded bar. *I hate it when she does that.*

I looked around the bar and caught a woman standing in the crowd, looking at me. It was a fleeting glance, then she was lost in the crowd. But her eyes…

"What is it?" Maggie asked.

I laughed and scratched my head. "I don't know. I need a beer."

Waiting for our table, we sat at the bar. I noticed Ed Samson sitting at his usual spot. He grinned when we sat at his end of the bar.

"Kate. How's the cabin?" he asked as we ordered drinks.

"Coming along just fine, Ed. Hey, you remember my sister, Teri. And this is Maggie, a very good friend of mine."

Ed leaned across and shook Maggie's hand. "Are you the doctor Kate is constantly yammering about?"

I felt my eyes bug out and I looked at him.

"What? Wrong girl?"

"No, I'm the right girl," Maggie said with a smug grin. "Dr. Winfield," she said and shook his hand.

I know I blushed horribly as I glanced at Teri who only smiled innocently.

"Good, then when she comes in here all banged up, *you* can do the first aid," Fran said. She and Ed laughed as I glowered at them.

"Banged up?" Maggie asked and leaned forward. So did Ed.

"When Kate first started building, she'd come in here all dirty and sweaty and either bleeding or scratched. We got to the point that when we saw her pull up in that Jeep, we'd place our bets as to what happened," he said, still laughing.

I drank my beer and ate from the peanut bowl. Nothing had changed in two years.

"I've won the most," Ed said proudly, "although Henry is a close second."

"Hey, I'm up there, too," Fran protested as she cleaned the bar.

Maggie and Teri laughed along, each sharing stories of my klutziness. By now, the peanut bowl was empty. I was on my second beer when Ed brought up the story about the…

"Raccoon," Ed said, and Fran laughed heartily.

I hung my head and felt Maggie lightly pat my shoulder. She then bought Ed a beer as if urging him to go on with the story while Fran replenished the peanut bowl.

"Tell me all about it, Ed," Maggie said in a solemn voice.

"Well, it seems Kate had a visitor in her loft right after the cabin was finished," Ed started and looked at me. "Ya don't mind me telling this story, do ya?"

"As if it would matter," I said seriously.

Ed laughed and continued, "Anyway, Kate figured that she didn't want to go into the loft, which was a good idea, so she thought she'd entice the critter out through the window. She got it with—what was it again?" Ed asked, knowing full well what it was.

I glared at him. "Leftover barbequed chicken."

Teri had heard my story before, but Maggie was completely enthralled. She gave me an odd look. "Leftover chicken?"

Ed was still laughing. "So there was Kate on a ladder, holding the chicken, which she warmed up…"

Maggie glanced at me and raised an eyebrow in question.

"So the raccoon could smell it," I said, as if it wasn't obvious. For some reason, I felt the need to explain further. "He'd smell the barbeque sauce and come out."

"I see," Maggie said, sounding like my hospital psychiatrist. "Continue, Ed."

"Anyway, it worked. This raccoon was huge, by the way," he said.

I nodded emphatically to Maggie. "Enormous."

"The raccoon waddled out onto the window ledge. Kate had the barbequed chicken dangling from a rope, and as the critter reached for it, Kate swatted at it with a golf club."

Maggie gave me an inquisitive smirk.

I hid my grin. "A five iron."

"Good choice," Maggie concurred. "So what happened? That cannot be the end of this story."

"Why not?" I asked indignantly. I looked at Teri who was now eating the peanuts. She wasn't about to enter this conversation. Over the years, she had witnessed far too much.

"Because I know you, Kate. Now what happened?" Maggie asked as she dipped into the peanut bowl.

We're never gonna eat dinner.

Ed looked at me and I shrugged. "Oh, tell her."

"Kate opened the window and the raccoon came out as planned, but not before Kate broke it with the golf club. Glass went flying. She lost her balance and dropped the chicken while she nearly fell off the ladder. She was holding on for dear life as our little friend, unscathed by the way, grabbed the chicken and dashed off into the woods. Thank God I was there to save her."

"Save me? You nearly let me fall, you were laughing so hard," I said seriously. "I could've broken my neck and all you could do was laugh like a fool."

Ed started laughing, as if remembering the whole incident again. Maggie laughed along with him and Fran.

"Ed, I think you and I will be great friends," Maggie said and lifted her beer.

"Oh, no you won't. You're never coming back up here again," I advised them both. "And it worked. I got the raccoon out of my cabin. You should have seen what that little beast did to my loft."

When their laughter finally died down, I noticed Martin Reese had entered the bar and was sitting in the corner. I leaned over the bar. "Fran, see that guy at the end of the bar? Buy him a drink for me, would you?"

She raised an eyebrow. "A little young for you, isn't he? And the wrong sex?"

I glared at her. "Just buy him the drink."

Fran set the beer in front of Martin, then looked over at me. He looked and smiled grudgingly, then he did what I hoped—he felt as though he should make an appearance and came over to us.

"Good evening, Mr. Reese," I said cordially, and he smiled.

"Hi. Thanks for the beer," he said and stood there awkwardly.

"Have a seat." I pulled out a chair.

He sat and said hello to Maggie. "Evening, ma'am," he said to Teri.

"Ma'am?" she asked and gave him a wary glance. I saw her looking him over, then she smiled. "You're a Marine, aren't you?"

Maggie and I were shocked when Martin blushed and nodded. "Yes, ma'am."

"I knew it," she said triumphantly and looked at me. "Your detective skills are rubbing off on me."

I gave her a warning look, and she returned it with a sick smile. It's not that I don't want anyone knowing about my now-defunct private investigation business. However, with these weird things going on, I'd prefer it were kept under wraps.

"Another Marine?" I asked and saw the confused look on Martin's face.

"My husband was a Marine. Well, he's retired. He's waiting for his orders," Teri said affectionately. "So I can spot one a mile away."

For the first time, Martin seemed at ease, as much as he could, anyway. He and Teri talked for a while. Maggie was giving me her opinion on Ellen. Sitting in the middle, I tried to listen to both conversations.

From what I gathered, Ellen's Marine basic training was in Quantico, Virginia, and Martin was a materialistic snob. I shook my head to clear the cobwebs.

I had an enormous headache and grabbed Fran. "Please get us a table," I begged, and she laughed.

"Twenty minutes." She slid another beer in front of me as I listened to Martin Reese.

"I was overseas for eighteen months, two weeks, and three days—"

"But who's counting?" I asked with a grin.

Martin nodded. "I'm on leave. I have two more weeks, then I report to San Diego."

"So will you have time to visit family before you go?" I asked, watching him.

He looked at his beer. "I don't have much family, Miss Ryan. So I decided to take it easy while on leave." He looked as though his thoughts were far away.

"How did you find out about my little piece of heaven?" I asked, breaking his thoughts.

He hesitated as if caught off-guard and answered too quickly. "Brochures, ya know, that sort of thing. Looked like a quiet lake." He shrugged and I watched him curiously. He didn't seem quite certain how he found out about it. It would be easy enough to corroborate. I'm sure the real estate office in town would know. Maybe the next day I'd go and talk to Jane, who sold me my property. If anyone would know, she would.

Finally, we got a table. Dinner was wonderful and the conversation was enjoyable. I found that we could talk about something other than what was happening on Deer Lake as we laughed and enjoyed the evening. So did Martin Reese, in his brooding way because shortly afterward, he excused himself and left.

"So what did you find out about Mr. Reese?" I asked as I drank my coffee.

Teri said with a grin, "Sergeant Reese to you, and not much. He was stationed in Japan for two years, got back ten days ago. He seemed preoccupied, though. Something…"

"What, Teri, what are you thinking?" Maggie asked slowly.

She shrugged. "I don't know. He unnerved me, that's the only word I can think of. He looked as though he was always thinking something else...you know? He looked through me, not at me," she said seriously and drank her coffee.

"Do you think he's up to something?" Maggie asked.

"I've been on this lake for four years, no problems. Now I have a prowler, and I'm knocked on the head. Mr. Reese has been here for about a week or so. Maybe he's up to something, maybe not. However, I will find out," I said with determination.

"Our little bloodhound, equipped with binoculars. Batteries not included."

Both women laughed—I ignored them.

Chapter Ten

After dinner, I decided a little early evening fishing was in order, so I gathered my trusty rod and reel. As I sat on the small bench on my pier, I heard the romantic music of Glenn Miller's "Moonlight Serenade" coming from Ben's cottage. It was just loud enough to hear, and as I listened, I smiled as I remembered my parents. When my father took my mother in his arms, you'd have to be blind not to see how much they loved each other. I remembered my mom saying that dancing was the most intimate thing you could do—with your clothes on. I smiled at the memory as I tied the lure onto my line. We grew up on music from the forties, and I loved it. "God, I'm showing my age," I said wistfully.

As Ben romanced Hannah, as I was sure he was doing, I thought of the line from a Shelley poem, "Nothing in the world is single."

"Then what the hell am I doing on this pier alone?" I asked stupidly. *It's the way things turn out.* After Liz almost killed Bob and me, I guess I'm afraid of sticking my neck out again, even figuratively. "Shelley was a brooding sap," I said and cast out my line.

Across the lake, I heard Jackie arguing with Phil, who was probably wishing he were something in the world that was single. I shook my head sadly. Somehow, you're not supposed to be listening to the romantic sounds of Glen Miller while arguing. I do believe there's a law prohibiting that.

As Nat King Cole's voice started with "The Very Thought of You," Jackie's very thought was to slam the screen door and go inside. I saw Phil standing on his pier, then he hopped in his boat. As the motor started, completely disrupting the quiet, he sped through the lake, then out of sight toward the cove.

While I concentrated on my fishing, I heard Hannah and Ben laughing; it echoed over the lake. Now this would be nice, a little vacation romance, I thought happily, and reeled in my line.

As I listened to Nat singing, *I see your face in every flower, your eyes in stars above,* I thought of Maggie and our loon lesson the other night. The grin spread across my face; I couldn't stop it if I tried.

"Still fishing?" Maggie asked as she walked up the pier.

I looked up and smiled. "Have a seat. There's a huge bass in this lake I've been trying to nab for two years." I cast my line one more time.

Maggie sat next to me on the bench. "Why don't you try barbequed chicken?" she asked seriously.

I continued to concentrate on my line. "I'm never going to hear the end of that, am I?"

"No, not for a while, I'm afraid."

We sat for a few minutes, staring at the calm lake, listening to the loons.

"Sorry about Ellen," I said as I looked out over the lake. Though she was the enemy, Ellen was still Maggie's friend.

"Thanks. I probably should have gone with her." She sighed and leaned back.

"Why didn't you?"

"B-because of Aunt Hannah. I just didn't feel right leaving her," she said in an unconvincing voice.

"Just Hannah?" I asked with a shrug. My fishing rod became very interesting.

When Maggie said nothing for a moment, I glanced up to see her watching the lake. "Okay," she said with a deep sigh and continued, "One of us has to be honest."

My stomach instantly knotted. *Do we have to?*

"No, not just because of Aunt Hannah. Kate Ryan, left to your own devices, you'd run like those mustangs of yours."

I glanced at her. "Maggie I—"

She put her hand up. "Let me finish. When we were in Ireland and you told me about Liz, I could see the weight of it lifted from your shoulders. I know it'll take time for you, truly, I do. I'll wait for you, but you have to meet me somewhere in the middle. You worried about me dating Ellen?"

"Yes, and I wouldn't blame you if you did. I'm such a—" I stopped short.

All of the sudden, I felt inadequate. In the next second, I was angry. I couldn't recall ever being this angry.

"Kate," Maggie said in a calm voice and reached for my arm.

I stood and reeled in my line so fast the lure flew out of the water and got hooked on the pier. "Damn it," I hissed and yanked the rod, trying to dislodge the lure. I was so angry and didn't know why, so I took it out on my fishing rod.

"Kate," Maggie quietly insisted. "You're going to give yourself a stroke."

I stopped yanking on the rod long enough to give her a helpless look. "Oh, no, *that* happens every time I look into your eyes," I assured her, then continued with my tirade. I yanked and pulled on the helpless fishing rod. That lure was really stuck.

"It does?" I think I heard the incredulous soft tone in Maggie's voice, but I was too intent with the irrational anger I had for my fishing rod.

"I'm pathetic, Maggie," I said with a low growl as I struggled. It never occurred to me to cut the line—that would've been far too easy. "I don't want you to be with anyone else," I continued, angrily and loudly, "but I'm too fricking petrified to make sure that doesn't happen!"

Then as the gods wiped the tears of laughter from their eyes, I pulled on the rod so hard, the line snapped and I went reeling backward. The fishing pole flew over my head and landed with a solid *plop* in the lake behind me. I heard Maggie call out and grab my arm. We both staggered backward and fell onto the bench with a resounding thud.

We sat there for a moment in silence. I was breathing like a bull and staring at the treacherous lure that was *still* lodged in the wooden pier. I didn't even want to look at Maggie. "Okay," I said while I gasped for air, "I'm a raving lunatic."

Maggie laughed and I reluctantly joined her. She reached over and placed her hand on my forearm. "I hope that wasn't an expensive rod."

I reached over and took her hand in mine as we stared out at the calm, peaceful lake. In the background, Nat King Cole sang "When I Fall in Love." This was Hannah's doing, I'm sure. The soft strings started and I took a deep breath. I glanced over at Maggie who had tears in her eyes.

"What's wrong?" I asked. I tried to swallow—impossible.

"Nothing, actually. Right now, I am completely content," she said wistfully and looked at me. She blinked, her tears fell, and I felt a physical pang deep in my chest.

Our eyes met as we listened to the soft music echoing over the lake.

Or I'll never fall in love...

"Maggie, if—" I stopped. What was I going to say? If things were different? If I wasn't such an idiot? And do what? *Take a chance on an emotionally detached fool like you, Ryan? Why don't you just ask her to throw her life away, you selfish idiot?*

"Kate, you're thinking far too much," Maggie said. Once again, she was in my head.

When I give my heart, it will be completely, or I'll never give my heart...

She stood, and as I looked up, she opened her arms. Without a word, I stood and gently took her into my arms. I felt her body tremble, or maybe it was mine, as we slowly danced in the confines of the small pier.

As the evening breeze blew, I closed my eyes—lost in her embrace, lost in her kindness and compassion. I felt her hand caressing the back of my neck, lightly tracing the scar; I tensed for an instant.

"It's all right," she whispered against my cheek. "I'm right here, and nothing will ever happen to you."

I swallowed the lonely sob that stuck in my throat and held onto her as if she were a lifeline; perhaps she was. Maggie held me so incredibly close I swear I could hear her heart pounding. *Who am I kidding? It was mine.*

I pulled back, looked down into her blue sparkling eyes, and watched as she swallowed convulsively and lightly licked her lips.

"What are you thinking?" she whispered.

I felt her hand lightly caress the back of my neck as she looked up and searched my face.

"I'm gonna kiss you, Maggie," I said in a coarse voice. It sounded like a threat. *God, Ryan, how romantic.*

"And I'm gonna let you," she whispered, and I heard her voice tremble.

I gently pulled her closer once again and held one hundred ten pounds of trembling doctor in my arms, amazed at how perfectly she fit against my body. What was she thinking? I had no idea, but there she was, looking up at me with a comical look of astonishment.

I grinned slightly. So did Maggie as she slipped her hand behind my neck and caressed the scarred area again.

As I lowered my head, I hesitated for a moment. I don't know why, probably to give her one last chance to run off the pier and back to Chicago. Maggie seemed to feel my hesitation because she gently pulled me down to her.

"Kiss me, Maggie," I whispered. I could feel her warm sweet breath against my lips. "Just one kiss."

I closed my eyes and kissed Maggie Winfield. My heart nearly leapt out of my chest. I couldn't swallow…I couldn't breathe…I couldn't do a thing but kiss Maggie—this woman who cared for me as no one ever had. Her lips were incredibly soft and warm. I have no idea how long that kiss lasted when Maggie gently pushed me away and gulped for air.

I was breathing heavily, my lips feeling wonderfully bruised, and I know I was grinning. Maggie had her hand against my shoulder, seemingly holding me at bay. She had a bewildered look on her face. "Good Christ, Kate," she whispered in a ragged voice.

Uh-oh. "What's wrong?" I asked, trying to find some moisture in my mouth. "I—should I not have—"

Maggie placed her fingertips against my lips. "Shh, no, you

should. You—God, Kate, kiss me again, please."

Hearing the soft plea in her voice sent my heart pounding. Listening to those damned violins didn't help, either. I pulled her so close I thought I'd snap a rib as I kissed her once again.

When I felt her warm lips leave mine, I looked down into her eyes. It was as if I had looked into those blue eyes for the first time. I was sick to my stomach. "Hey, Maggie," I whispered. I know she heard the quiet amazement in my voice.

She grinned, the dimples cutting deep lines into her cheeks. "Yes, I agree," she whispered and gently caressed my cheek.

And the moment I can feel that you feel that way too is when I fall in love...

"That's when I'll fall, Kate," she whispered and pulled back.

I looked down into her smiling eyes. "Maggie—" I stopped. The old fear would not let go; perhaps I wouldn't let it. I still felt safe in my pain. "It's unfair of me to ask you to wait—"

"*Are* you asking?"

"I, um…"

"Because if you'd ask me, I would," she said quickly. I heard the hopeful tone in her voice and my heart ached at the possibility. "If you'd ask," she whispered and ran her fingers through my hair—a ritual I looked forward to now. "Thanks for the dance. I'm not sure I'll listen to that song the same way from now on." She grinned, and with a wink, she walked up the pier.

"Kate, there are no fish in this lake," Ben said as he and Hannah walked up.

Maggie kissed her aunt on the cheek. "Thank you, Aunt Hannah," I heard her say and she walked away.

"I'm glad Margaret is here," Hannah said.

I watched Maggie as she walked off the pier and up to the cabin. "I am, too," I said calmly, but my heart was still racing and my lips still tingled. "I wouldn't feel right if there was a mystery to solve and she wasn't here," I said almost to myself.

We turned and walked up the pier toward the cabin. Hannah glanced my way and said absently, "I didn't trust that Ellen. I don't know why, but she's gone now."

The happy tone in her voice was unmistakable. "Vito, you

don't think anyone is good enough for your niece."

She laughed outright and slipped her arm in mine. "Oh, I don't know. I have hope for you," she said with a smile.

She stopped and we faced each other. Ben slapped my back and walked up to his cabin.

"Nat King Cole was your idea, wasn't it?" I asked in a stern voice.

She gave me an innocent, shocked look but said nothing. I looked down at her and grinned slightly. "You're a hopeless romantic, Hannah Winfield, and I love you."

"I am a romantic, and I believe you are, as well, or more accurately, you used to be. You're afraid of romance now, but I see the way you look at Margaret. I see the way she looks at you." She smiled and reached up to place her small hand on my cheek. "Now tell me what put that grin on my niece's face. A grin, I might add, I have never seen before."

I closed my eyes and winced. "I kissed her."

"You did? I missed it," she said, and I heard the disappointment in her voice. "But how wonderful!"

I opened my eyes and looked down at this little woman. Visions of Maggie thirty years from now flashed through my mind. "It's all your fault. All your talk of Vito and enemies and mattresses." I ran my fingers through my hair. It then dawned on me. "Oh, God, Hannah, I *kissed* Maggie."

"I know! And I'm so happy for both of you." She pulled me down and kissed me on both cheeks…twice.

I pulled back and knew I had an incredulous look on my face. From Hannah's reaction, I knew she saw it, as well. "What's wrong, dear?"

"I'll tell you what's wrong, Mama Corleone," I replied sternly and ignored her laughter. *This woman was insane.* "Now what?"

Hannah waved me off and slipped her arm in mine. "Oh, don't be such a worry wart." She giggled liked a little kid. "But now you *will* have to do more than grunt."

My stomach knotted again as I stared down into the calm lake. Hannah gently pulled me along. "No, darling, you can't jump."

Chapter Eleven

Later that night, I sat on the front porch listening to the crickets chirping. It got very annoying. I couldn't think of Maggie anymore or the image of her alone in the loft…in bed. I wanted to kiss her good night as she walked down the hall, but instead, I stood there and gave her a short wave. Trying to ignore my idiocy, I ventured out into the kitchen—rocky road was calling me. I looked into the freezer, pushing the unwanted healthy food out of the way.

"Ah!" I exclaimed. I grabbed a spoon and sat at the kitchen table. I was about to have a spoonful when I heard the stairs to the loft creaking. I shook my head and fondly gazed at the ice cream in the carton.

I looked up to see Maggie standing there in a white tank top and shorts and barefoot. *Hmm.*

"I can't sleep," she said and spied the ice cream. Her eyes widened and she grinned. "Is that rocky road?" She quickly sat across from me.

"No, you won't like this, Maggie," I said and looked into the blue pleading eyes. "Are you pouting?"

"Yes. For rocky road, I'd—"

"Ah, ah." I wagged the spoon, then handed it to her. She gleefully accepted and dug in. I retrieved another spoon, hoping there would be some remaining upon my return.

"This is orgasmic," she exclaimed with a mouthful.

I laughed. "It's been so long I wouldn't know," I blurted out. *What in the hell made me say* that? I quickly dug in, as well, both of us eating out of the carton.

After a moment of me thinking about kissing her—again, I felt her watching me. "It's been a rough time back for you, hasn't it, Kate?" she asked.

Visions of that night once again flashed through my mind like a never-ending horror movie. *I don't want to think about it, goddamn it. I want to push it so far back in my mind that...*

"Kate?"

I looked up into the soft blue eyes filled with concern. I don't know if my heart was racing from that look, the terror I was trying to forget, or the sugar buzz from the rocky road. "I'm fine, Maggie. It was tough for a time, I'll admit, but I just don't want to talk about it." I dug my spoon into the ice cream carton and my heels into my stubbornness.

"Okay, we don't have to talk if—"

"I just want to forget it."

Maggie nodded. "I understand, and I—"

"When I think of how easily I was taken in. She didn't care about me. Shit, she was nuts!" I exclaimed and ate a spoonful. "I don't wanna talk about it."

"That's fine—"

"I mean, I was nearly decapitated, Maggie. Bob nearly had his leg blown off." I took a deep breath. "I can't get over the visions in my head sometimes. They wake me up in the middle of the night. I'm in a pool of sweat and feel like I've just run a marathon," I said and laughed. "Without any rocky road at the end."

"I have noticed the anxiety attacks are less frequent, though," Maggie reminded me as she ate the ice cream.

I shrugged in agreement and gave her a stern look. "You just got me to talk about this, didn't you?"

She smiled and shrugged. "Inadvertently. Sometimes you need a nudge, ya noodge."

"Hmm," I grunted and took another spoonful, then sat back. "I'm done. Have at it, Dr. Winfield."

Maggie happily took the carton and started to stir the ice cream with the spoon. I gave her a curious look as I watched. "What are you doing?"

She looked up and sported a look of pure delight. You know how you read those sappy romance books and they say, "It took my breath away"? Well, the look on Maggie's adorable face did just that. I caught my breath and said nothing.

"Be quiet. This is a fond childhood memory," she said and laughed.

I joined her as I rested my chin on my hand. "Now what?" I asked, completely fascinated.

"Now this," she said and drank right from the carton. When she was finished, she licked her lips and grinned. "Ahh, just like a milkshake."

"Why don't you just make a milkshake?" I handed her a napkin. "You, um, have a mustache, Dr. Goofball."

"I do?" she asked and leaned forward. She did not take the napkin as she smiled slightly.

I leaned forward and lightly wiped her lips with the napkin all the while my heart was racing. "You just want me to kiss you again." I tried to control my shaking hand.

"I do not," she countered with a nervous chuckle and pulled back. I was grateful I saw her hands shaking, as well.

I laughed and picked up the empty carton. "You do, too, you ice cream-drinking demon." I tossed the carton in the trash.

She laughed that damnable contagious laugh, and once again, I joined her. We quickly grew silent. I glanced at Maggie, who seemed deep in thought. I really wanted to know what she was thinking but was too damned afraid to ask. I was thinking of the kiss. *Oh, God, did I make a fool out of myself?*

"I thoroughly enjoyed it, Kate."

I looked into her smiling blue eyes and grinned. "Ya did?"

Maggie nodded happily and blushed. "And if it happened again, I wouldn't mind it at all."

"Ya wouldn't?" I felt my heart racing once again. For the first time, Maggie blushed like a teenager. I was amazed at how I found that so endearing.

"Well, I'm going to bed," she said and stood. I noticed her hands still shaking.

I stood, as well, and followed her out of the kitchen and down the hall. "Well, g-good night," she said and ran her fingers through her hair in an adorable, nervous gesture.

As she turned and started up the stairs, I gently grabbed her elbow and pulled her into my arms. *Oh, boy...*

Maggie gasped but put her arms around my neck. She was breathing heavily; I thought I might hyperventilate. "Good night, Maggie," I whispered and kissed her.

One of us was moaning. It had to be Maggie because I was too stunned to utter a sound.

As I pulled back, Maggie's eyes fluttered opened. I looked down into the confused blue depths. "My God, Kate," she said breathlessly.

"Mag—"

Maggie's urgent kiss stopped whatever I was about to say, which I couldn't remember to save my life. Her arms tightened around my neck as she deepened the kiss. I let out a groan as I felt her tongue lightly flicking across my lips. When I felt her fingers run through my hair, I nearly had a heart attack.

I pulled back from the heavenly kiss, with a resounding *pop*. We were both gasping for air. I let out a small breathless chuckle as I pulled her close. "Holy crap, Maggie." I sighed.

"I know," she replied and kissed my neck. "I can't believe this is happening."

"You?" I countered. We both laughed as I reluctantly pulled back. Maggie looked up and grinned. "What are you grinning at?"

"I knew you'd be a good kisser."

"You did, huh? Why didn't you tell me I'd enjoy kissing you so much?"

Maggie sported a smug grin. "As if you'd have listened."

I laughed and kissed her forehead. "Well, there is that. Now get to bed before—" I stopped as the mental picture flashed through my mind.

I looked at Maggie. The blush started in her neck and quickly rose to her face. She looked like a thermometer.

"I-I..." She stumbled backward. She then grabbed my shirt and pulled me down for a scorching kiss. "Good night," she said hastily and ran up the small staircase, leaving me standing there like a dummy.

"Kate?" I heard Teri's voice through my stupefied haze. I slowly turned away from the staircase.

"What's wrong? You're all flushed," Teri said.

I leaned back against the wall and banged my head a couple of times. "I kissed Maggie."

I heard Teri laugh. "But did she kiss you back?"

I looked at her then and grinned. "Yeah, she did."

Teri laughed again. With that, Hannah opened her bedroom door. "Is it safe?"

I groaned with embarrassment and banged my head against the wall again.

"Kate kissed Maggie, and Maggie kissed her back!" Teri whispered with excitement.

"I knew it would happen!" Hannah exclaimed.

I looked back and forth between them. "I'm going to bed," I said evenly and left them giggling in the hallway. I must admit I was smiling when I finally fell asleep.

The next morning over breakfast, Maggie, Teri, and I decided to go into town. They wanted to shop; I wanted to see Jane at the real estate office. So we stood in the middle of town, synchronizing our watches.

"Okay, you two, go off and have fun. Buy me something, then we'll meet at Sutter's for lunch at high noon."

I put my sunglasses on and walked across the street. Looking in the window of the real estate office, I saw Jane sitting behind her desk. She looked up as I gently rapped on the window. She recognized me and waved me in.

"I don't believe it. When did you get here?"

"On Wednesday. Got the family and some friends up for the week," I said and sat down.

"You're not alone? That's different."

That's the third time someone had said that to me. *Good grief, do I spend that much time alone?* I thought, scratching the back of my neck.

I asked her about the three cottages on Deer Lake. She gave me a curious look. "Another purchase?"

"God, no. I'll be paying off my log cabin until I'm old and gray. Well, older and grayer anyway. No, I'm curious as to how the owners advertise for that. You know, brochures, the Internet, that sort of thing."

"Mr. Jenkins doesn't advertise at all. As a matter of fact, the gentleman staying in there now was a walk-in."

"A walk-in? I don't get it."

"He came in last week and wanted to know if there was anything for rent on Deer Lake. I told him about the cottages, and he snapped one up, sight unseen. Paid cash, two weeks."

"Martin Reese *asked* for Deer Lake?" My mind raced.

"Yes, I assumed he knew someone. Do you know him?"

"Just from seeing him on the lake. I was curious." That was almost the truth. For some reason, I thought of Lucas. "Do you know anything about Henry renting out his house?"

She frowned. "I didn't know he did. Isn't he there?"

"No, some guy is renting it. He made it sound like he got a call that it was available. I assumed it was through you."

Jane shook her head. "Nope. I'm surprised that Henry left. Last time I talked to him, he was looking forward to the summer. Must have changed his mind and went to his niece's in Minnesota."

"When did you talk to him last?"

"Oh…end of last month, about two weeks ago. But like I said, he must have changed his mind."

"Must have," I said and stood. "Well, thanks, Jane. It was nice to see you again." I stuck out my hand and she shook it.

"Don't be such a stranger," she said with a smile as I walked out the door.

Waiting for Teri and Maggie, I had time to think about Martin Reese. So he's on leave from the Marines and he comes to Deer Lake? He comes into town and specifically asks for a cottage on Deer Lake. Why? Then I thought about the day before, seeing him with Sandy. They looked like they were having an argument.

As I lazily window-shopped, something I loathe doing, I got that same feeling that I had in Sutter's that crowded night. I scratched the back of my neck. It was then, as I looked into the store window, I saw the reflection of a woman standing across the street looking my way. In a quick study, I noticed she was tall with very short dark hair and wore sunglasses. When I turned around, she was gone—or was she even there?

In the next instant, my senses were assaulted with a wonderful aroma. I sniffed the air like some bloodhound and followed my nose. There at the corner, I found a short portly fellow who was grilling bratwurst. The aroma was mouthwatering, and I couldn't resist.

I took my appetizer, walked down the street, and across to the park. As I sat on a park bench under a nice huge shade tree, I took a healthy bite and spilled mustard down my shirt.

"Good grief," I said and took the napkin to it, which only made it worse. *Maybe Maggie is right. I need a keeper.* Deciding the shirt was a lost cause; I got back to Mr. Reese.

Why would Martin Reese want our lake? He lied about the brochures–why, for what purpose? I wondered, shaking my head and savoring yet another bite.

It was then I heard Teri's exasperated motherly tones and felt like a kid who got caught with her hand in the cookie jar. "You've got mustard all over your shirt. Couldn't you wait, for heaven's sake?"

Looking up with a mouthful, I gave her and Maggie a sick smile. "It called to me. Its will was much stronger than mine." I quickly finished and tossed the bag in the trash. "It's an old shirt anyway. Okay, to lunch."

The three of us stood at the bar waiting for a table; it was unbelievably crowded for lunch. As I waited for Fran, someone slapped me on the back. "Why didn't you come and get me?" It was Ben.

"Sorry, Ben. What was I thinking?"

"You weren't, you're a typical woman. Speaking of women, where's Hannah?" he asked absently as he ate peanuts from the bowl.

"She's at the cabin."

"See ya," he said, and as he turned to go, I grabbed his arm.

"Ben, before you go and woo Hannah, I'm still trying to

figure out why someone would knock me on the head. What do you think?" I asked seriously.

"Maybe to knock some sense into it?" Ben offered, equally serious. "And who says I'm wooing Hannah?"

I glared at him and bounced a peanut off his forehead. "What do you think of Lucas Thorn?"

He shrugged. "Nothing really. Nice guy, quiet, which is a big plus in my book. A lady-killer, I'd say. Why?"

"I don't know. Doesn't it seem odd that Henry would rent his place? He never has." Then I told him about Jane.

"I do remember last month Henry mentioning his niece. However, I will agree, I was under the impression he wasn't going. He must have changed his mind. Renting the house for the month seems like a good idea."

"I suppose," I said, but something still didn't ring true. I couldn't figure it out.

"What's on your mind?"

"I don't know." I sighed. "There's too much going on at the lake for my liking. Something's happening. I have a gut feeling."

Sometimes, I hate my guts.

Chapter Twelve

Once back at the cabin, we found Ben and Hannah sitting at the kitchen table. Ben had an icepack on his head, which Hannah was holding.

"What happened?" I asked as Maggie rushed to his side.

"I don't know. I was by Kate's shed, and I thought I heard somebody. I thought it was Hannah. As I went in and turned around, something hit me on the head. That was it."

"I found him lying on the ground," Hannah said in a worried voice.

Maggie lifted the icepack. "Just a bump. The skin isn't broken." Maggie checked his eyes. "Follow my finger, Ben, and no jokes." She moved her index finger across his line of vision and Ben silently did as he was told.

I, of course, couldn't resist. "Now, follow my thumb," I said over Maggie's shoulder and got a glare from the good doctor.

"How do you feel?" Maggie asked.

Ben shrugged. "Fine, just a little woozy."

"Well, just sit still for a little while. I don't want any trips to the hospital," Maggie said and gently held the icepack in place. "I'm sure Kate personally knows everyone in the emergency room, though."

I sneered in her direction, to which she responded with a slight bow.

For the remainder of the afternoon, under Maggie's scrutiny, Ben was quiet and seemed no worse for wear. Hannah was still fussing over him, which I thought was adorable. After making sure his hard head was all right, we went down to the lake. I followed behind Hannah and sang, "Hannah's got a boyfriend, Hannah's got a boyfriend."

I heard Maggie and Teri chuckling behind me. Hannah turned around and glared playfully. "Grow up."

I pulled a face and laughed. "You first."

Maggie still watched Ben as he and Hannah chatted on the pier. I was curious about what hit Ben on the head. "He's all right, isn't he?"

"I'm sure he is. He's in fit shape, and his coordination seems to be fine," she said professionally and added, "better than yours."

I chose to ignore that. "I really hope it was just an oar or something that fell and hit Ben," I said as I watched him.

"First you, now Ben. Maybe your shed is possessed," Teri chimed in.

I stood and grabbed a beer. "One way to find out." I headed for the shed.

I looked around the shed and there seemed to be nothing out of the ordinary. The paddles and oars were still in place, the life jackets still hung on the walls. As I turned to leave, I tripped over the length of rope and fell headlong into the door of the shed. Only my stealth coordination stopped me from crashing through the door. *Maybe that's what happened to Ben.*

A relaxing uneventful afternoon turned into a quiet peaceful evening. We sat on my porch lazily drinking coffee and listening to the crickets chirping and the loons wailing their song. The fireflies blinked happily, looking like a million little lights over the lake. For now, all was still peaceful and relaxing. I feared it wouldn't last long.

Ben had gone to his house and came back up on the porch grinning like the goof that he was. "Try these out, Ryan." He handed me a pair of field glasses.

"Night vision?" I asked with delight and Maggie groaned, which I ignored.

"Yep, be careful, you can't look into the light with these, you'll blind yourself."

I put them up to my eyes and was amazed. Everything was

illuminated and had an eerie green aura to it. "Amazing," I said as I scanned the lake.

"My turn," Teri said childishly, and I handed them to her.

"Wow. You can see everything. Oops, I see Martin."

Hannah seemed appalled. Well, being the mother figure, perhaps she thought she should be. I watched her; she was itching to take a look.

"Wanna look, Hannah?" I enticed her.

She frowned and waved her hand, then said slowly, "Well, just for a moment."

Teri eagerly handed them to her. Hannah cautiously put them up to her eyes. "I don't see anything."

Ben let out a manly huff and pulled his chair closer. "Here, you silly woman." He put his arm around her shoulders, then adjusted the glasses. "How's that?"

"Better, better," she said.

I could see her smiling behind the field glasses. I glanced at Maggie who rolled her eyes.

"Good Lord!" Hannah exclaimed. "Does he have a gun?"

I quickly took the glasses from her. "Where were you looking?" I asked impatiently.

"The little cottages," she said and pointed.

Putting the glasses to my eyes, I adjusted and scanned. In the eerie green illumination, there was Martin Reese with the door wide open sitting shirtless at the table.

"Oh, boy." I sighed nervously. "This cannot be good."

"What's he doing?" Teri asked.

"He's got a rag and, I'll be damned, he's cleaning a gun," I said as I continued watching. If memory served me, it was a forty-five caliber. It reminded me of the one I carried when I had my P.I. business.

He finished cleaning it, then checked the clip. He put the bullets in, then slammed the clip home into the butt of the gun.

I put the glasses down and saw Ben frown deeply as he looked across the lake. "Ben," I said, answering his confused look, "Martin is a sergeant in the Marines. He's on leave."

Ben raised a curious eyebrow and I nodded. "I know," I said

and answered his questioning gaze. "What's he doing on Deer Lake?"

"A gun, huh? I'm sure if it's his, he has a license. The service won't allow a serviceman to carry a weapon, not off base. Although it's probably his, the Marines will frown on him displaying it. Damn it, what does he need a gun for?"

I looked through the glasses again. I could see him sitting on his front porch in the dark looking out at the lake. He was watching my cabin, and though he did not know it, he looked directly at me. My heart raced as he sat there and watched.

"This can't be good," I said again and shivered uncontrollably. "He's just sitting there. He's cleaned his gun and staring right at us."

With that, he wiped his brow and took a drag on his cigarette. In the eerie green illumination, the smoke lazily hung around his head. He was still looking across the lake at us.

"What should we do?" Maggie asked and leaned into me.

"What can we do? Nothing. He hasn't done anything." I put the glasses down.

"Well, it's late," Hannah said and stood. "Good night, all."

"I'll be going, too," Ben agreed.

Maggie stood and kissed the top of my head. "Get some sleep," she whispered and pulled me out of my chair. "No more tonight, Kate."

I could not have been asleep for more than an hour when I heard the screaming and Chance barking and bolted out of bed. I ran into the living room to see Ben coming onto the porch holding Teri. Ben was soaking wet and in his swimming trunks.

"What the hell happened?" I asked as I opened the front door. Hannah had come from her room and stood there white as a ghost. Maggie was right behind.

"Good heavens, what is it?" Hannah exclaimed as she put her hand over her heart.

Ben came in with Teri, who was crying and couldn't catch her breath. He gently set her on the couch, then knelt in front of her as did Maggie.

"Take it easy, Teri. We're here," Maggie said.

Hannah got her a glass of water, and with trembling hands, Teri took a drink.

I sat next to her and put my hand on her arm. "What happened, Ter?" I asked gently.

Taking a deep breath, she started. "I couldn't sleep, so I thought I'd go outside. It felt like the storm was coming and you know how I love a good storm," she said in a quivering voice and looked up at me. I smiled and nodded. "I didn't intend to be out long, but I found myself walking the shoreline. On my way back, that's when I heard, or thought I heard, laughter. With the wind blowing, I couldn't tell where it came from," she said and looked at all of us. "The wind was blowing, I was petrified. I must have imagined it." She looked at Ben and chuckled. "Sorry, Ben."

"You scared the hell out of me. I was swimming, and I heard you scream. When I came over to her, she looked terrified. I put my arm on her shoulder, and she turned around and slugged me," Ben said and flexed his jaw.

"I'd have slugged ya, too," I added. "Teri, was there anything but laughter?"

"No, whoever it was just kept laughing. Like…"

"Like what?"

"Like they knew I couldn't see them. The laughter turned to giggling. I was so scared. I looked all around and…" She stopped and put her hands to her face.

I put my arm around her. "Okay, Ter, it's okay. I think that's enough for now."

Maggie put her arm around her as Teri stood. "C'mon, let's get you to bed."

My heart was now pounding and I was wide awake. Hannah kissed my cheek. "You look exhausted, Kate. Go to bed."

"Ben, thanks. Sorry Teri slugged you," I said.

"No, you're not. Good night, everyone," he said with a chuckle and walked out.

Maggie came out of Teri's room and I met her in the hallway.

"Is she okay?" I asked.

"She's fine, just scared. I would be, too."

I flipped off the lights. "Do you think she imagined it?" she asked as we walked down the hall.

"I don't know. Teri is not one to imagine things. With the wind and all, maybe she thought…I don't know," I said and ran my fingers through my hair.

Maggie put her hand on my shoulder. "Get to bed, Kate," she said.

We stood in the dark hallway for a moment. "Sleep is a 'highly unlikelihood,' in the words of Maynard G. Krebs," I said and frowned. "I have no idea what made me think of 'Dobie Gillis.' Ya know that old TV show?"

"I don't pretend to know how that brain of yours works, Miss Ryan," Maggie said, and we both laughed.

"What kind of name was Dobie anyway? And what was the name of that short girl with the ponytail? She had a crush on him, remember?"

There was another moment of silence. "You're insane," Maggie said. "Go to bed. Good night." Maggie stifled a yawn.

"Can I walk you to your room?"

"That would be very chivalrous of you. I'd hate to get lost."

I smiled as we walked down the hall and pulled down the staircase. We stopped there.

"Well, here we are," I said.

Maggie leaned over and kissed my cheek. "Thanks. It's Zelda," she whispered.

I pulled back. "Who?"

"The girl who had a crush on Dobie."

I laughed. "That's right."

"Can you sleep now?" Maggie asked. I heard the sarcasm in her soft voice.

"No," I said and cupped her face. I bent down and kissed her. "Now I think I can. Good night, Maggie."

Maggie sighed and grinned. "God, Kate, what you do to me. Good night."

I lay there dozing off and heard the floor in the hallway creak.

Hannah's up, I thought half-asleep. Feeling as though I was in a dream state, I thought I heard my door open. I was lying on my stomach, and as I lifted my head and looked over my shoulder, the door was closed. Then I heard the creaking again.

Maybe Teri was up again. It was hot and perhaps she couldn't sleep. Then I thought for sure I heard the back door. I sat up in bed listening in the dark. Once again feeling vulnerable, I reached for my robe and quickly put it on. I walked to my door and opened it. The hall was dark as pitch, but the moonlight shined in the living room. Cautiously, I walked out into the hallway. Hannah's door was closed tight. I put my ear to it and heard only the whirring of the fan. Then I walked out into the living room.

In the moonlight, I saw nothing out of the ordinary. I turned and went into the kitchen and found nothing unusual. Both the back and front doors were locked. With a wide yawn that nearly cracked my jaw, I made my way back to my room.

Slipping into a pair of lightweight boxers and a T-shirt, I crawled back into bed. At least if I'm going to be murdered in my bed, I'll be clothed.

I trembled violently. *What in the hell made me say that?*

Chapter Thirteen

The storm was coming and I couldn't wait. Soon it would cool off and the ungodly humidity would be gone. I woke early as usual and did my morning ritual of putting on the coffee first, then going out on my front porch to greet the day. The day was gloomy and overcast as the storm clouds rolled across the sky.

Thinking about Teri and what happened the previous night, I went to her door and put an ear to it. I breathed a sigh of relief when I heard Teri snoring peacefully. *Christ, I hope she imagined hearing a voice last night.*

I stood on the porch and took a deep breath and noticed Ben's boat out on the lake. He noticed me, waved, and held up a string of fish.

"Damn it, if he catches that bass," I said, and as I grabbed my gear, I remembered I no longer had my favorite fishing rod. Remembering our dance on the pier, it was well worth the loss.

I hopped in my rowboat and started the trolling motor. As I neared Ben's boat, I heard him laugh. "Good morning, Ryan. Hurry up before I catch 'em all. How's Teri?" he asked as I cast out my line.

"Still sleeping. Ben, that scared the crap out of me last night."

"You? Kate, she looked petrified. She was running down the shore, looking over her shoulder like someone was chasing her."

"Did you see anything?" I asked and watched him.

"No, nothing. I hope she imagined it."

"So do I."

We fished in silence for a while when I asked him about Martin Reese and his gun.

He sighed. "He's a Marine. They're taught well, but they don't carry firearms with them."

"It was eerie seeing him watching the cabin. This is worrying me."

"I don't blame you."

"Hey, how's your head?"

"I'm fine, Ryan," he assured me and lightly rapped his knuckles on his forehead.

"What do you think happened?"

"I don't know. I didn't see anyone, if that's what you're thinking—"

"It was."

"I figure something fell in that mess you call a shed," he said with a grin and glanced my way.

"Very funny," I grumbled and looked up at the sky. "Radio's calling for heavy rain for the next couple of days."

"How are you fixed?"

"I'll check when I go back, how about you?" I asked, and he nodded. He was frowning and I could tell he was worried about all of this, as well. "What are you thinking?"

"Ryan, someone is after you. I don't know why. Someone knocks you out. I would assume he wanted something from your cabin, but nothing's missing. I'm stumped."

"I don't think he wants me dead. He could've done that on Saturday. Martin Reese worries me now. It made me nervous when he jacked that bullet in the chamber."

Ben gave me a curious look. "You seem to know about guns."

"I read a lot," I lied and continued fishing. Glancing at him, I knew he didn't buy it.

We continued to fish for the elusive bass in silence.

When I walked back to the cabin, without any fish, Teri was standing in the living room with her hands on her hips. Maggie and Hannah looked as though they were on an Easter egg hunt. I set my fishing gear against the wall. "What are we looking for?" I asked and joined the hunt.

"I swear to Christ, Kate, you have a poltergeist," Teri said, scratching her head. "I can't find my cosmetic bag."

"Good, I agree with Mac. You don't need it," I said. "I'm starving."

"You're always hungry," Maggie said absently as she looked under the couch. "Ha! Here it is. How did it get there?"

Teri looked shocked and relieved. "It must have fallen out when I first got here." She opened it, then frowned again. "Nuts, I forgot my favorite cologne. Where has my head been?"

I heard the exasperation in her voice and by their look, so did Hannah and Maggie. I put my arm around her and gave her a reassuring hug. "You okay? How did you sleep?"

"I feel like it was a dream, Kate," she whispered.

"Are you all right?"

"Yes, it was just so scary." She took a deep calming breath.

"You need breakfast."

As I stood at the sink, I looked out the window and caught a glimpse of something moving. My first thought was that it was a deer. I ran out of the kitchen.

"Where are you going?" Maggie asked as we bumped into each other in the hall.

"This is becoming a ritual," I said with a laugh. "I'm getting my camera. I think there's a deer out there."

"You've never taken a picture of a deer?" I heard her ask as I retrieved my bag.

"Very funny. Hundreds of them, but you never know when you're going to get the right one. If I play my cards right, this photo might pay for the walls in my loft." I headed out. "Start breakfast!" I laughed at the stunned look on Dr. Winfield.

I stood on the back porch looking through my lens. Then I saw it—rather, him—Martin Reese. He was wandering through the woods, my woods. "What the hell is he doing?"

He hadn't noticed me. He was looking at the ground, as if trying to find something.

Slowly, I made my way off my back porch and walked to the edge of the woods. Suddenly, he looked up and saw me. He looked as though he might run when I called, "Good morning, Mr.

Reese. Are you lost?"

I tried to sound friendly, but I was getting edgy. *I'm going to get to the bottom of this if it kills me,* I thought and grimaced. *I wish I'd quit thinking about killing.* This whole week had me completely baffled.

He stopped and waved as he made his way over to me. I watched him, trying to see if he was carrying his gun.

"Good morning," he grumbled. "I was going for a walk. I didn't mean to intrude." He sounded sincere enough.

"Well, how about a cup of coffee? Have you eaten breakfast?"

"N-no, I—"

"Good, consider yourself invited." I turned and he stood there. "Mr. Reese, it's just breakfast. C'mon for chrissakes."

He shoved his hands in his pockets and followed me.

"Have a seat." I motioned to the kitchen table.

"Good morning, Mr. Reese," Maggie said, hiding the surprise on her face. She was standing by the stove with a spatula in her hand. It was an odd sight.

I peered down into the cold frying pan, which had bacon it in. Maggie leaned into me and whispered, "We watched him cleaning his gun, and you invite him to breakfast?"

For an instant, we looked in each other's eyes. Well, that's not entirely true. I was looking at her lips, trying to avoid the urge to kiss her. She must have read my mind because she grinned and raised her eyebrows.

"Is it self-frying bacon?" I asked, ignoring her question. She glared at me as I turned on the burner. "Voilà!" I whispered. "We have fire!"

"This is a nice place," Martin said as he glanced around the kitchen.

"Thank you, it took me long enough to afford it. It's all mine, though. Well, the Bank of Steven's Point may argue, but you know what I mean." I handed him a cup of coffee.

"So where are you from, Martin?" I asked as I watched Dr. Winfield flounder at the stove. She looked completely out of place in a kitchen but still adorable.

"St. Louis. I grew up there," he said and drank his coffee.

That's as good a city as any.

Maggie absently pushed the bacon around in the pan with a spoon. I hid my eyes. "Mother, father?" I asked affably. Good grief, it was like pulling teeth to get him to talk about himself. *He's worse than I am, and that's saying something.*

"Both died when I was eighteen, car accident. Then I joined the Marines," he said as I watched him. He was staring at his coffee cup with a faraway look in his blue eyes. I felt bad for him.

"I'm sorry," I said. I watched as Maggie now picked up the carton of eggs. This had disaster written all over the carton. She held one as if it were a hand grenade and tentatively cracked it on the side of the pan. The egg and shell fell into the sizzling pan. She nonchalantly looked over her shoulder, then moved as if to hide her culinary expertise from me.

I was quickly at her side. "That poor egg did nothing to deserve such a fate," I scolded and guided her to a chair next to Martin. "So no sisters, brothers?"

He sighed heavily. "One sister, she died about eight months ago."

I was shocked and all at once felt like a nosy PI. Sometimes I hate myself when I get in that Dragnet—just the facts, ma'am, just the facts—mode.

"Forgive me for being a nosy Irishwoman," I said lamely, and he looked up at me and smiled, sort of.

"It's okay. So have you found out who your prowler is, if there is one?" he asked, changing the topic.

"No, I haven't a clue. I suppose it was someone who thought I had something of value. When they saw I didn't..." I shrugged. "He's probably terrorizing some other lake as we speak."

Teri and Hannah came into the kitchen smiling. "I thought I smelled something wonderful..." The smile faded when she saw Martin.

Hannah's reaction was well, Hannah.

She was humming as she came into the room. When she saw Martin, she stopped dead in her tracks. "Good Lord—" she exclaimed, looking at him and quickly recovered without missing a beat, "—what a beautiful morning." She gave me the eye as she sat down and reached for the coffeepot.

Throughout the meal, Martin glanced at Teri every now and then.

Teri put her fork down and looked across at Martin Reese. "Mr. Reese, since I've met you, I've noticed you've been staring at me on occasion. I am flattered, truly. Do I remind you of someone?" she asked, smiling.

Martin immediately turned bright red. "I meant no disrespect. It's just that you look remarkably like my sister. Everything about you, especially your hair...it's a little unnerving. I apologize." He put his head down and drank his coffee.

Knowing his sister had died, I didn't want to pursue it further. "So where did the Marines place you?" I asked, changing the topic. It was better than asking him about cleaning his gun.

"Nowhere special. I fix tanks. I'm basically a mechanic," he said and drank his coffee.

With that, the thunder rolled. "Here it comes," I said and collected the breakfast dishes.

"I should be going. Thanks for breakfast." Martin quickly stood.

I looked up into the late morning sky, which was now an ominous dark gray. *The rains are coming.* It was humid and very still as the storm clouds hung low over the lake. Off in the distance, the lightning streaked across the sky. Soon, too soon, it would be right over the lake.

"You're welcome. Can I give you a lift across the lake?"

We slowly made our way across the lake to his cabin. As he jumped out of the boat, he stood on the little pier and looked me right in the eye. "Thanks. Be careful," he said. He then turned and walked up his pier to his cabin. I watched him as the screen door slammed.

"Be careful?" I repeated. "Was that a threat? A Marine sergeant with a gun tells *me* to be careful?" Martin gave me the creeps. I quickly motored back to my safe log cabin.

Ben was in my living room again. He sat there, frowning as he listened to the radio. Clad in a red flannel shirt, it struck me that he looked like something out of a Norman Rockwell painting. He was the weary logger, all alone in a little log cabin, leaning with one ear to the radio waiting patiently for the baseball scores. I laughed and shook my head.

"What's the scoop, Ben?" I picked up an apple and took a healthy bite.

"Rain, lots of rain. Wind, hail, the whole enchilada, Ryan."

Now he scared me. So I prepared for the worst. With Maggie's help, we brought all the firewood in and stacked it up against the fireplace. Teri and Hannah checked the food. We had plenty, and I had six or seven gallons of bottled water, just in case. All the flashlights worked, and I had plenty of batteries. I counted them and checked them as I lined them up on the table.

A generator—that was the one big thing Mac told me to buy that I hadn't yet. I really should listen to him more about these things. However, I had plenty of candles, lanterns, and matches.

Confident we could ride out any storm, I left them to continue in the cabin, and I went down to the lake to clear out the boats.

As I battened down the hatches and secured all the beach toys, I disappointedly closed the shed and bolted it. This was to be a relaxing fun week, I thought, shaking my head sadly. The thunder rolled and I looked up, "Okay, okay. You win."

The mid-morning was still, too still for my liking. It was hot, humid, and annoying. The radio was on, and every ten minutes was a weather update. We still weren't expecting the big blow until late that evening. Waiting for this storm left me with an eerie feeling.

"So we're all set for the big blow, if we get one," I said confidently.

Ben called from the porch, "Do you have a generator?"

"I have plenty of water, food, flashlights, and candles—"

"So you didn't buy one. Typical woman." Then I heard him grunt out loud.

"Thanks, Hannah," I called out to her.

By mid-afternoon, Ben had gone to secure his house. I stood on the porch and watched the dark sky. *Something's about to blow, and it's not only the storm.*

Teri was standing there watching me. I looked at her, and as our eyes locked, I knew she felt the same thing.

"You feel something, don't you?" It really wasn't a question. Teri has a sixth sense. I believe this and don't question it.

She nodded and looked out at the lake. "Something, Katie…" Teri only calls me Katie when she's really serious or really emotional.

"Teri, what's going on?" I asked helplessly as we watched the lightning streak across the distant sky.

I looked over at Hannah who looked decidedly pale. Maggie put her arm around her and kissed her head. "We'll be fine, Aunt Hannah. We're all together and we'll ride out any storm," she said confidently and looked at me.

"Maggie's right, Hannah. We're together," I said.

"I know. I trust all of you," she said, smiling, but I could tell she was nervous.

We turned to see Ben coming up the trail. He was dirty and his hands were full of grease.

"What the hell were you doing?" I asked as he passed us with a grunt. I looked back at his house, then smiled triumphantly as I followed him into the kitchen.

"What's the matter?" I asked happily. "Is there something you couldn't fix?" I continued and stood behind him as he washed his greasy hands. "Is there, huh?"

"Did your generator blow?" I asked horrified, and he grumbled. "It did. Gee, Ben, do you have candles? No? How 'bout some lanterns? No? Poor baby."

He turned and took a menacing step toward me, then playfully grabbed me around the throat.

"God, Ben, don't hurt her." Hannah laughed.

"I'm a doctor, Ben. Go right ahead," Maggie urged with a wide grin.

I ran out the front door and Ben followed.

"Help!" I yelled at Teri, who stood there laughing.

Like an idiot, I ran to the pier. I was cornered; I put a threatening hand up. "Be careful, I know judo," I said jokingly, as he walked toward me. "I'm not kidding, Captain Harper. I had to have these hands registered. I'm warning you."

I was unceremoniously picked up and thrown into the water.

The girls were on the porch laughing as I scowled at them. "Go ahead, laugh, but I think Ben threw his back out," I said and dripped all the way to my room.

Chapter Fourteen

By late afternoon, the rains came. By seven, it hadn't stopped. I could see the lake rising.

"This is unbelievable," Maggie said as she looked out the huge picture window in the front room.

It was relentless. The thunder rolled; the lightning flashed; the wind blew. *Good grief.* Hannah stared out the window, and I knew she was worried about Ben. He had gone back to his house after dinner.

"I hope he's all right," she said.

"He'll be fine. Hell, Hannah, he's Navy. They love the water," I said, and she chuckled halfheartedly.

The gale force wind started. The four of us sat at the table in front of my picture window. Chance was hiding underneath it, lying atop Hannah's feet.

"Okay, let's play cards," I said, trying to ease the tension as the thunder cracked and rattled the window.

Every now and then, lightning would flash and illuminate the lake. We aimlessly played poker and watched the storm. The fire was roaring, and the only other light was the lantern on our small table. A cozy comfortable glow seemed to engulf my log cabin while outside the torrential rains fell.

"Okay, how about iced tea or something since I've about lost all my matchsticks?"

"I'll help," Maggie offered as I started for the kitchen.

I pulled the iced tea out of the refrigerator and stared out at the unforgiving rain and wind. Maggie stood next to me and watched, as well. "Some rain," she said.

I snorted. "Some week," I said, disgusted with it all.

Maggie put a hand on my shoulder. "Kate, don't get discouraged. We'll be fine."

Thunder cracked and I jumped. "My nerves will be nonexistent after this week." I picked up the pitcher of tea.

Maggie smiled and stood in front of me. "What?" I asked and couldn't help but smile, too.

"Nothing." She reached up and cupped my face in her warm hands. "Just this." She gently pulled me down for a soft brief kiss. I groaned like a dope.

I really did lose all my matchsticks, and the Las Vegas girls wouldn't let me borrow any of theirs, so while they played a hand of poker, I stared out at the darkness. The lightning flashed and I jumped. For an instant, I thought for sure I saw someone standing on my pier. My heart was pounding in my ears and I waited for another flash. Yes, down on the pier... Someone was standing, their legs apart, bracing themselves against the torrential winds and rain.

"Guys..." I said in a warning voice and swallowed slowly as I watched the pier. My heart pounded in my chest.

"What?" Teri asked. Hearing the tone in my voice, her eyes got as big as saucers. She looked at me and would not look out the window as I did.

Maggie, however, looked out into the darkness. "What is it, Kate?"

Now we all looked out the window into the pitch dark. When the lightning flashed again, he was gone. We sat there in silence, watching.

Grateful that my heart was still pounding in my chest and not in my throat, I stared out the window. It scared the hell out of me. *I'm not nuts, I know I saw someone, or did I?*

"Nothing. I thought I saw someone on the pier as the lightning flashed..." I was saying as we looked out the window.

Then suddenly, the blinding lightning flashed and a man's face, contorted with pain, was pushed against my window, his hands clawing, trying to get in. We all screamed in terror as the lightning illuminated the pain-stricken face. Cards went flying through the air as grown adults screamed like banshees and clung to one another. Chance was still under the table.

It was Ben...laughing.

Never have I used such foul language in my entire life. Hannah almost had a heart attack. Teri was holding her chest and poor Maggie looked like she might faint.

"Geezus Christ!" I bellowed and threw down the only card that hadn't been tossed in the air. "You *ass*," I hissed angrily, as I looked around for my stomach.

"Good heavens, Ben. You fool," Hannah exclaimed, holding her chest. "What in the world were you thinking?"

Teri shook her head. "Good grief, Ben," she said and chuckled.

"I-I'm sorry. I..." he stammered apologetically. Then he sneezed violently twice, and all was forgiven. Hannah and Teri ran to him, stripped the wet slicker off, and ushered him to the fire.

Maggie and I were not easily swayed. We both glared at him as Hannah ran to get a towel for his poor stupid wet head.

Teri got him a cup of coffee. "You are an ass, Ben," she whispered kindly and handed him the coffee. Teri was a far better person than I was.

"A *colossal* ass, Ben," I added with a growl.

"Huge," Maggie concurred in a grave voice.

Maggie and I decided to forgive Ben since we couldn't kill him. "So what were you doing on my pier, Ben?" I asked as we sat around the fire.

"I wasn't on the pier, Ryan."

"Ben, you were standing on the pier looking at us. I saw you when the lightning flashed. Now cut it out."

"I was not on the pier. I came from my house and walked directly up on the porch. I was not down on your pier," he repeated, and I looked at Maggie and Teri.

Hannah whispered, "Then you did see someone on your pier?" The poor woman swallowed with difficulty. "I need a drink," she said slowly and went into the kitchen.

Ben watched Hannah. "I'll take a scotch and water, if you

please." His hands were shaking as he looked back at me.

"You saw someone on your pier? In this downpour? Who was it?"

"I have no idea. I only saw him when the lightning flashed. When it flashed a third time, he was gone." I sighed and rubbed the back of my aching neck, then glared at Ben. "Then as we all know, Mr. Hardy-Har shows up," I said to the rest of them while jerking my thumb in Ben's direction.

Maggie glared at Ben, as well. "What were you doing on the porch?"

"I got lonely. So I thought I'd come back," he said sheepishly.

I gave Ben a suspicious look. "Lonely?"

He winced. "My electricity went out."

"Well, you can stay here and sleep on the couch. Right, Kate?" Hannah offered. Ben grinned hopefully.

"Hmm. No electricity, no generator, no candles, no lanterns?" I asked. "What does that mean, Ben?"

He closed his eyes and took a deep breath. "It means I am unprepared for an emergency."

"Now that wasn't so hard to admit to, was it?" I asked with a happy smile.

"Taking shrapnel in Nam was less painful," Ben said through clenched teeth.

Feeling vindicated, I graciously offered Ben the couch.

Once again, I stared at the ceiling. It was 2:30; sleep was impossible as I tossed and turned and fought the feeling I had all week. I got the creeps thinking of someone in my house. What could they possibly be looking for?

Frustrated, I sat on the edge of the bed and looked out the window. It had been raining on and off for almost ten hours. It wasn't the heavy torrential rain from earlier in the evening. This was a steady rain and seemed like it would never stop. I was surprised the electricity hadn't gone out. *That'll be next.*

Walking into the kitchen, I heard Teri's door open. She came out and whispered, "Can't sleep either?"

"An impossibility." We then heard the snoring from the living room. "Well, it's not impossible for Ben," I said and put the kettle on the stove. "Maybe some tea will help."

We sat at the kitchen table. The only illumination was the small light above the stove. "So what gives with Martin Reese?" Teri said thoughtfully as she drank her tea.

"I don't really know. Part of me likes him. However, and this is a *big* however, I don't like the way he looks at you. I don't like his brooding moods, and I am not that fond of seeing him with that gun. The way he cleaned it unnerved me, Ter."

"Well, he's a Marine. Mac can still take apart a rifle and put it back together. That part doesn't bother me as much as him doing it in the dark. That unnerves me."

"At least we know now why he stares at you," I said and explained about his sister.

Teri's eyes widened. "She's dead? I remind some gun-toting Marine sergeant of his dead sister?"

It did strike an eerie chord. Martin was an unusual character indeed and now, with his dead sister looking like Teri. "I've got to keep my eye on him. All this seems to be happening since he's been staying on the lake. I don't know him. He's totally unfamiliar to me. If he's the prowler, what in the Christ is he looking for? What do I have? Damn, I don't get it. And what the hell was he doing in my woods? He appeared to be looking for something. No, I don't trust him. Something is up with Martin. I only hope he's not a Section Eight on the loose."

I laughed and so did Teri. Our laughter quickly turned to frowns as we realized that possibility.

"Like I'll ever sleep tonight," I said and raised my teacup. Teri nodded in agreement.

The rain stopped and everything was underwater. I know I only have a hundred feet of beach frontage, but my small beach was almost nonexistent. Because of the heavy rains, the lake had risen at least four inches. It was right at the top of my pier. Out on the lake, there were tree branches and a few scattered lawn chairs floating near the shore; debris was everywhere. My lawn chairs that I thought were secure had been tossed into the woods.

"Well, I don't think I'm in Kansas anymore," I said, scratching my head. Thank God, the boats were still moored to the pier; they had taken a beating in the wind, but they were intact. I was glad I had remembered to cover them.

It had turned cooler as I walked out onto the porch to survey the damages. Looking at the sky, it was still extremely overcast. Although it was windy, it was nowhere near the gale force of the day before. I turned when I heard Ben call out a good morning.

"Good grief, what a mess. It looks like a bomb hit the beach." He chuckled and stood next to me.

"Iwo Jima has nothing on us, aye, Captain?" I laughed as we made our way down to the beach, what was left of it.

The early morning was spent cleaning up my beach and Ben's. By ten, I decided to take my Jeep and check out the others on the lake.

Ben offered to stay with Hannah and Teri. Maggie came with me—more to the point, she wouldn't let me go alone. So my shadow and I drove to Henry's first to check on Lucas Thorn.

"Well, good morning. Weathering the storm?" Lucas smiled but looked extremely tired. Dark circles under his eyes darkened his otherwise clear blue eyes. His hair was uncombed and he looked at though he slept in his clothes.

"So far so good," Maggie said.

He looked at me. "How's Curious George doing this morning?"

I turned red and smiled. "Fine…"

He stepped back and invited us in. I looked around the house. It was warmly decorated. The living room had a couch in front of a fireplace and a small table and armchair in front of the window.

A door led presumably to the basement or cellar, and a hallway led to the kitchen and bedrooms. There was a huge oval rug near the fireplace but was not centered. It looked completely out of place lying off to the side. Men, I thought. That would drive me nuts. I suppressed the urge to straighten it.

"This was awfully neighborly of you. I think I have everything I need," he said.

"I'm glad someone is here to keep an eye on Henry's house for him," I said.

"I'm glad to do it. I was lucky to get this at all," he said, looking out the window. "Again, it was nice of you to drop by. How is the rest of your family enjoying the vacation? I hope all of you are having a good time. Now if the weather could only cooperate."

I agreed. "It would surely help, although my sister could use a day at a mall. She gets a little itchy when she's not by a store."

Lucas laughed. "Well, that's a woman—" He stopped abruptly when he saw the glare from Maggie. "Thanks then for stopping by. Perhaps if it doesn't get too bad, I'll return the favor and stop by for a visit. I'd like to meet the rest of the family."

"That sounds fine, Lucas," I said. "Let us know if you need anything."

"I certainly will."

Our next stop was Martin Reese. He looked surprised when he came to the door.

"Good morning. We're making the rounds. How're you fixed with this storm?" I asked nicely.

Maggie and I stood on his porch feeling foolish; he hadn't invited us in.

"I'm fine, thanks. I've got what I need." Like Lucas Thorn, Martin looked exhausted. I knew this storm was taking its toll on all of us.

"I wanted to make sure my neighbors were safe. We're supposed to get hit again. If there's anything you need," I said and pointed across the lake to my cabin. "You know where I live. I have plenty of supplies."

"Thanks, but I'm pretty well fixed," he said simply.

"Sorry to bother you," I said awkwardly.

"You didn't. Thanks." And with that, he closed the door.

"What a grump," Maggie said as we climbed into my Jeep and drove to the Hendersons'.

Jackie Henderson answered the door. "Hello, Kate and Maggie, is it?"

"Yes, Kate and I are checking on everyone," Maggie said.

Jackie Henderson nodded emphatically and invited us in. Phil was sitting at the kitchen table reading the paper. "Hey, there. Some storm, huh?" he asked and stood.

"I'm checking on everybody. There's another storm on the way. Have you seen Sandy Meyers?" I asked. I glanced out the window at her house. It looked quiet.

"Actually, I haven't seen much of her. Maybe she went home," Phil said logically.

Jackie mumbled, "I hope so." He gave her an exasperated look and angrily folded the paper.

"If you need anything, give me a holler," I said quickly. Maggie and I bumped into each other trying to get out the small kitchen door. Neither of us wanted to be part of whatever ongoing argument these two had.

Sandy Meyers's house was empty. I looked in her window and noticed the chair was no longer overturned as it had been the other day.

"Maybe she went home," Maggie shrugged as she looked around Sandy's property. Her beach was also nonexistent. The water was up to the grass, completely covering the beach.

"If she did, someone took her. Her car is still in the back." I walked down her pier and noticed her speedboat had at least six inches of water in it.

"My God, that was a lot of rain," Maggie said, shaking her head as we walked back to my Jeep.

It suddenly occurred to me. "Shit, Maggie. You know what's going to happen now?"

Maggie stopped and gave me a curious look.

"Deer Creek is probably cresting as we speak. How could I have forgotten Deer Creek? It runs parallel to my only access road—the only way in and out of Deer Lake. We'd better figure out whatever we need and get it fast. If this keeps up…" I looked up at the dark clouds swirling in the sky.

"This isn't over, Kate. Is it?" Maggie asked and grabbed my arm.

I held on to her hand, knowing she was exactly right.

Chapter Fifteen

Hannah, Ben, and Teri were waiting for us on the porch when we came back. Teri sighed with relief. "You were gone so long. We got a little worried."

"The road is getting pretty muddy. It was slow going, but thank God for Kate's Jeep," Maggie said.

"We need to figure out what we need and go quickly," I suggested and told them about Deer Creek.

Everyone agreed, and once again, we checked our supplies. Satisfied we were prepared for anything, we sat on the deck listening to the weather report on the radio. They were calling for more rain and unfortunately, I was right, the creek would be a problem in a day or two. I looked over at Hannah who looked tired and worn.

"Sorry, Hannah. This week was a bust." I patted her hand.

"Nonsense. I'm having the time of my life. I'd be sitting at home staring at the four walls and feeling sorry for myself." She watched Ben, who was down at the dock looking over my boat. "Besides, I wouldn't have met Ben," she said, smiling, and winked at me.

"Well, there's that anyway," Maggie said happily.

Hannah looked at Teri. "You promised you would show me how the Ouija board works."

My eyes flew open. "You did? A Ouija board?" I groaned. "Why?"

"Don't be a ninny," Teri said. "Hannah's never seen one in action. Maybe, and I mean *maybe*, we could try it later. You have a Scrabble game, don't you? And I know you have a wineglass."

"Yes and yes…" I said hesitantly. "Count me out. Wasn't it

enough that Ben scared the life out of us last night?"

Hannah laughed and Teri gave me a disappointed look. Maggie gave me those damned blue eyes and I groaned helplessly. "Okay, okay. I'm in."

Hannah kissed my cheek and said, "This will be fun."

"Says you," I grumbled and looked at Teri. "See what you started."

Maggie laughed. "It'll be fine," she said halfheartedly.

With that, the thunder rolled in the distance. "Perfect," I said and glared at my redheaded sister.

After dinner, we sat at the table in front of the window as Teri arranged the Scrabble letters in alphabetical order in a circle on top of the table. The words "yes" and "no" were spelled out with the remaining letters and put on opposite sides, bisecting the circle. I was getting nervous already. Hannah watched with quiet amazement as did Maggie, who was sitting close to me. *Well, maybe this wasn't too bad of an idea.*

"You mean this wineglass will move by itself?" Hannah asked.

Teri shook her head. "No, the idea is to put your finger on it, maybe it will move, maybe it won't," she said seriously and looked at me.

Right. This thing is going to be jumping all over the table.

Teri seemed to read my mind and laughed, then looked at Hannah. "Hannah, really, this isn't a game, not to me anyway. So you'll have to trust me if we need to stop."

Hannah nodded and stopped smiling. "What's going to happen?"

"Probably nothing," Teri said and took a deep breath. She turned the small stemmed wineglass upside down and set it in the middle of the circle of letters. "Who wants to start?"

I shook my head vehemently. "Don't even..."

Ben, the disbeliever, said, "Hell, I'll do it," and looked at Maggie. "C'mon, Maggie. Let's show 'em."

"Ben, you have no idea how real this is and neither do I. However, I've seen Teri at work. Although I may not be convinced of its capability, I know Teri's. Keep an open mind, Captain Harper," she warned with a smile.

Ben and Maggie placed their fingers on the bottom of the glass. We all waited and nothing happened; it didn't move. Hannah looked completely deflated.

I was grateful. "Okay, all done. It's not working. Let's play cards," I said quickly and was told by all four of them to shut up and keep still. I shut up and sat back.

The quiet was deafening. Ben snorted sarcastically, "Well, I'm impressed." He took his hand off the glass, and reluctantly, so did Maggie.

"Hannah, put your finger on the glass," Teri instructed, and she did. Then Teri placed hers on it, and immediately the glass moved in a circular motion. Hannah gasped as she tried to keep her finger on the glass as it moved around the inner circle of Scrabble letters. Teri gave Ben a superior look as he watched in disbelief.

I sat back. *Here we go.* My stomach was in knots. This type of thing always spooked me. Teri is used to it because she truly has some psychic abilities. How much, we don't know. And if it scares her, she hides it well.... She's a freak.

The glass moved and Teri looked at me. "Kate," she prodded with a grin.

I let out a sigh of resignation, knowing what she wanted—I got a pencil and paper.

Watching the glass move, Hannah asked, "What's it doing?"

Teri smiled with anticipation. "I don't know."

Ben was still frowning and Maggie gave him a sidelong glance. "Told ya," she leaned over and whispered.

The glass moved quickly now. Teri called out the letters as the glass stopped by each one.

"L-" she started, "E-A-V-E."

"Leave..." Hannah said.

"Leave what, my heart on the floor? I've already done that," I whispered, and Teri glared at me.

The glass moved again and spelled the same word.

"Leave where?" Teri asked, and the glass quickly slid across the table.

"L-A-K-E," Teri called all the letters again. "Why leave the lake?"

"C-O-M-I-N-G. What's coming?" Teri watched the letters. I looked at Hannah, she was amazed. Ben still sat there with his mouth open.

"S-O-O-N. What's coming soon?" Teri persisted. Her calm was a constant amazement. I, on the other hand, needed a drink.

Ben whispered, "Maybe another storm."

The glass slid across the table, "NO"—it stopped there. We all looked at each other. Ben turned a lovely shade of ash.

"Then what's coming?" Teri asked again as she and Hannah tried to keep their fingers on the glass as it started moving again.

"Who are you?" Teri asked, and Hannah caught her breath again. The silence around us was deafening. Well, I heard my heart drumming in my ears.

"Is someone here?" Hannah asked Teri. The poor thing looked like she was going to faint.

I smiled weakly and whispered, "Unfortunately, Hannah, there's always a 'someone.'"

The glass was sliding all over the circle of letters as if it were impatient to find the right ones. Quickly, we tried to call out the letters as the glass touched them. I frantically wrote down the letters as they were called out.

"C-H-A-S-K-O-T-E." The glass furiously slid into the letters as they in turn slid all over the table.

As Maggie and Ben quickly tried to place the letters back on the table, the glass stopped and Teri and Hannah took their fingers away.

I gave my paper a curious look. "What the hell is chaskote?" I looked at all of them.

Maggie chuckled and Teri laughed. Hannah and Ben were still in shock.

"Well, I'd like to find out," Hannah said with determination and looked at Teri, who nodded. They both placed their fingers on the glass and it started moving again.

"Okay, let's try this again," Teri said casually as though she was talking to a friend. That alone scared the hell out of me. "Who are you?"

The glass slowly moved and we all leaned forward as it slid into the letters.

"L-E-A-V-E." Hannah sighed and we all sat back.

"Whoever it is, they're awfully persistent," Maggie said, and for the first time, Ben chuckled.

"Okay, what's coming soon?" Teri asked patiently, trying a different tact.

My mind started racing. I thought of the prowler, of Ben and me being knocked out, and of certain things that happened to my cabin.

I looked at the glass on the table. "Not what…" I said. "Who."

The glass slid quickly across to the opposite side "YES" and kept banging into the letters. "YES-YES-YES," the glass seemed to scream out repeatedly.

Suddenly, the glass started teetering back and forth. Teri and Hannah no longer had their fingers on the glass. It moved on its own, making a clinking noise against the table. Then, just as quickly, it toppled over and broke in two. Hannah jumped, as did Ben.

We all stared at the broken glass in horror waiting for it to do something else.

"That went well," I said dryly. "Now that we've pissed off our ghostly guest, I'm sure we can all retire to our bedrooms for a night of peaceful slumber. Now can we play cards?"

No one was in the mood for a game of poker, so we cleaned up the table. Hannah picked up the broken wineglass and examined it. "Nothing like a good scare before bed."

"Speaking of bed," Ben said and grabbed the sheet and pillow I had laid on the couch for him. Hannah helped him with the sheet.

"I agree," Hannah said. "I'm exhausted. Tomorrow we can figure out what all this means, right, Teri?"

"It may mean nothing, Hannah. We'll see," Teri said and grinned, "but I told you it might happen."

"Wait a minute," I said in astonishment. "Doesn't anyone

want to talk about this?"

Ben stretched out on the couch and sighed. "Nope."

Hannah laughed and kissed my cheek. "Go to bed, Kate." She kissed Teri and Maggie. "Good night all."

I looked at Teri who patted my cheek. "Enough scare for one night. We'll talk in the morning." She headed down the hall.

Ben was already snoring. "Good grief," I mumbled and noticed Maggie putting the Scrabble letters back in the box. I also noticed her hands shaking.

"Maggie, I know you hate storms and if…well, between the storms and the spooks and you being all alone in the loft. If you—"

"God, Kate, thanks!" Maggie exclaimed, letting out a relieved breath, and dashed to my room.

I laughed quietly, and when I found her in my bed, the memory of last spring in Ireland when we comforted each other on that stormy night flashed through my mind. I got into bed and pulled the sheet up over us.

"I hate to be such a baby," Maggie whispered.

"It's okay. I'm a little spooked myself, Dr. Winfield. I don't know how Teri does it."

"Aunt Hannah looked like she was going to faint. The poor thing," she said and laughed.

I joined her. "Ben looked like somebody kicked him in the gut."

We laughed for a moment or two, then I yawned and looked over at Maggie. She was lying on her back and staring at the ceiling. I turned on my side and watched her for a moment.

"You're staring," she whispered.

"I can't help it. You have a nice profile."

She laughed and turned on her side, mirroring my position. "Thank you."

I reached over and gently brushed the dark hair off her forehead. "So what happens now, Maggie?" My body ached for her in a way I never thought possible.

"What do you want to happen, Kate?" she asked and held my hand.

"I'm afraid to think about it. I never thought I had the nerve to kiss you."

Maggie chuckled and pulled my hand close to her breast. I instinctively shivered as she held my hand. "I was having my doubts, as well. If you hadn't kissed me on the pier, I think I would have pushed you right off it."

I laughed at the idea and sidled closer to her. I reluctantly removed my hand, but it found a happy home lightly caressing her arm. I grinned when I heard the short intake of breath.

"God, Kate," she whispered and reached over, placing her hand on my neck. Her soft fingers caressing, her nails gently scratching.

Through the darkness, we stared into each other's eyes. I never wanted to kiss someone as badly as I wanted to kiss Maggie. I was staring at her lips and listening to my heart pounding in my chest.

"Kate Ryan, if you don't kiss me this instant, I—"

I slipped my arm around her waist and pulled her close. "You're so bossy," I whispered against her lips. Then I kissed her…and I kissed her again. When I opened my eyes, I realized Maggie was on her back with me looming over her. I pulled back. "Okay, how did we get in this position?"

Maggie let out a small laugh and wrapped her arms around my neck. "Oh, who cares, kiss me like that again."

As I lowered my head, we both jumped when Chance bounded up on the bed. Maggie let out a small shrieking laugh. I rolled out of the way, as my insane canine wedged her way between us.

"Chance!" I said through clenched teeth. "Get the hell—"

"Don't yell at her," Maggie insisted through her giggles as Chance tried to lavish her face with kisses.

"Those are my lips, Chance. Go get your own girl." I moved out of the way to give her more room. "Better yet, go bother Ben."

Chance happily lay between us. I glared at her through the darkness—she offered her paw as Maggie laughed.

"Don't get used to this," I warned my happy dog. "Canine interruptus."

Maggie laughed and leaned over Chance to kiss me deeply. "Good night."

"Whatever," I grumbled.

Chapter Sixteen

In the light of day, the Ouija board incident was forgotten. Well, let's say Hannah and Ben didn't want to talk about it. Teri, Maggie, and I decided we would discuss it later.

"Well, Hannah, how about a stroll along the shore before it starts raining again?" Ben asked.

We watched as Hannah and Ben walked down the shore and out of sight. I noticed Maggie smiling.

"He's adorable, Kate. I'm so glad Aunt Hannah's got her mind off Doc for a while," she said.

"So do we leave or do we stay?" Teri asked.

"We could ask the Ouija board," I said sarcastically. Maggie picked up a pillow and tossed it in my direction. I plucked it out of the air with a laugh. "What? I was being serious."

Maggie rolled her eyes. "That'll be the day, Kate Ryan."

I narrowed my eyes. "One kiss and you think you know me?"

With that, Hannah came running up from the beach, completely breathless. "Come quickly, Ben found…" She couldn't catch her breath.

I set her in a chair and looked at Teri. "Watch her and stay here."

Maggie and I ran down the shoreline. As we got to Ben, he was leaning against the rocks, bent over, looking like he was about to vomit.

"Ben, what is it?" I called out to him and abruptly stopped with Maggie bumping right into me.

There was something lying half on shore and half in the water. It was a woman's body; the lifeless eyes stared at the sky. I was shocked, and for a second, my stomach lurched.

"You didn't touch anything, did you, Ben?" I asked, quickly recovering.

He shook his head and looked at me. "It scared the life out of Hannah and me." He sagged against the rock. All at once, he looked old and tired, and my heart ached for him.

"You're sure you haven't touched anything?" I asked again.

"Yes."

Maggie was already squatting down next to the body. "Is this who I think it is?"

I squatted down to take a closer look. I was shocked and felt my stomach churning once again. I looked again to be sure.

"Christ, Sandy Meyers," I said sadly, putting my hand to my forehead. I heard Ben suck in his breath; he really hadn't looked.

"God help her," he said.

"Ben, go back and call Dan and please stay with Hannah and Teri," I said.

He nodded and jogged back down the shoreline.

"Shit, Maggie," I said in a worried voice. "Can you tell anything? I figure it's safe to assume she's dead."

Maggie was examining as much as she could without touching anything. "I never like to assume. However, in this instance, you're dead on."

We glanced at each other. "You have an irreverent streak, Dr. Winfield," I said gravely. "So what do you think killed her?" I looked around the area.

"Without an autopsy, I have no clue, but it does look like there's head trauma. With all the debris in her hair and around her, I can't be sure. There's no blood, no wounds," Maggie said as she looked over Sandy Meyers's body. "There are scratches on her legs, though. I don't know forensics, but it looks like she might have been in the water for at least a day. Her body is bloated."

"She's wearing a bathing suit and a top over it. Could she possibly have been swimming?" I asked, not believing it. Her raven hair, wet and tangled, made her almost look like Medusa.

"I can see no trauma to her neck or the surrounding area, but I can't tell from this. Your sheriff will have to…"

With that, we heard the sirens in the distance.

Soon the police were there combing the area. Dan Jackson's tall frame came into view.

"Kate, this is getting monotonous." He squatted down by Sandy's body and tried to figure out what had happened without disturbing anything.

He stood, adjusting his glasses, breathing heavily, and took out a pad. "Okay, from the top." He sounded as though he was controlling his urge to empty his stomach all over the beach.

"There's not much, Dan. Ben and Hannah found her. We called you and stayed here," I said.

He nodded and scribbled. "It looks like she went for a swim, and that was all she wrote. She could have easily been out on the lake when the storm hit. That wind was something. Maybe she was thrown overboard," he said calmly as we watched two young deputies put Sandy's body in a black bag and zip it.

"I don't think so, Dan. Her boat is still moored to her pier."

Just then, one poor kid ran to the woods and heaved his lunch. He came back a little shame-faced and the two took the bag.

Dan sighed as he watched his deputy. "Ugly, very ugly." He shook his head. "Well, that's all. If you think of anything, let me know."

"Wait," I said. "There is one thing. When we checked on Sandy, we saw a chair in her living room overturned."

Dan nodded and scribbled in his notebook. "Okay, I'll be back to scout around, but I think it's obvious, though, an autopsy will definitely be done."

"How long?" Maggie asked.

Dan shrugged. "I have no idea. Deer Lake is a small town. I'm sure the state police will be called in."

"Will you let us know?" I asked. He nodded as we walked back to my cabin.

"I hope this doesn't put too much of a damper on the vacation, folks," Dan said as we stood by my porch. Hannah was still pale and shaking. Ben stood behind her with his hands on her shoulders.

"It looks like we're in for more rain," Dan continued. "The creek might crest. If it does, your road will be completely underwater. You might want to think about leaving the lake. It's coming soon."

Teri and I quickly looked at each other at his last statement. Our eyes locked and we knew.

"Thanks, Dan, we might," I said firmly.

"A damper," Hannah repeated when Dan and the deputies left. She continued angrily, "I literally stumble over a dead body, and he hopes it doesn't put a damper on the week."

Off in the distance, the thunder rolled once again. I watched Hannah cautiously.

"I'm sorry you had to see that, Hannah."

Ben reached over and patted her hand. "It was macabre, I will admit."

"Do you think she drowned?" Teri looked at Maggie.

"I don't know," Maggie said. "I couldn't tell much, but I did notice a head injury. To what extent, I have no idea. Dan said they'd do an autopsy. How quickly I'm not sure. As he said, it's a small town."

Maggie continued, "I couldn't see any wounds, though there were scratches on her legs. Maybe she got a cramp while swimming. They can be very severe. God, that was ghastly."

"Yes, it certainly was," I said sadly and rubbed the back of my neck, which started to ache. "I hope she drowned and nothing more, the poor woman."

"Dan could be right. She could've been out on the lake when the storm hit. Anything could have happened to her," Maggie said.

I had to agree with her, but something didn't sit right with me. My mind raced as my instincts started to kick in. I looked up to see Ben watching me.

"You know, Ryan, you handled yourself too confidently out there, checking the area and the body. Then, the other morning, your familiarity with firearms. Is there something you haven't told me about yourself?" he asked frankly.

I figured he had a right to know. "I was a private investigator for nearly ten years. Now I seem to find myself in these odd situations. I don't know how, but I'm grateful I can help, if I can help."

"Why did you quit?" he asked the logical question.

For an instant, I instinctively put my hand to the back of my neck, feeling the scar. I was going to do what I usually do—joke and be sarcastic and evasive. However, for the first time, I told a relative stranger the truth. I looked at Maggie, who was the reason for this, and smiled gratefully. I saw a tear well in her sparkling blue eyes.

"We had a nightmare of a last case. The woman we were helping turned out to be a murderer. I had gotten emotionally involved with her and lost all perspective. Because of that, she nearly blew off my partner's leg and almost beheaded me. So we figured to limp away with whatever body parts and dignity we had left," I said and looked around the table. My hands began to shake, as they always do and probably always will.

Teri was amazed at my honesty. I could tell by the look on her face. She glanced at Maggie who wiped the tear off her cheek. I had never talked so openly about it. Maggie made that possible, for without her friendship and understanding, I seriously doubt I would have ever told anyone.

Ben must have seen quite a bit in his life. He didn't look shocked or amazed. He nodded but said nothing. Then all of the sudden, he reached down and pulled his pants leg up and put his leg on the edge of the table. There was a scar from the back of his knee and across his calf muscle. I looked at it, wondering how I never saw it before.

We all stared and he said, "Vietnam, 1968. I was aboard an aircraft carrier. One of the jets came back and exploded on deck. I should've been watching, but I was exhausted and nodded off. This is from shrapnel, almost lost the leg. I blamed myself for ten years," he said sadly and put his leg down. Then he reached over and patted my hand. "Guilt is the most worthless emotion, Ryan."

A tremendous wave of emotion swept over me. I swallowed back the tears and nodded. Maggie put her hand on my head and smoothed back my hair.

Hannah let out a loud sniff and went to the stove to make coffee. Ben watched her anxiously and went over to her. He put his hands on her shoulders and guided her back to the table. "I'll make it, cutie."

Getting back to the matter at hand, I said, "I hope in a couple of days we'll know what really happened. It looks like an accident: She went swimming, got a cramp, and drowned. Dan said he was going to come back and check out the shore where we found her. I'll tag along."

I smiled confidently and looked around the table. No one returned my feeling. I was about to say something when Dan knocked at the back door as he opened it.

"I made the rounds to the other houses on the lake. Looks like the Henderson's are leaving; they heard the weather report. I told them about the Meyers woman, and as you'd suspect, they were both shocked. Bad business, this..." he said, shaking his head and continued. "The Reese fella isn't around, but that guy renting Henry's place was shocked, as well. I told him everybody was pretty much considering leaving the lake. Looks as if he might, too. So if you see Reese...fill him in, will you?"

"Dan, I don't want to be an alarmist, but Martin Reese worries me a little." I told him about my suspicions.

"I want you all off this lake as soon as possible. I'll drive around and look for Mr. Reese..."

"Dan, I have no proof or anything. It's just a feeling," I warned him.

"I know, but there's too many odd things happening. I'd feel better if you were off the lake." He took a deep tired breath. "I'm gonna check out the shore again."

"Mind if I come with you?" I followed him out the door.

I watched Dan as we walked to where we found Sandy Meyers. He had the area roped off. He squatted and looked around, then scratched his head. *Poor guy*, I thought. It's not that he wasn't a good sheriff, but I could see by the look on his face that he knew he was out of his league.

"How's everybody doing?" he asked seriously.

"Scared shitless. Otherwise, they're doing all right. So what are you thinking?" I folded my arms across my chest. The wind had picked up; it cooled off and I started shivering.

"Kate, I'm gonna level with you," Dan started, and I heard the apologetic tone. "I've never had a dead body to contend with. They're doing the autopsy as soon as possible. Sandy Meyers is in the deep freeze. Sorry, don't mean to joke…"

I shrugged him off and he continued, "I thought I noticed blood on the top of her head, but I couldn't tell. Damn it, I hope this was an accident."

"Wait till the autopsy is done, which may take a while," I said and looked around. "So what do you think?"

He shrugged. "I don't know. I don't see anything out of the ordinary. I don't know how long she'd been in the water. She looked bloated to me."

"That's what Maggie said, too," I said and saw his curious look. "She's a doctor."

Dan nodded and looked up at the sky. "I suggest you leave in the next couple of hours. The rain will start again and the creek is gonna rise fast."

I looked up at the sky, as well, and shivered. Fast was definitely the right word.

Chapter Seventeen

The five of us sat in the living room, drinking coffee and staring at the fire. We were discussing whether to leave or stay.

"If it wasn't for all the rain we got, I'd say the hell with it. However, that creek will crest, and we'll lose the only road out of here," Ben said, and we all agreed.

"Okay, it's unanimous—we leave. If we all get packed, we can be out of here in an hour or so."

Hannah looked at Ben. "You'll be coming with us?" she asked.

He smiled down at her. "Cutie, I wouldn't dream of staying behind. I'll be ready in an hour." He kissed her forehead and walked out the door.

What a bust of a week, I thought as I packed my bag. *Someone knocks me out. And I'm still not sure if Ben was knocked out or an oar fell on his head. Sandy Meyers is dead. Teri reminds Reese of his dead sister. What else?*

I absently looked out the window into the woods and thought I saw movement by Henry's house. Then there was nothing. I was sick of getting glimpses of whatever, or whoever, in these woods. It was best we were leaving, although I wished to hell I knew what the prowler wanted from me.

We packed the cars and I made my final run-through of the cabin. I looked by the kitchen door and noticed the peg where my spare set of house keys usually hung was empty.

"Hey, did you take my spare set of keys?" I asked Teri.

"No. Why would I take your keys?"

Scratching my head, I said, "I thought for sure they were

hanging there when I got here. Damn. I must have left them at home. I thought for sure, though…"

I looked around the entire cabin and found nothing. A crack of thunder boomed overhead along with a streak of lightning. "Okay, Hannah, you go with Teri. Maggie will ride with me. Let's get the hell out of here," I said and for some reason felt an urgency to scram.

As if they all felt the same, we hurried to our cars and as had been our luck for the week, it started to downpour just as we got into the car.

I waited for Teri to pull away. "C'mon, Teri," I said nervously. I wasn't going anywhere without her. I couldn't hear her car start and it wasn't moving.

"God, Kate, don't tell me her car won't start," Maggie said and wiped the rain out of her face with one hand and held onto Chance with the other.

I grinned evilly. I couldn't help it. "Do I *look* like a mechanic?"

She shot me an angry look, and I tried not to laugh. She shook her head. "God, sometimes I just hate you."

I laughed while we waited for Teri. "Hell, the van's not going to start. Stay here." I let out an exasperated sigh and got out of my Jeep.

I didn't like this. My instincts once again took over as I looked around the woods. I wanted everyone out of there as soon as possible.

"I can't tell what the hell is wrong," Teri said as she opened her window.

By now, I was completely soaked. Ben pulled up in his car—his very small car. He rolled down his window and I explained.

"Damn it. What do you want to do?"

I looked around through the pouring rain. "Okay, here's the plan. Ben, please take Hannah. Maggie and Teri will come with me. We'll call a tow truck from town. We're out of here now," I said decisively. "Ben, you go, we'll be right behind you."

The lightning streaked and crackled overhead. I ducked instinctively. "Geezus, this lightning is getting too close! We need to get the hell out of here."

Teri ran to my car, and as Hannah ran to Ben's car, Chance leapt off Maggie's lap and ran to his car and jumped on Hannah's lap. She laughed and waved me off as I started for his car. "I'll take her, dear!"

Ben and Hannah took the lead, and I followed down to my entrance driveway. The flooding had already started. My wipers couldn't keep up with the torrential downpour, and I couldn't see a thing in front of me as I wiped the rain from my face.

"Geezus, Kate. This is bad," Maggie said.

As I drove, my hands were sweating as they gripped the wheel. The rain that pelted the ragtop of my Jeep was annoyingly loud.

"I can't see Ben. I don't want to run into him," I said.

Then it happened. There was a flash of lightning, and we actually saw it hit the tree in front of us. I slammed on my brakes, and we watched in awe as a huge tree split and fell across the road, no more than forty feet or so in front of us.

"Good Christ!" Teri exclaimed.

"Stay here," I said and jumped out of the Jeep.

Hannah and Ben were on the other side, thank God. Ben waved and yelled, "Are you all right?"

I nodded and gave the thumbs-up sign. "Go on ahead! We'll double back and try the other way. We'll meet you at the hotel in town," I yelled back.

Ben nodded and jumped back in his car. I watched as he drove safely down the muddy road.

I turned my Jeep around, hoping to God I wouldn't get stuck in the mud. There was at least six inches of water in the road.

"We've got no choice now," I said and put the Jeep in gear and started the other way. We got no more than a half-mile and the road was even worse. I stopped and looked ahead. Once again, I got out and this time Maggie came with me. The water was more than ankle deep.

We stared at the road, which was covered with tree limbs and debris. The water had to be rising with each minute.

"Sonofabitch. There's no way I get my Jeep through that," I

said sadly, and Maggie agreed.

"Let's get back to the cabin," she urged and pulled at my arm as I cursed under my breath.

There we stood in the kitchen, dejected and wet. "Well, I'm freezing," I said and headed for my room and dry clothes.

When I returned, Maggie was kneeling on the hearth and had a nice fire going.

"Who taught you how to build a fire?" I lightly kissed the top of her head.

She looked up with a smug grin. "A pyromaniac ex-P.I."

"She taught you well."

"At least we have enough of everything and we're together," Teri said, trying to keep things in perspective.

She was right. However, I wished they both were safe with Hannah and Ben.

"Well, there's nothing to do but wait this out," I said and turned on the radio. It was more of the same: rain and more rain and damaging winds.

"Good grief. Okay, I've had it." I uncorked a bottle of wine and poured three glasses.

We stood in front of the fireplace and toasted. "Here's to being together. I wouldn't want us split up for anything," I said, and we all touched our glasses.

Mine broke…

"And that's my life," I said dryly, standing there holding the stem of the glass and with wine down the front of my shirt.

Hannah and Ben called from hotel; at least they got out. "Good heavens, we couldn't believe the noise," Hannah exclaimed.

"We're all safe. You two relax, there's no way you can get to us. Both ways out are blocked, and Deer Creek is cresting. The only thing that can happen is the electricity," I said.

"I'll call you in a few hours," Hannah said.

"That's not necessary."

"I insist, now you take care of each other. I love you, now let me speak with Margaret, dear."

After Maggie talked to Hannah, we sat in relative silence staring at the fire.

Teri broke the silence first. "What do you think that Ouija board was trying to spell out?"

"I don't know, Ter. It was definitely not a name. *Chaskote*—it wasn't even a word. What is that?" Maggie asked.

"It's got to be something," Teri said positively.

"You really believe that?" I asked her.

"Yes. Kate, you and I have had this discussion before. There's too much that goes on to dismiss it as fancy. I know it scares you, but I know you believe that."

I let out a sigh of resignation. "You're right. It was weird that Dan said that this morning about leaving the lake because 'it was coming soon.'"

"I know, that was much too weird," Maggie agreed.

"I've got to get a common thread there." I got up and paced in front of the fire.

"After all that has happened this week, now Sandy Meyers turns up dead. Is she part of this or a coincidence?" I looked at Teri.

"We both have Dad's opinion on coincidence—no such thing. It was not my imagination that all the men at Ben's barbecue had eyes for Sandy Meyers one way or the other. You noticed it, too. There was tension whenever she opened her mouth," Teri said.

"Then the other day when we were fishing," Maggie chimed in, "she and Martin were arguing by his cottage. We saw them through the binoculars. Something's going on, Kate. I can't wait to hear from Dan. Do you think he'll know anything tomorrow?"

"I haven't a clue." I thought of Martin then and the binoculars. "I wonder if Ben left—"

I ran past the confused women and onto the front porch. There they were... Thank God, Ben's night vision field glasses, he had forgotten them.

"Maggie, turn off the lights, will you please?" I asked.

Now only the soft glow from the fireplace illuminated the cabin. Teri and Maggie came up behind me as I sat in the window and looked out. The rain had mercifully stopped, but the wind continued.

"What are you looking for?" Maggie asked.

"I'm going to get to the bottom of this. I'll watch all night if I have to."

"Watch for what?" Teri asked, looking into the darkness.

"A murderer covering his tracks," I said and settled down into the chair and watched.

"Maggie, what do you think about Sandy Meyers? You saw the body," Teri asked.

"It was a horrible thing," Maggie said.

"Do they think it was an accident?" Teri asked.

"I don't know. My gut says no, but Kate's guts are better than mine," she said, and Teri laughed.

I continued to scan the lake with the night glasses as Maggie and Teri discussed Sandy Meyers. So far, no activity.

"I'm glad Aunt Hannah and Ben got out because with this creek cresting…" Maggie stopped and looked at Teri and me. She didn't finish my sentence.

I knew what we were all thinking, but I fought the sick feeling that Maggie, Teri, and I were now at the mercy of whoever was out there and we had no way out.

Chapter Eighteen

Teri had gone to bed after nearly falling asleep in the chair. Maggie had fallen asleep on the couch in the living room. I was still looking through the night vision glasses and drinking far too much coffee. I sat in the darkness of my porch scanning the lake, seeing nothing but the green illumination of night. I did see a deer, though, which was interesting with night vision glasses.

"Kate, go to bed," Maggie whispered from the doorway.

"Not gonna happen, too much coffee."

I heard her yawn and chuckle as she sat next to me on the small couch. Her body felt warm next to mine, and I fought the urge to lean into the comfort. "Why don't you go to bed?"

"Am I interrupting?" she asked and yawned again.

I set the glasses down and reached for the afghan. Handing it to her, I said, "You know you're not. It's getting a little cool, cover up." I continued to scan the lake.

She snuggled the knitted quilt around her and put her head back. "I'm not afraid to admit I'm a little scared," she whispered.

"I'm not a little scared—I'm petrified, and I'm not afraid to admit *that*," I said seriously. The phone rang. I jumped and picked it up quickly. "Hello?"

"Hey, Ryan, Ben. How you holding up?"

"Fine, Ben. You sound way too wide awake for midnight," I said, now stifling a yawn.

"I can't sleep. I talked to Dan. The autopsy will be done tomorrow. So that's good. Anyway, I'm worried about you womenfolk," he said, and I heard the smile in his voice.

"Shut up, Ben," I said, and Maggie laughed.

"Ask him to put Aunt Hannah on," Maggie whispered in my

ear. I shivered violently. *I wish she'd quit doing that.*

"Maggie wants to talk to Hannah, Ben," I said and glared at Maggie's sleepy grin.

"She's sound asleep. Left her an hour ago."

"Oh, okay. Good. Go to bed, Ben. We're all fine, Captain," I said.

"Smart-ass, good night."

"Hannah's sleeping," I said and set the phone down. Maggie was sitting close to me with her head against the back of the couch. She moved restlessly as if trying to get comfortable. "You can use my shoulder if you want," I said and once again picked up the binoculars.

"Thanks," she mumbled and nestled her head against my shoulder. "Try to sleep, Kate."

"I can't sleep. It's impossible."

"God, this is awful. That poor woman." Maggie sighed.

"What do you think, Maggie?"

"I think somebody hit her and killed her. I think you believe that, as well."

I looked down at her and saw only a mass of auburn waves. "Get out of my head."

She laughed and snuggled closer. "Let's go over what we saw again," she suggested with a yawn.

I laughed, put the glasses down, and picked up my cup of coffee. "Okay, time for a bedtime story. Once upon a time, there was a woman named Sandy Meyers, who was found on a shore, lying on her back, half on shore and half in the water. Her eyes were opened and she was covered with debris. Leaves, twigs, muck, all sorts of lake stuff," I said with gruesome relish. Maggie stifled a hearty laugh as I continued, "Dan, the local sheriff, had suspected she was out on the lake and was caught in the storm."

"But the heroine, Kate Ryan, was not convinced," Maggie interjected and slipped her hand through mine and nestled against my shoulder.

"Hey, shush, you're supposed to be sleeping. However, you're right. Kate Ryan was not convinced. She's just sitting here waiting patiently."

Maggie snorted in disbelief. "Patiently?"

"Hey, it's my story. Now where was I? Oh, the crime scene. Now, according to Dr. Maggie Winfield, of Cedar Lake, Illinois, Sandy Meyers's body was bloated and distended. With no visible wounds except scratches and bruises, which she surmises are from the victim's time in the elements," I said and heard Maggie's even breathing. "So what does Dr. Winfield think the autopsy will show?"

"Dr. Winfield thinks if she drowned, she will have lake water in her lungs."

I thought for a moment. "And if there is no water in her lungs? Then she was dead before she hit the water, correct, Dr. Winfield?"

"Absolutely, Miss Ryan," she mumbled and yawned.

"And what about that overturned chair? I mean, you knock over a chair and don't pick it up?" Maggie's yawn was contagious. "Unless you didn't knock it over or you were in such a hurry…" I stopped and shook my head. "Christ, Maggie, this is sad. She was somebody's daughter. Who's going to tell her parents?"

"Kate, you can't do everything. Wait till you hear from Dan. You need to sleep. Now put those glasses and that coffee down and lie back."

I did as I was told. In a moment, I was on the verge of sleep as I gazed out at the dark quiet night.

"Thanks for the bedtime story," Maggie mumbled against my shoulder.

"You're welcome, you ghoul," I whispered and looked down into her sleepy eyes.

She smiled as her eyelids slowly closed. I leaned over and gently brushed my lips against hers, smiling as I pulled back. *I love kissing Maggie Winfield!*

If the grin on Maggie's face was any indication, I think she felt the same. "G'nite, Katie," she whispered and opened her eyes. "Is it okay if I call you Katie?"

I reached up and brushed the dark wayward strand off her forehead, then placed a small kiss on her brow. "No."

Maggie laughed and snuggled closer. "Too late."

I woke in relatively the same position at 6:30. My back and neck were killing me. I was half-sitting, half-lying and half-freezing—I hated math. I looked down to see the comatose doctor, comfortably sprawled out on my lap, covered, warm, and snoring peacefully. I glared down at her and quelled the impish urge to buck her right off the couch.

"Good morning," Teri whispered from the doorway. "My, she looks comfy."

"Doesn't she though?" I agreed as Maggie stirred. She then made a noise that sounded like a little squeak. I raised a curious eyebrow as she stretched like a well-fed cat and nuzzled once again into my lap, falling back to sleep. "Amazing," I whispered. "I believe she can sleep through anything."

"Maybe she's just comfortable with you," Teri suggested and ruffled my hair on her way out.

I paced back and forth all morning waiting for Dan's call. I couldn't call him again; he'd strangle me. When the phone rang, I nearly killed myself getting to it. It was Ben.

"G'morning, Ryan. I'll get right to it. The road is completely closed. It's under at least three feet of water. No way in and no way out. And to top it off, the power went out on the next lake. The lines were down, and they had to wait for the utility company to repair the damage. Thank God, you still have power," he finished, taking a deep breath.

"Shit. How's Hannah?" I asked and sat at the kitchen table.

"She's fine. Worried sick but fine."

"Take care of her, Ben," I said sincerely.

"Of course I will, Ryan. You do the same. Dan said the coroner is doing an autopsy now. It's ten, he figures to be done and the preliminary report finished by mid-afternoon, if not by early evening, so hang in there."

"I can't believe they're doing the autopsy this quick," I said.

"I have no idea, but it's a good thing. Have you seen Reese?"

"No, I haven't seen him or Thorn all morning or last night. By the way, you left your night vision glasses. Hope you don't mind my using them."

"Not at all. Use 'em all you want."

"Thanks. Call me later."

With the rain stopping, we decided to cruise the lake. According to the radio, the storms were moving south and another batch wasn't expected for a few days. So I locked up and we got into the speedboat and slowly motored around the quiet lake.

It was eerie to say the least. We motored by all the houses, not stopping. Martin's cottage looked deserted, and we assumed he left. As we left that part of the lake, I looked across at my cabin. Nothing looked different except there was no beach. The lake was still high, very high. Even the loons were gone and the only sound was the low revving of my motor.

"Boy, it looks spooky," I said, and Teri nodded.

Maggie was looking through the binoculars. "No sign of anyone, Kate. If nothing else, we can pick up any debris we find. Maybe Reese and Lucas left."

"I wonder..." I said almost to myself as I steered toward the cove. I motored around the point, getting as close to the shore as I dared and followed it slowly. There were a couple of downed birch trees recently uprooted by the wind and lightning lying under the surface of the water.

"In a couple of years, that'll be a good crappie bed," I said.

Both women looked completely confused. "I need Ben," I said and explained, "A crappie is a fish."

"Ah, thank you," Teri responded and looked at Maggie. "The Great Outdoorswoman."

Maggie laughed. "Complete with her own first-aid kit. Watch out for filet knives."

"All right, you two, cut the crappie..." I said as I trolled around the banks of the cove.

As we got closer to the cove, we saw several items floating in the water.

"We might as well get this junk out of the lake," I said and cut the engine when we got close. I pulled out the long net and we went to work.

We picked up a couple of lawn chairs and a Styrofoam top of a cooler. Then I noticed it, wedged in the felled birch tree—a shoe. No, not a shoe, a hideous three-inch stacked sandal.

"Christ, look," I said and pointed in the direction.

Teri scanned for a moment, then her eyes flew open. "Good Lord," she hissed.

"What? What?" Maggie asked impatiently as she looked.

There was no way we could get to it with my boat. I knew I had to get out of the boat and swim to it. So I decided to leave my sneakers on as I started over the side.

Teri gave me a worried look. "What do you think you're doing?"

"I'm going to get it. Teri, it's Sandy's silly sandal," I said. "Say that ten times."

"Oh, no, you're not," Teri said.

"Oh, yes, I am," I countered and stepped onto the ladder, then lowered myself into the water. It was chilly, I'll admit.

"Kate, why are you doing this?" Maggie asked, and I heard the helpless tone and laughed.

"Because I must," I said emphatically.

Teri groaned. "Be careful, watch out for sharks."

I slowly made my way over to the downed birch tree, grateful I didn't take off my sneakers. I stood on the tree and cautiously reached for the shoe. Grabbing it, I steadied myself, then looked around. Up on shore, I saw the other one.

I made my way past the downed branches and limbs and got the other sandal. It was about twenty feet off the shore. I looked around trying to think, something didn't seem right, but I found nothing else out of the ordinary. Then I looked farther into the woods, and about two hundred feet in the clearing, I saw the back of Henry's house. I had no idea we were this close to his house.

Once back in the boat, Maggie and Teri looked relieved. With a wide smile, I held up the hideous sandals. "I saved Sandy's silly sandals," I said triumphantly.

Maggie rolled her eyes. "Let's go, Jacques Cousteau."

As we went back toward my cabin, we passed Henry's and saw no signs of life. There was no smoke from the chimney, no lights, no car.

"Must've gone," I said as I steered the boat past his dock.

"Good grief, isn't the public boat launch supposed to be right here?" I asked as we motored by the area. It was completely gone. The entire area looked like another lake. The launch was recently opened to the public and had seen a good deal of action that summer. Now, however, you couldn't tell where the lake ended and the launch began.

"If this water gets much higher, and I think it will, I bet we can get the rowboat through there," I said absently.

Maggie and Teri looked at me curiously. "You think we could?" Teri asked.

I shrugged. "Never can tell, if the water rises."

Teri was making lunch as we sat around the kitchen table. Maggie sipped on a cold beer, and I could tell she was thinking about something. She was eyeing the sandals by the back door.

"You're wondering how her shoes got all the way across the lake—right?" I asked them both as Teri set the plate of sandwiches on the table. I reached over and snagged one, taking a healthy bite.

"Now who's in whose head, Miss Ryan?" Maggie asked. "But you're right."

"Well, the unfortunate thing is, in this severe weather, anything is possible. We took lawn chairs out of the lake for chrissakes. That wind was gale force, remember," I said and ate my pickle.

I looked at the clock—1:30. *That preliminary report should be almost done.*

With that, the phone rang, and I quickly reached for it. Maggie and Teri leaned in, as well. It was Dan. My heart was pounding in my chest when I heard the tone in his voice. He sounded vague and hesitant. *Great, this should be interesting.*

"Kate, you'd better sit down," he started.

"I am sitting. Shit, Dan, should I stand up for this? Is it that bad?" I rubbed my forehead. There was silence for a moment before he continued.

"Here's the prelim. It appears that Sandy Meyers received a

blow to her head before she went into the water. There was no water in her lungs, so, according to Dr. Greer, she was dead before she took a swim. Now he doesn't necessarily think there's reason to suspect foul play. It could be anything. Her skull was...well, crushed." Dan hesitated.

"Crushed?" I asked, amazed. I immediately looked at Maggie who nodded. She was right.

Dan went on quickly, "He thinks she fell and hit her head on a rock or maybe she got caught in the storm, hit her head, and died. Then with all this rain and wind, her body fell into the water." He cleared his throat. He didn't sound like he believed that. "That's the preliminary..." His voice trailed off.

"Dan," I started and took a deep calming breath. "Why was this preliminary report done so quickly?"

There was silence on the other end. "Dr. Greer is going on vacation."

I let out an impatient growl. "So Dr. Greer was about to go on vacation and Sandy Meyers's death was more of a hindrance." I tried to remain calm. "Dan...crushed. Her skull was crushed, and he thinks she *fell* on a rock. Good grief, to have her skull crushed—what, was she dropped from a hundred feet?" I asked sarcastically.

Maggie and Teri listened and Teri gave me a warning look, about my sarcasm probably.

"Kate," Dan said tiredly. "I know what you're saying—"

It wasn't Dan's fault, but I was exhausted and lashed out at him anyway. "What does Dr. Meatball think the cause of death was...suicide? She aimed, then threw herself against a rock, thus ending her tragic life?"

Sarcasm was winning the battle. *This was Maggie's influence, I'm sure.*

There was silence on the other end once again. "I'm sorry. I know you're only the messenger. So what happens now?"

I could hear him take a long deep breath. "Dr. Greer is leaving tomorrow. He and the...mayor are going to Canada, fishing."

Groaning, I stood up and began to pace back and forth, while Teri and Maggie watched patiently.

"It's his medical opinion that Sandy Meyers was killed accidentally. He'll state what I said and put that in his report. I can't even get to her place to get her belongings or to see who the next of kin might be." He sounded tired and sad and helpless. You can't do much when you have an imbecile for a coroner.

"I can take the boat and look, Dan. There's got to be something in her house. I'll call you later in the afternoon," I said and took a deep breath.

"Kate, we both know this girl was murdered."

That he admitted it was to his credit. That he scared the hell out of me and I didn't soil myself was to mine.

"Please, please be careful. Have you seen Reese or Thorn at all?"

"No, nothing today, but while we were out on the lake, we found Sandy Meyers's sandals."

"You found them all the way across the lake?" He sounded incredulous. "I guess with this storm, that's not unusual. Damn, I hate being cut off from you."

"Believe me, I agree."

"Do you have a gun?" he whispered into the phone.

"No...Do you?" I whispered back, trying to keep things on an even keel.

To my surprise, he laughed heartily. "Okay, be careful. Thank God, the electricity hasn't gone out. There are power outages all over the area. I can't believe your lake is still up. That's something anyway." He tried to sound uplifting.

"Yippee," I said flatly.

"Call me after you go to Sandy's. Please be careful."

"Will you quit saying that?" I pleaded and hung up.

Chapter Nineteen

Maggie and Teri waited patiently while I ranted. "What a colossal idiot!" I spat and opened the fridge, taking out two beers. "Crushed!" I bellowed and handed Maggie the unasked-for beer. She took it without saying a word.

"Can you believe it? Her skull was crushed, and he says it's an accident." I took a long drink.

Teri asked, "What happened?"

"Happened?" I exclaimed. "I'll tell you what happened..." I started, then closed my eyes.

I sat down and took a deep breath, then calmly explained the autopsy. Maggie frowned deeply but said nothing.

Teri was incredulous, her redheaded temper started. "What? Is he an idiot? He calls himself a coroner. Maggie, who isn't a forensic specialist, could do better. God Almighty!"

I raised my beer bottle to her. "Agreed, sister mine." I watched Maggie who was deep in thought as she picked at the label on the beer bottle. "What's on your mind, sweetie?"

She took a deep breath, then shot me a wide smile. At first, I didn't know why she was smiling. I then realized what I had said and felt my face get red hot. I drank my beer.

"Well...*sweetie*," she started happily, and Teri laughed. "It would appear—to me anyway—that someone with a good deal of force hit Sandy and killed her. I'm sure they must run a test on her blood gases. Perhaps she was drunk and fell, Kate. She was drinking very heavily at the party. However, I don't believe the trauma I saw was from a fall. I think someone hit her and that killed her."

"I agree. We need to go over to her house. Dan needs her

purse and belongings, next of kin and all," I said sadly.

We decided to all go together. "No one stays alone from now on until we can get the hell out of here. I don't know what's going on, but someone killed Sandy Meyers. We stay together," I said unwavering, and they both heartily agreed.

The wind picked up as we motored to Sandy's house. The wind would surely take the boat as we pulled to Sandy's pier. I sat Maggie behind the wheel and said, "Just cut the engine when I say."

I went to the bow of the boat with the mooring line in hand. As we got close to the pier, I called over my shoulder. Maggie cut the engine and steered us close enough. I jumped off and landed on the pier, pulled the boat in, and tied us off. I looked at Sandy's boat. It was filled with water; no cover had been put on it.

We had to break the pane of glass on her back door to get into her house. Feeling like trespassers, we quickly looked around. Teri and I looked in her bedroom. Her bed was unmade and clothes lay on the floor as if dropped as they were taken off. I felt like a ghoul and wanted to leave quickly.

Maggie was looking in the living room. "I don't see any kind of papers or anything," she called from the doorway.

Teri came out of the bedroom with a purse. She grimaced as she opened it. It was crammed to overflowing: wallet, checkbook, everything that a woman's purse holds. Safety pins, lint-ridden Lifesavers, a lace hanky, receipts from a year ago. *If Jimmy Hoffa jumps out...*

I saw a black phone book by the phone in the living room and leafed through it. Teri shivered as she looked around. "I don't like this. Let's go, quickly."

I only needed to hear that tone in Teri's voice once. Maggie agreed. We quickly took the purse and the book and skedaddled.

He watched as they pulled away from the dock. He couldn't believe they found her. He was furious with himself as he watched them pull away from her house. "Stupid, stupid, stupid," he repeated as he walked in circles, hitting himself in the head with his fists. "Will someone tell me why this is so...much...trouble...?"

Then he stopped and cocked his head. "Wait. It's not my fault. I had her crammed under that tree so tight. This frickin' weather. This stupid, stupid," he sighed, "stupid weather."

They found her, but it didn't matter. Soon, nothing else would matter. They were cut off. No one would be able to get in. He straightened his shirt, took a deep breath, and looked around. Hell, he ditched the car. Now he had to walk all the way. He didn't care, though, as he made his way through the mud and water keeping deep in the woods. Soon...

Dan listened as I gave all the information I could find. "So that's it," I said tiredly. There was a pause. "Dan? Are you there?"

"Yeah," he said slowly. "I didn't know you were a private investigator."

"Hannah and/or Ben?" I asked, trying to figure out why they would tell him.

"Ben. After I told him what the situation was, he thought I should know. I guess I was a little worried. I'm glad he told me. Why didn't you?"

"I'm not a private investigator anymore. That was a long time ago. What difference would it make?"

"No difference, I guess. Maybe I feel better knowing it. I don't worry as much," he said. Gratefully, he changed the subject. "So I have all the phone numbers. I'll start making calls. Still no sign of Reese or Thorn?"

"No, nothing," I said and I yawned so, I thought my jaw would crack.

"Well, get some rest. I'll talk to you tomorrow. The creek is still flooded and the power lines are still down. Looks like another day, Kate. Hang loose. We'll get to you as soon as we can."

After hanging up with Dan, I called Hannah and Ben, who didn't apologize for telling Dan. "He was worried and making a pain in the ass out of himself, Ryan. I figured if he knew you could take care of yourself, he'd relax and it worked."

"Fine, fine, I don't care. How's Hannah?" I asked anxiously.

"She's holding up just fine. Get some sleep, you sound like

hell. Probably look the same, too."

I took the phone away from my ear as he laughed. "Thank you for your consideration. We'll talk to you tomorrow, good night," I said sweetly and hung up on his laughter.

After a quiet dinner, Teri, looking very pooped, said her good nights, leaving Maggie and me sitting at the kitchen table. I reached over and took her hand in mine. "I really wish you and Teri would have gotten out of here."

Maggie lightly ran her fingers up and down my forearm. "I don't. Well, I wish Teri would have gotten out, but I wouldn't have left you anyway."

I smiled slightly and looked into her blue eyes. "You're not gonna leave me alone, are you?"

Her dimples started when she grinned. "Nope. You're stuck with me now." She then yawned.

"You need to get some sleep," I said as once again my heart raced.

"So do you," she replied in kind.

We sat there for a moment looking at our fingers entwined. The ache for her started again. As I looked into her eyes, I saw it—that look of want and desire.

"Maggie," I said and stopped.

"Yes, Kate?"

I let go of her hand. It was distracting me to no end. I picked up the saltshaker. "I—" I stopped and cleared my throat and looked up.

She was grinning slightly. "Yes?"

"We're both adults," I said hastily. Maggie raised an eyebrow but said nothing. "Well, at least you are." I played with the saltshaker.

"Yes, we're adults," Maggie agreed and sat back. "Now that we have that established."

"We've kissed and so forth."

"And so forth."

I looked up and chuckled. "Yes, well…"

Maggie took a deep breath, and I could tell she was getting impatient.

"You see," I said logically, "I want…"

"You want?" I saw the little artery pulsating in her neck. I was not sure if it was from arousal or anger. In this infancy stage of our—whatever this was—it was hard to tell the difference.

When I didn't say anything further, Maggie slowly stood. I looked up as she stood between my legs and ran her fingers through my hair. "I want, too, Kate." She then lowered her head and kissed me.

I groaned like a fool as her tongue snaked past my lips and into my mouth, all the while her fingers held a tight grip in my hair. When she pulled back, I tried to focus. "Good night," she whispered and walked out of the kitchen.

I sat there staring at the empty doorway. I realized I wasn't breathing when I gulped for air. My mouth was dry, my lips felt bruised, and my scalp tingled. "Holy crap," my voice squeaked out as I tried to swallow.

When I was sure I could walk, I turned out the light above the stove and made my way through the pitch darkness. I paused and looked at the staircase leading to the loft before I walked into my room.

I yawned as I slipped out of my shirt and unhooked my bra.

"Do that slowly, please."

I quickly looked at my bed to see Maggie, bathed in the moonlight, lying on her side, the sheet pulled up to her waist. She was naked under that sheet; that was the only thing I was certain of at that moment—that and I was about to have a stroke.

I realized then there was no more doubt, no more questioning. I wanted Maggie, and she wanted me. I suddenly remembered the way we danced on the pier, how we kissed, and how I felt from that one kiss.

All at once, I knew—it was time, time to let go of the past, or at least try to. Time to take that scary leap and get back into life. Time to love again. Time to love Dr. Maggie Winfield of Cedar Lake.

My heart drummed in my ears as I slipped my bra off, then pushed my shorts down my hips and stepped out of them. You have no idea how grateful I was I didn't trip. I listened to her breathing hitch as I walked to the bed. I stood there naked, feeling *very* vulnerable, yet perfectly natural before Maggie. Now I'm not in the best of shape, age and gravity have certainly taken its toll—

"You're beautiful, Kate," she whispered in a coarse voice. *Good, I'm not the only one whose mouth feels like the Sahara.*

Standing by the bedside, I reached down and gently pulled the sheet away, revealing her lovely body. It was as I imagined. Lying on her side, I noticed her small breasts, her long auburn hair, and the sensual curve of her hip.

"So are you," I replied and easily lay beside her, mirroring her position.

I reached over and brushed the hair off her shoulders and lightly caressed her cheek, down to her neck to the top of her breasts. "My God, you're so soft." I was amazed at the silken feel of her. I ran my fingers down to her breasts and leaned forward. Maggie sighed deeply as she now lay on her back.

"Just let me look at you," I whispered.

"God, Kate—"

I ran my fingertips between her breasts, listening to her breathing. She sighed and stretched out, placing her hands behind her head. Her small breasts were firm and her nipples hardened immediately as I raked my fingers over them. She caught her breath again and closed her eyes.

"So beautiful," I whispered. "I can't believe I'm touching you like this. Can't believe we're gonna make love." *We are, aren't we?*

Maggie nodded but said nothing. I cupped her breast, feeling the small weight of it in my palm. "Perfect." She moved, and I quickly held her hands above her head. "Please, just give me a minute, sweetie."

"You're driving me crazy," she said in a whimper.

"Sorry," I said. "I'm just amazed at the feel of you."

I ran my fingers down her torso, feeling her stomach muscles fluttering beneath my fingers. "It's been so long for me." I slipped farther down to the top of her thighs and smiled as she parted her legs.

"Please," she whispered as her body trembled.

"What? Tell me," I found myself saying. I wanted so much to please her. I gazed at her breasts and my mouth watered. "Tell me," I mumbled against her breast. She arched her back and let out a small gasp as I bathed her nipple with my tongue. I was in heaven, still trying to wrap my mind around the fact that I was making love to Maggie.

I groaned as my fingers slipped through her damp curls, her arousal coating my fingers. I looked up. "Is this what you want, sweetie?"

Maggie nodded furiously. "Yes, touch me, please."

I took her breast into my mouth once again as I felt her swollen clitoris throb against my fingers. "My God, Maggie," I mumbled against her breast.

"Ohgodohgod," I heard her whimper. "Yes."

I pulled away from her breast. "Maggie, please look at me."

Her eyes shot open and tried to focus. "You've been so patient," I whispered and swirled my fingers through her wetness. She arched her back once again. "So loving," I murmured and kissed her deeply. I slipped my tongue deep into her mouth and heard her soft moan as she eagerly accepted it. She whimpered as I moved my fingers lower. Our tongues darted and danced as I entered her. I couldn't help myself; my body shivered and I groaned into her mouth as I added another finger. I pulled back, breathless. "So warm," I whispered.

An inexplicable feeling of contentment wafted through me as I moved within her. I felt as if I were part of her. Her warmth felt like a safe haven. When I felt her walls contract around my fingers, I pulled back. "Come for me, Maggie," I murmured against her lips.

"Yes, Kate. For you." Her arms flew around my neck and pulled me into a crushing embrace. Our breasts compressed against each other, my heart beat wildly out of control as I loved her. "Kate! Please!" she cried out as I continued.

I buried my head in her neck as her fingers entwined in my hair, holding me close. Her body stilled for an instant before it shook with the force of her orgasm.

I continued to thrust deeper as she shook uncontrollably. "Kate!" Maggie cried out and frantically grabbed at my shoulders.

After a few moments, Maggie was panting, her body glistening as she writhed through her orgasm. A thought ran through my brain at that moment: I may not be able to love Maggie the way she deserves, but right now, right at this moment, I loved her with everything I had in me. I knew I could give her this pleasure and my heart ached at wanting to give her everything she desired.

I felt her body begin to relax as she whimpered and caressed my back and shoulders. As I slowly withdrew my fingers, her thighs tightened around them. I looked up into her smiling blue eyes.

"I didn't want it to happen so quickly, but I couldn't help it. Stay inside, please," she whispered.

I heard the disappointment in her voice. "I think we're both a little overwhelmed," I said and kissed her dry lips. "You're so warm, Maggie. You feel like heaven."

Maggie sighed happily and held me close to her breast. "My God. That was unbelievable."

I shrugged slightly. Maggie gently pushed me back and cupped my face. "You don't believe me?"

I shrugged again, not knowing what to say. This was a whole new ballgame to me. "I dunno."

She breathed heavily through her nose. If it wasn't dark, I know I'd see the left eye twitch. "So you think I say this to all the girls?"

Was she angry or hurt? Ryan, you dumb-ass. "Maggie, no, I don't think you say this to all the girls. I-I suppose I never thought this would happen for me." I stopped and took a deep breath.

Maggie caressed my cheek. "I never did, either."

I must have been staring at her like a dope. "Are you nuts?"

Maggie laughed and shook her head.

"You're a beautiful woman and sexy. Geezus, Maggie, I—"

She pulled me up to her and wrapped her arms around me. "You're talking too much, Miss Ryan," she whispered against my cheek.

I kissed her lovely neck, my tongue lazily slipping up to her ear. "Maggie?" I whispered.

"Yes, Kate," she replied and moaned deeply, as my tongue bathed her ear.

"Can I have my hand back now?"

Maggie let out a small laugh. "As long as I can have it back."

I kissed the top of her breast. "Whenever you like." I withdrew my hand as Maggie groaned deeply.

With a quick move, I didn't think she had in her, Maggie had me on my back and she was looming over me. "Hello," I said with a grin.

"Hey," she whispered with a grin of her own. "My turn, Miss Ryan."

I heard a tone in her voice that I had yet to hear. It sounded positively sultry. I swallowed convulsively. "Well, isn't it too soon?" I questioned, trying to ignore how I immediately started trembling.

"Nope," Maggie said and kissed me. Her long hair cascaded down, tickling my shoulders.

"Aren't we supposed to wait twenty minutes or something?" Now I tried to ignore the squeak in my voice.

"Uh-uh." Maggie grinned and shook her head. "I've been thinking about this moment since last fall."

"You have?" I asked. I groaned as I felt her fingernails lightly raking across my breasts. *Oh, God...*

"When I first opened my eyes and saw the worried look in your green eyes, I knew you had done more than knock me off my horse—you sent my heart into a tailspin."

"I did?" I tried to peel my tongue off the roof of my mouth. "Th-that was almost a year ago."

"Yes, but that's all going to change right now."

"You seem pretty sure of yourself, Doctor," I said breathlessly. I arched my back and I felt her warm lips against my breasts. "Ya know I'm not in the best of shape, and…" I stopped short and groaned when I felt her tongue flicking across my painfully hard nipple.

"You're beautiful, Kate," she mumbled against my breast. I closed my eyes and sighed as her fingers danced down my stomach and across my hips.

"Okay, I give," I said and parted my legs. "I'm all yours."

She looked up from feasting on my breast and grinned. "At last," she said with a wink.

Her tongue was incredibly soft as it flicked across my nipple, first one breast, then the other, until I whimpered like a small child. I ran my fingers through her long hair. "God, Maggie, you feel so damned good. Don't stop."

She didn't. Her tongue danced across my breasts, her fingers ran up and down my torso, turning me into a mass of quivering flesh.

"I need to taste you." She kissed her way down the length of my torso before settling between my legs.

It had been so long for me, I nearly came right there. So many sensations bombarded my poor brain: the feel of Maggie's soft skin and her long hair flowing across my thighs. The idea alone of Maggie making love to me this way was overwhelming. I knew I was very aroused as I parted my legs for her. She moved from the top of my thighs down to my knees and back up again, leaving a trail of moist kisses in her wake. I shook with anticipation and could almost feel her tongue against me.

"Maggie, please," I begged as I reached down and ran my fingers through her thick hair, pulling her against me. I heard a deep groan and I jumped as she placed a small kiss against my overheated flesh. Skyrockets went off in my brain as I cried out and nearly arched right off the bed when I felt her cool tongue slip through me. It was heavenly. "Oh, Maggie," I groaned.

The thought of Maggie loving me this way, caring for me in a way no other woman ever had, had my heart thumping and my body aching for more. Again and again, Maggie teased and licked while I bucked and writhed against her warm, wet tongue. Never had I been so thoroughly loved.

My body broke out in a cold sweat, my heart continued to race as I felt the onset of my orgasm building deep in my belly. "Maggie!" I cried out my warning as she continued.

I was on the edge, and she knew it. She entered me with two fingers and that was it. The orgasm rippled through me and my body convulsed uncontrollably. I was speaking in Swahili—and I don't speak Swahili—as Maggie thrust deeper and batted her tongue against my sensitive clit.

After a moment, I began to see stars. I thought my heart was going to burst as my body continued to spasm. *I just may have a stroke*.

"No more," I cried out. I reached down and easily pulled her small body away from me and pulled her up, where she lay atop of me. "Good God, woman!" I cried out and wrapped my arms around her.

She kissed my neck. "Incredible," she murmured and kissed up to my chin, then to my ear. Her dastardly tongue flicked around my sensitive earlobe. "I knew it would be like this."

"Stop it, please!" I begged in earnest as I twitched. "I'm gonna pass out. I'm not kidding."

She laughed and relented, then shared the taste of my arousal in a sensual kiss, which she ended it by sucking on my bottom lip, then kissing my chin.

"Okay, Dr. Winfield," I said breathlessly as I held her close. "I hope you're a cardiologist."

Maggie laughed quietly and slipped next to me, cuddling close to my side. She then nuzzled for a moment, seemingly trying to get comfortable. When she tossed her leg across my body and wrapped her arm around my waist, I smiled happily. "All settled in?" I asked and kissed the top of her head.

"Hmm, yes," she whispered.

I lay there for some time, listening to the crickets chirping. I knew Maggie was awake since I felt her eyelashes fluttering against my chest. "Thank you," I whispered into the darkness.

Maggie shifted slightly and I felt her lips kiss the top of my breast. "Same here, Kate. I love the way I fit so perfectly against you. We do fit, don't we?"

I smiled and pulled her closer, my fingers lightly running up and down her back. "We fit, Maggie," I assured her.

For an instant, my stomach knotted as the image of Liz

Eddington flashed through my mind. "I hope you know what you're getting into with me."

I felt her arm tighten around my waist. "I know what I want, Kate Ryan. You've got that demon you're chasing. I'll help you anyway I can, baby."

I kissed the top of her head and sighed.

"That was a big sigh," Maggie said with a yawn.

"I kinda like it when you call me baby," I said and reached down to pull the sheet over us. "I love the feel of your body against mine, Maggie. I can't believe we just made love."

Maggie looked up then, and through the moonlight, I saw tears in her eyes.

"Hey, what's wrong?" I asked, thinking the worst. *Fine, one night with me and she's crying.*

She reached up and touched my face. "Nothing, absolutely nothing. Good night, Katie."

"G'night, Maggie," I whispered.

For an instant, we looked into each other's eyes. When I kissed her tenderly, I knew no matter what, kissing Maggie Winfield would be the most heavenly thing I could imagine. Her lips were so soft; her soul was right there, right in that kiss.

I prayed with all my heart that I could be true to Maggie and the love she felt for me.

Chapter Twenty

I woke with a start and found myself alone in bed. Glancing at the clock, I saw it was nearly 8:30. I never sleep this late. I grinned like some teenager and put my hands behind my head and let out a huge contented sigh as I remembered our night. My body was still thrumming.

"You look awfully pleased with yourself."

I opened my eyes to see Maggie standing there wearing a short white robe. Fresh from the shower, her long thick hair was wet and combed and her face flushed. She was drinking a cup of coffee and leaning against the doorjamb.

"I am actually." I eyed the coffee cup. "I'd kill for a cup of coffee."

"No more murder, please, Miss Ryan." She sat on the edge of the bed and handed me the steamy cup.

I sat up and took the offering. "Why didn't you wake me?" I asked as I blew into the cup.

"You looked too adorable sleeping and you needed the rest," she said and ran her fingers through my hair. My heart started to beat out of control again.

I set the cup down and reached for her. Maggie chuckled and ruffled my hair as she kissed me. "Good morning," she said as she pulled back.

"G'morning," I said, still grinning.

Maggie shook her head. "Will you get that ridiculous grin off your face?"

"You put it there." I reached for her again.

She quickly scooted off the bed. "Teri is up and in the kitchen."

I had completely forgotten that we were not alone the previous night—and we were loud. I closed my eyes and winced as I flopped back against the pillows. "You think she heard us?" I heard her contagious laughter and opened my eyes.

"I think we woke up every loon on this lake," she assured me.

I let out a deep groan and covered my face with a pillow. "I can't believe my sister heard me having sex with you," I said in a muffled voice.

"We're adults, remember?"

"Says you."

"Good morning!" I took the pillow away to see Teri standing in the doorway, grinning. "I am so happy for you!" she nearly squealed and held her hand to her heart.

I was stunned. I glanced at Maggie who was five shades of red—very adorable—as she sat on the edge of the bed.

I put the pillow back over my head. "I give."

I couldn't eat breakfast—a first—mainly because Maggie and I exchanged sappy lovesick glances. Well, mine were sappy. I know this will sound stupid, but when Maggie looked over her cup of coffee and winked at me, my heart hammered in my chest and the aching for her started again. *Good grief, just from a wink.*

So after picking at my breakfast, I decided to take the Jeep and check out the roads. Of course, Maggie came with me. We drove as far as we could. When we got to the end of my entrance, we were shocked. There was water everywhere. The woods were flooded with at least three feet of water, but hell, we found the loons. They lazily swam and dove in the floodwaters. Tree limbs and branches floated by as we watched.

"We woke them up last night. At least we didn't scare them off the lake," I said dryly, and Maggie laughed along.

"But I think I was right yesterday. I bet we could take the rowboat and get out it if wasn't for that tree." I looked down the road. "We'd have to use the rowboat with the small motor. My speedboat sits too deep in the water. Well, let's get back."

As I started back, Maggie gently grabbed my arm. I looked

down into her blue eyes. "What?"

She smiled and my heart stopped. "Nothing, just this," she said and stood on her tiptoes and kissed me. "I love to be able to do that now."

"I do, too," I said and returned her kiss. I pulled her close and she moaned into the kiss. Thank God the Jeep was behind me as I leaned against it. As I lightly flicked my tongue against her lips, I felt her body sag against me. I pulled back and looked down. With her eyes closed, she sighed as I kissed the corner of her mouth, her cheek, then her forehead.

"God, Kate," she whispered as she rested her forehead against my chin. "I can't believe how sensual you are."

I ran my hands up and down her back. "You make me feel that way. I can't seem to stop touching you," I said and blushed furiously.

The grin spread across Maggie's face. I tried to ignore those dimples. "We, um, we'd better get back."

Teri was sitting at the kitchen table drinking her coffee when Maggie and I returned. I noticed she was looking at the paper I had scribbled on from our Quija night.

"What are you doing?" I asked cautiously, as if I didn't know.

"I'm still trying to figure out what that name was that was spelled out the other night," Teri said thoughtfully.

"That seems like a year ago." Maggie poured two cups of coffee.

"I think we should try again," Teri said.

"You're kidding," I said hopefully.

Maggie chuckled. "Kate, look at her face. Is that the face of someone who's joking?"

Teri had already gotten the Scrabble letters and I grudgingly retrieved the trusted wineglass. "I was hoping." I groaned and put the glass on the table.

With the letters in place, Teri smiled. "Here we go. We're all doing it this time."

I reluctantly put my finger on the glass along with theirs.

"Don't be a ninny." Teri sighed and the glass happily started its circular motion, as if it was waiting for us.

Teri cleared her throat. "We can't leave, whoever you are, so think of something else to say."

"Sing a few bars of 'Swanee River,'" I suggested as I leaned over it. Maggie nudged my ribcage.

"V-E-R-Y S-O-O-N. Very soon," Maggie repeated. "Someone is coming very soon?"

Great, now Maggie is into this.

The glass quickly slid across the table and knocked into the letters that spelled YES. It slid back into the middle, as if waiting for another question.

"This is like playing twenty questions with a ghost," I whispered to Maggie, who tried to give me a stern look as she shook her head.

Teri ignored me. "Who's coming?"

Teri looked at the table and the glass started to move rapidly. Once again, Maggie and I had a hard time keeping up with it.

"Teri, I think you've upset it. Ask something else." I was not joking. I felt a vibration coming from this glass run all the way up my arm.

"Okay, okay. Who are you?" Teri asked quickly and the glass slowed. It almost looked confused, if that were possible. The glass aimlessly touched almost all the letters, not stopping at any one in particular.

I shook my head. "This doesn't make sense."

Maggie nodded but said nothing.

"It spelled out C-H-A-S-K-O-T-E last time. Is that a name?" I asked Teri, and the glass slid across to YES, then to NO.

We all stared at the wineglass as it moved across the table, back and forth from YES to NO.

Suddenly, I felt as though there was someone, something in the room with us. A shiver sliced through me as I looked around my cabin.

"I feel it, too, Kate," Teri said and looked around for God knows what.

Great, now I have a ghost in my log cabin. So much for

solitude.

"What can we do?" Teri asked, looking at the glass. It slid back and forth.

Once again, it spelled, out L-E-A-V-E. We all groaned.

Maggie got a little aggravated and took a deep breath. "Let me try."

"Uh-oh." I groaned and looked at Teri, who shrugged.

"Look, we can't leave. We're stuck, so if you've got something to say, say it," Maggie said firmly.

I could tell she felt a little ridiculous talking to a wineglass. I bit my lip in an effort to hold back the barking laugh at the serious look on her face. However, the wineglass was doing a little talking of its own. It almost angrily teetered and rammed itself into the letters. We tried to keep up and read aloud as it touched them.

"M-" Teri started, "U-R-D-E-R."

"Murder…" I repeated flatly and gave Maggie a scathing look. "Fine, you've annoyed chaskote."

"Who's murdered?" Teri asked quickly, trying to keep it moving while ignoring me.

"S-I-L-L-Y S-A-N-D… Silly sandals." Teri looked at both of us. "Sandy Meyers." Teri caught her breath. The glass flew to YES.

I cleared my throat and said nicely to the wineglass, "If you could find your way to tell us who murdered her, I'd be awfully grateful."

Maggie chuckled and the glass moved in its circular motion. The glass looked as though it was gearing up for another spelling lesson. We all leaned in and once again tried to keep up.

Teri called out the letters, "H-E, who he?"

"He who…" I corrected her as she impatiently waved me off. The wineglass spelled out once again.

"M-E… Me?" I asked stupidly and Teri glared at me. I was all confused. *He, me, who?*

The glass was rapidly moving in a circular motion. It got faster and faster until I thought it would cut right into my kitchen table. The scraping noise it caused was unnerving to say the least. I gave a helpless look at Teri, as did Maggie. Then Teri's eyes widened as if something dawned on her.

"He killed Sandy and—you," Teri said confidently.

Then the glass slid, almost flew, across the table, knocking into YES.

The glass slowed down but still looked as though it was searching for something. I gave Teri a questioning glance. She shrugged.

"Was there something else?" she asked.

I glanced at Maggie who looked as confused as I was. The glass then spelled out something more.

"B-O-A-T, boat," Teri said. "What boat?"

"Maybe the boat we're going to use to get out of here," I suggested.

The glass quickly shot over to NO.

"Okay, what boat then?" Maggie questioned as she watched the glass.

"I-R-E-L-A-N-D... Ireland?" Teri asked and looked from me to Maggie.

"What has Ireland got to do with this?" Maggie asked.

I sat back while Maggie and Teri still had their fingertips on the glass. It moved so slowly that we all just watched it.

"T-" Teri started as the glass slowly moved through the letters. "R-E-A-S-U-R-E."

The glass stopped completely.

"Treasure?" Maggie repeated and looked at me.

"What do Ireland and that treasure you found last spring have to do with this?" Teri asked, and I could see something in her eyes that looked very much like fear. I nearly soiled myself.

"Teri? W-what's wrong?" I asked and glanced at Maggie who looked just as scared as I felt.

"I-I don't know," Teri said. "It's just as if there was someone else here."

I shivered violently. "What do you mean, here? Like here, here?"

Maggie rolled her eyes. "Teri, you mean another spirit?"

Teri nodded and stared at the wineglass. "Really, I'm not sure."

Really, I think she was...

We all sat at the table staring at the wineglass. "I will never be able to drink out of that glass again," I said. I was numb, overtired and now, thank you, we had not one but two murders to think about. That is, if you believe Scrabble letters and an overturned wineglass.

"Well, that was interesting," Maggie said.

"Very," Teri said. She looked at me. "Do you believe?"

"In Tinkerbell? Yes. In this?" I pointed to the table and sighed. "I would be more convinced if I knew who or what chaskote was." I rubbed my forehead. I walked into the living room and looked out at the lake.

"Do you think we're alone on this lake?" Maggie asked from behind me.

"No. I don't," I said sincerely. "I believe we're being watched. I've had a feeling of that all week. I can't explain it, but I don't think we're alone. What next?"

I've been saying that all week. I really didn't need an answer.

Chapter Twenty-One

It was 11:30 when I saw him. I was standing on the porch in the dark, looking through the night vision glasses. Martin looked around, then looked across at my cabin. Then he opened his door and stepped inside. He hadn't closed his door and I could see him through the screen door. Once again, he was sitting in his kitchen in the dark. *Where the hell had he been?* I thought as I watched. He put his head down on his arms for a moment, then sat up and rubbed his hands over his face as if to rouse himself. He then stretched his neck as if it bothered him.

"I know the feeling..." I whispered as I continued looking through the field glasses. "Martin, Martin. Where have you been?"

He stood up and stretched and I lost him as he walked down the hall and out of my line of vision. I sat in my rocker for a few minutes and watched his cottage. Then I scanned the lake and saw nothing, but hey, the loons returned.

Smiling, I saw a few of them; the eerie green illumination of the night glasses gave them a haunting glow. I continued to scan and stopped at Henry's house. No movement there, either. I really couldn't see in the house; all the shades were drawn.

I took the glasses away from my face. Were the shades drawn the day before as we passed the house? My mind raced as I frantically tried to remember. We had motored by and I thought... *What did I think?*

"Damn it," I said irritably. I stopped rocking and looked through the glasses once more. I wondered if Lucas Thorn had left the lake. I hadn't seen him at all.

The clouds were breaking and a gentle breeze had started.

Good, that'll get these annoying rain clouds moving off the lake.

As I watched the clouds drift by, I thought of Sandy Meyers. What an awful way to die. My guess is that she was hit from behind, and I hoped she was killed instantly. From what Maggie said, if there was no water in her lungs, which there wasn't, then she was dead before she even went into the lake. Then I remembered the bruises and scratches on her legs. Maybe she was killed in the woods, then dragged to the lake. That could explain the scratches. I wondered, though, who hit her and with what and more importantly—why.

I ventured back into the living room to find Maggie asleep on the couch. I wished she and Teri had been able to get out the other day. Hell, I wish we all could have.

I thought how close we came to getting out of here, if Teri's car had started. What are the odds of that happening just when we wanted to leave? What a coincidence. Coincidence—no such thing in a homicide, my blessed father used to say.

Then I looked across at Martin's cottage. What did he say he did in the Marines? A mechanic, worked on tanks, he had said. How hard would it have been for him to sabotage Teri's van? That was stupid. If Martin were somehow involved, why would he want us to stay? Maybe I'm reaching.

Suddenly, I started to shiver, even though it was a warm evening. I looked around the lake. This is my little piece of heaven, and I'll be damned if I'll let anyone take it away from me. Somewhere out there, someone has killed one, possibly two people. That's if you believe chaskote, I chuckled inwardly. However, I still don't know what it has to do with me or if in fact, it does. Now the Ouija board brings up Ireland last spring—why?

I put my head back and my feet up on the porch railing and watched the clouds quickly move as the moon faded in and out, illuminating the lake every now and then. It was wonderfully quiet as the crickets chirped. That's when I heard it. The noise sounded familiar. I raised my head but kept very still. The wind had died and not a leaf was stirring. I strained, trying to listen. There it was again. What the hell was that? A faint, clicking noise, like metal on metal.

I looked around the woods and saw nothing, of course. Then I looked down by my beach, nothing. Sitting there completely still, I strained once more to hear. *Click,* click. I heard it again. Slowly, I got up and tried not to make any noise. I walked off my porch and down toward the pier. Completely in the dark, I looked all over as I heard it again—*click*, click. I looked out toward the lake. It sounded like it was coming from all directions. Noises carry and are distorted over water, so I couldn't tell where it was coming from now. My senses were leaving me; I was overtired and my mind was shutting down.

I grabbed my phone and the field glasses and went inside. I had just locked the doors when Maggie woke.

"What time is it, Kate?" she mumbled and sat up.

"A little after midnight, sweetie."

She stood and brushed the hair away from her face. "You need to sleep," she ordered and pushed me down the hall.

"God, I'm tired." I groaned as I stretched out.

Maggie chuckled as she lay next to me. "The honeymoon's over."

I laughed along and pulled her close. "We'll talk about that when we get home."

Maggie lifted her head and looked at me. "We will?"

"Well, yeah," I said, suddenly feeling confused. "Won't we?" I was out of the relationship loop for quite some time. *Relationship?* My stomach instantly flipped.

Maggie laughed again and nestled into my shoulder. "I can hear the wheels turning. No more thinking tonight," she said and kissed my neck. "Good night, Katie."

I sighed like a dope and held her close. "Good night, Maggie." I closed my eyes and was asleep within minutes.

I was awakened by the sound of my bedroom door creaking, the same way it did the other night. I was lying on my side, with my back to the door and spooned behind Maggie. Not being able to see the door, I felt extremely vulnerable.

I opened my eyes but didn't move. I don't know why. Half-asleep at first, I thought I might be dreaming. I couldn't keep my eyes open and thought I might have drifted off, then I heard the hallway creak. *Teri must be using the bathroom, as Hannah had used it the other night when I heard the same thing,* I thought sleepily. I opened one eye and looked at the clock, 3:15.

I will never sleep again. I groaned and rolled over on my back.

I felt it then—someone was in my room.

"Katie?" Teri's voice called.

After peeling myself off the ceiling, I exclaimed, "Geezus Christ, Teri!"

Maggie jumped up, as well, and flipped on the small lamp. Teri sat on the edge of the bed. She looked as though she'd seen a ghost.

"Oh, God, don't tell me chaskote made an appearance," I said half joking.

"Not funny. Were you up walking around a while ago?" she asked anxiously.

I looked around my room. "No, I thought it was you."

"No, it was not me."

"C'mon, let's check," I said and bounded out of bed.

"You're not leaving me in here alone," Maggie said and followed us.

Teri walked into the living room and flipped on the light. I turned on the small light above the stove in the kitchen. Maggie checked the back door while I checked the kitchen. "I'll check the spare room," Maggie said and disappeared down the hall.

After making sure both doors were locked, I turned and noticed my extra set of house keys were on the peg. My blood ran cold as I stared at them. Teri came into the kitchen.

"What's wrong?" she asked.

I pointed at the keys.

"So?" she asked confused.

"So they weren't there when we were leaving the other day. I remember distinctly they were not on that peg," I tried to convince her.

She cocked her head. "I remember you saying they were gone, yes. Honestly, I can't remember if I saw them or not. Maybe you were mistaken?" she asked, scratching her head.

She then stepped back and looked at me. I looked down and asked, "What?"

The corners of her mouth were twitching. "Are those...little fishes on those sexy boxers you're wearing?"

I looked down at my boxers, then I became indignant. "Yes. I like them."

"Between those fish boxers and that Hawaiian shirt... Kate, you're a fashion nightmare. Please let me or even Maggie buy your clothes from now on," she pleaded.

"What am I buying?" Maggie asked as she returned.

"Nothing," I replied firmly.

Teri laughed. "Check out Kate's boxers. I didn't know you wore boxers," she said to me.

"I only wear them to bed when I have to wear something," I said and turned bright red.

Maggie grinned evilly. "Not on my account."

"Oh, go to bed, children," I said wearily and turned off the light.

Teri kissed my head. "G'nite, you sexy thing." She chuckled all the way to her bedroom.

I don't know why I was embarrassed. I wear those boxers all the time. Perhaps, it was the way Maggie was grinning.

Maggie sensed my embarrassment. How couldn't she? I was as red as a beet, even in the darkness. "Well, now I know what to get you for Christmas," she said as she crawled into bed.

"Don't forget my birthday," I said and slipped in behind her.

We comfortably assumed our previous position. Spooning behind her, I wrapped my arm around her small waist. "God, I love the feel of you."

She let out a contented sigh and wriggled her body back into mine. "I do, too, Kate. I feel safe in your arms."

We lay in the darkness once again, and just before sleep overtook me, I mumbled, "Am I a fashion nightmare?"

I heard Maggie's soft chuckle as she pulled my hand up to her breast. I let out a deep groan, and I snugly engulfed her breast. She hadn't answered my question. "Am I?"

"Yes, Kate," she whispered and kissed my arm. "Now go to sleep."

I frowned deeply and grumbled something. "But I love those boxers," she whispered and held onto my arm. "They're sexy."

Hmm, Maggie thinks my boxers are sexy? Geesh, I hope she doesn't want me to wear them all the time. What if she does? What if she wants me to start wearing...

"Stop thinking and go to sleep," Maggie warned. "G'night."

"G'night," I whispered and kissed her shoulder. "Will you get out of my head? How is it you can do that? And don't think I'm wearing fish boxers all the—"

With the agility of a jungle cat, Maggie turned over and got me on my back. "There's only one way to shut you up, Miss Ryan," she said, looming over me.

I looked up at her in the darkness as I slipped my hand beneath her tank top and palmed her warm breast. She let out a helpless sigh as I smiled. "It's that easy, huh?"

I stood on my porch the next morning and stretched my aching body. The young Dr. Winfield was in far better shape than I; at least we didn't wake up Teri or the loons. The heavy fog had rolled in and settled over the lake. It's interesting how fog dulls the senses. It was completely quiet, except for my beloved loons, calling every so often and echoing around the lake. I could barely see Martin's cottage, but it was still early, the sun was just rising. Then I had an idea that I had to do before the sun came up and burned the fog off the lake.

There was another cove behind Martin's cottage. It was opposite the cove where we found Sandy Meyers's shoes. From that side, I could dock the boat and walk the two hundred feet or so of woods to the back entrance of the cottages, without being seen. Maybe, just maybe, I'd get lucky and Martin would be gone and perhaps I could get into his cottage.

Maggie was still sleeping from our late-night sexual escapades. It took more out of us trying to be quiet. Though I had more stamina than I realized, I ached in places I didn't know I had muscles. The younger Dr. Winfield will be the death of me.

Teri was still sleeping, as well. I should wait till they got up, but my gut told me to do this quickly. So I left them a note, then took the extra set of keys and locked the doors. When they woke up, they'd be angry. I knew that.

I decided to take the rowboat. At first, I was going to change motors and put the larger motor on the rowboat. However, it would make too much noise. There was no noise to the trolling motor. It would take longer, but at least I wouldn't be heard. I watched Martin's cottage as I trolled across the lake. Every once in a while, I stole a glance to my left toward Henry's house. I could see nothing through the fog, which was good—no one could see me. I hope.

I passed the cottages and saw no signs of Martin. Trolling around the point, I steered to the right and into the small cove. I pulled up along the shore and tied my rowboat to a felled tree stump. I made sure it was secured, as all I needed was to have my only means of transportation adrift in the middle of the lake. I walked inland through the mud and ankle-deep water. It took me almost twenty minutes before I made it to the back of the cottages. The fog was thick, which was to my advantage as I crouched down and watched his cottage.

Waiting for a few minutes, I saw no movement, so I crept up to his windows. I checked every one; he was not in the bedroom, even the bathroom was vacant. Confident that he was gone, I cautiously tried the back door. To my surprise and horror, it was open.

Fear gripped me momentarily, then my instincts took over and I opened the door. Walking in, I made sure the screen door did not slam as I walked into the kitchen. I looked around and found nothing out of the ordinary—the table was neat except for his cigarettes, ashtray with a couple of cigarette butts, and lighter. It was then the lighter caught my eye. It was one of the old Zippo lighters, the silver kind you had to refill. I remember my father had one and he always played with it... I suddenly remembered that clicking noise that I heard the night before.

I picked up the lighter, noticing the Marines emblem on it, and flipped it open, then snapped it shut. I did this several times; that was it—*click,* click. That was the sound I heard while standing on my pier. If it were indeed Martin, he had to be close for me to hear it that clearly. I put the lighter back in its place and felt the ashtray. It was cool, so I figured Martin hadn't smoked before he left or had been gone quite awhile. Whatever, I needed to get out of there quickly.

I crept into the living room. These cottages were cozy but very small. I walked down a hall to the only bedroom.

I breathed a sigh of relief as I cautiously pushed the door open. I looked on the small dresser and saw a few personal items: a shaving kit, comb, brush. Then I saw his dog tags and gingerly picked them up. I thought servicemen were supposed to wear these at all times. I'd have to ask Ben about that one.

Looking at them, I did not see what I expected. I looked for Reese, Martin, his serial number, USMC, and his birth date. I was shocked to see the name Andrews, Martin J.

I stared at the tags, completely confused, then I got very nervous. I quickly looked around and spotted his luggage. It was Government Issue—a green khaki duffel bag. His name was stenciled on it, Andrews, Martin J… *Crap, who is this guy?* Why change his name?

My gut told me to get the hell out of there. I replaced the dog tags as I found them, repeating his serial number over and over to remember it, and quickly made my way out the back door and closed it. Looking around and seeing nothing through the fog, I headed toward the woods.

I motored back to my cabin. I looked over my shoulder and saw someone standing on the shore shrouded in the dense morning fog.

Chapter Twenty-Two

After scaring the hell out of myself, I quickly headed back to the safety of my pier.

Out of the dense fog, I saw a most terrifying sight: Maggie and Teri standing there, scowling—so much for safety.

I maneuvered the rowboat behind the speedboat and tossed Maggie the line. She tied it off.

"What—" Teri started.

I put my hand up to stop her as I repeated Martin's serial number and ran past them to the cabin, leaving them scowling and confused.

I got a pencil and quickly wrote down Martin's dog tag number. Sighing with relief, I turned to see them both standing in the doorway.

"Okay, get angry. I deserve it, but let me explain first," I pleaded.

"Fine, go ahead," Teri said. She was more worried than angry, they both were. I explained what I did and why I did it. They listened and said nothing.

"So there you go. I'm sorry, I know I said no one goes anywhere alone, but honestly, I had to do this before the fog cleared. I didn't mean to scare anyone."

"I see your point," Maggie said with resignation. "But don't do it again."

"Maggie, I can't promise anything like that. Please don't ask. This is a very odd situation and I have to follow my instincts. If I don't, I'll never get to the bottom of this." I watched them both.

"Teri, you follow your intuition, your guts. So do I," I challenged her.

"You're right. Only something always happens to you," she said, exasperated and threw up her hands.

"What did you find?" Maggie asked as we sat at the kitchen table.

I explained what I found and Teri frowned deeply. "Mac and I had a discussion about that once. He said you're supposed to wear them at all times, no matter where you are."

"Sure, if you're who you say you are. However, if you're masquerading as someone else, you wouldn't," I said, and Teri nodded in agreement. "I'm starving," I said and started to get up.

Teri put her hand on my shoulder. "Sit, bloodhound. I'll make breakfast." She was still angry, I could tell.

Maggie leaned over to me. "Kate, you must know someone who can find out who—"

I thought for a moment and grinned. "I do. Why didn't I think of him before?" I ran to the phone and dialed Bob Whittier's number. "Bob can track him down..." I started, and Bob answered the phone.

"Kate Ryan. My God, how in the hell are you? I haven't seen you since last April at the airport." His voice sounded clear and happy. Bob Whittier, my partner. We were as close as two people could be. For almost ten years, we worked our P.I. business well. He had his own security business now in Arizona. It's the only weather that suits him since his kneecap was practically blown off.

After a few minutes of catching up, I briefly told him what was happening. He listened, not interrupting until I was finished.

"Holy cow, Irish. You got yourself in the middle of something. What do you need?" he asked, and I smiled knowing he would do anything for me, as I would for him.

I explained about Martin Reese, or Andrews. I gave him the serial number and any other information I could think of. I told him about Lucas Thorn, but I had no information on him.

"Lucas Thorn doesn't sound like an ordinary name. I'll see what I can dig up. Doesn't it strike you as curious, Irish, that you don't know anything about this guy and you've been around him for a week?"

"Now that you mention it, Bob, it's very curious," I said, cursing myself for not finding out anything more on Lucas Thorn.

"I know you. You're blaming yourself again. Look, keep your eyes open and get those cop instincts honed. This may take the day. I'll call you by late evening, how's that? I've got a friend who owes me a favor. I'm sure he can tell me what I need to know about this Martin. Don't worry, I'll get all the skinny on your Marine." We talked for a few more minutes, then rang off.

I put the phone down and smiled. It was good to hear his voice. "I need to call him more often. He sounded happy," I said, feeling much better that I called.

"Can he find out anything?" Maggie asked.

"Bob Whittier was Dad's partner for twelve years before Dad died. Bob and I learned a great deal from Dad," I said, as the memories drifted through my mind. "If anybody can find out, Bob can."

The heavy fog had lifted, though there was still a light fog that hung over the lake. The day had turned cool as we sat on the porch trying to fit all of this together.

"Why would Martin lie about his last name? I don't know him, no one does. Who would care what his name is?" I stood up and paced back and forth. "He must know someone or thinks someone would know him by name."

As I looked across the lake, the shroud of light fog gave the lake cottages a somewhat mystical aura. "What is your business here, Martin?"

"Maybe he knew Sandy Meyers," Teri said as she watched me pace.

"Why change his name?" I countered logically. "I'm sure he's from St. Louis. I'm sure his parents died when he was eighteen, and I'm sure his sister died eight months ago. My guts tell me this is all true. There's some reason he picked this lake—the same reason he's lying about his name. Same reason he's watching my cabin. He's probably watching it right now." I waved stupidly and Maggie chuckled. "Hi, Martin," I said, then glanced into the woods.

She's beginning to annoy me, he thought as he watched them on the porch. She looks in the woods far too much. She'll see me one of these times, he thought, smiling. His smile faded as Kate, once again looked into the woods, right in his direction. Yes, she's beginning to annoy me, he growled to himself. He stood perfectly still as she looked almost right at him. That's it, he said to himself, look all you want. Tomorrow... it will all be done by tomorrow.
The insidious grin lit up his face.

There was an eerie quiet on the lake. The light fog dulled my senses as the loons cried their mourning call. As we sat on the porch, we still couldn't see across the lake. Even Ben's pier that was only one hundred feet or so away was hard to distinguish.

Then we heard it. We all looked at each other, then looked at the lake. It sounded like a boat motor, off in the distance—the steady low humming of a motor.

"It's coming from the cove," Maggie whispered, looking straight ahead, and I shook my head, looking in the opposite direction.

"No, it's coming from our side of the lake, past Ben's house." I narrowed my eyes, trying to see through the fog.

The three of us looked in different directions, all believing the noise from the motor was coming from our direction. "God, this is too eerie," Teri whispered.

Then the motor was cut. It abruptly stopped, and once again, the deafening quiet took its place. We looked around, not knowing where in the world the boat was.

Through the numbing quiet, we heard laughter—quiet muffled laughter. My blood ran cold as Teri, standing between Maggie and me, reached over and grabbed my arm. Her nails dug painfully as her eyes widened in fright.

"Sweet Jesus, who is that?" Maggie whispered.

I had no answer as I stared out at the rolling fog.

After the fright of mid-morning, we decided to stay indoors, with the doors locked. We still had no clue who was out there, so caution was the order of the day.

I started a fire, as the weather had turned chilly. Christ, three days before, we were complaining about the humidity. Maggie and Teri sat on the couch watching as I paced in front of the fireplace desperately trying to piece this together.

"Okay, from the top," I said to them.

Maggie started. "Well, first you notice the cabin showed signs of a possible prowler. Then someone knocks you out and we find you."

"We meet all your neighbors at Ben's. And we all agree that Sandy Meyers is a flirt," Teri added.

"Right, they all looked like they had something to do with her at some point in time and for some reason or another," I agreed. "Then I go swimming, *sans* my suit, and someone scares the life out of me."

"Then what?" Maggie frowned as if trying to remember.

"Oh, I lost my nightgown," Teri said firmly. "Well, at least I forgot it."

"Don't forget your cosmetic bag and your favorite cologne."

"Hmm, and I misplaced that, as well. Kate, I think you *do* have a poltergeist," Teri said.

"God, please don't say that." I shook my head. "I'm having a hard time sleeping as it is."

However, I had a thought. "Now that you brought this up, we couldn't find that picture the other night, either." Things were beginning to fit, but I still couldn't figure out how. "And the chair in Sandy's house is overturned when we checked her house. Let's not forget Ben getting hit on the head. Also, my spare set of keys. I knew they were there when I arrived." I scratched my head. "At least I think they were. Then they were missing when we tried to leave the other day. Now they're back."

Something was missing, and it was staring me right in the face.

With that, the phone rang. It was Hannah. "Hello, dear, how is everything?" she asked, worried.

"Everything is fine, Hannah. How's Ben?" I asked wickedly,

and she huffed.

"Don't be childish." Then she chuckled. "He's fine. He's been very attentive."

"Hannah, have you seen Lucas Thorn or Martin Reese in town at all? Has Ben?" I asked, not sure what answer I was hoping for. If they were in town, then who was on the lake that morning?

"No, dear, I haven't. Wait, though, let me get Ben." She put the phone down.

"Ryan, you all right?" Ben asked, and I heard the smile in his voice.

"Fine, Ben." I asked him the same question.

"No, I haven't seen either one. I've been sticking close to Dan. He hasn't seen them, either. By the way, the creek is rising. By tomorrow night, you'll have water in your backyard."

"Great. Is the access road completely flooded? No one comes in or out?"

"That's right, kid. They're not calling for any more rain, just this fog for another day, then a cooler front."

I told him of my idea about the rowboat. He agreed it might work. "But you'll need more water. Wait till late tomorrow, maybe even the next day. Then you'll be able to paddle or even troll your way down the access road."

I felt a little better as I hung up the phone. "Bob should be calling," I said absently.

"Kate, you looked tired," Maggie said. "Go lie down for a while and see if you can get some sleep."

Maggie pushed me toward the bedroom. "Ya nag," I mumbled and stretched out.

"Take a rest, then we'll figure this out," she said reassuringly.

"Thanks." I closed my eyes and immediately fell asleep.

The same old dream gave me a fitful sleep: faceless people chasing me. Everyone was in it, including Liz. She was unrecognizable, but in my dream, I knew it was her. She chased and I ran. The faster I ran, the slower I got, until I felt as though I was sinking in quicksand. My hands were stuck, and I couldn't get free as I slowly sank. Just as the Liz-thing was about to ax my head off, I jumped and woke up.

Maggie was instantly sitting beside me on the bed. "A dream?" she asked as she ran her hand up and down my back.

I was sweating and instinctively put my hand behind my neck and felt the scar. "Will this never end?" I sighed and looked at the clock, 5:30.

"Same dream?" Maggie asked.

"It's nothing—"

"Tell me, please."

"Yes, it's the same damned dream over and over and over again. Just when I think I'm over it—" I stopped. "I'm fine, Maggie. It's just a dream. I'm gonna jump in the shower. I hope Teri made dinner, I'm starved," I said lightly and stood.

Maggie pulled me down again. "It was not just a dream, sweetie," she said and held my hand. "It still haunts you and it's okay to admit that."

I looked into her blue eyes, knowing she was right but hating myself at the same time. She grinned slightly. "It's good to admit it."

"Oh, I know," I grumbled and held her hand. I grinned, as well. "You called me sweetie," I said with a shrug.

"Oh, I know," she grumbled, mimicking me as she stood. She then stepped between my legs. I looked up and swallowed with difficulty when she ran her fingers through my hair. "I kinda like calling you sweetie," she whispered and kissed me.

I closed my eyes and whimpered like a fool. "Go take a shower," she murmured against my lips.

"A cold shower," I said with a groan.

I stood under the warm spray, and my mind drifted and I thought of all the times I had come to my cabin alone. While I loved my solitude, I was getting weary of being alone. It is however, a hard habit to break; even now with Maggie, it still haunts me. Even the hospital psychiatrist's words haunted me— *You feel comfort in your pain, Kate. Someday you'll feel comfort with your happiness.*

God, I hope she was right.

When the phone rang, I scrambled over to it. It was Bob. "Hey, Irish, wanted you to know I haven't forgotten about you. I'm still waiting on Camp Pendleton, however, here's what I've got. His name is Martin James Andrews, twenty-nine, single, rank—sergeant. Been a Marine for almost ten years, more to follow. Bureaucracy at its worse. My guy promised a call by five, so he's got about an hour."

"Thanks, Bob."

"You sound done in. Take care of yourself now. Have you seen either of these guys yet?"

"No, not yet." Then I told him about the boat that morning.

"Good grief. Look, you stay close to your gal and Teri. By the way, this Lucas Thorn. I came up with quite a few. I've been able to check on two. One's in New England. I spoke with him; the other is in Florida. Retired, I spoke with his wife. I'm working on the other two. So sit tight. I'll call you back in an hour or so."

"Thanks. Hey, wait, take this number down." I gave him the phone number of the inn, then the police and gave him Hannah and Ben's names. "Just in case our electricity goes, the creek is rising. Just a precaution."

"Good idea. Now give your mind a rest. I'll call you. Love ya, Irish."

I walked onto the porch; the fog had dissipated as twilight approached. The skies were overcast and the air cool. I got the night vision glasses, thanking God once again that Ben had forgotten them, and sat on the front porch.

Bob called back, true to his word. However, he had no more information. He told me not to worry, he'd have it all by morning. I sat on the porch rubbing my forehead, praying for a break.

Maggie and Teri joined me on the porch. "Is he there?" Teri asked as she looked across the lake.

"I see no movement," I said, scanning the cottages. Then I concentrated on Henry's house.

For the first time, I noticed that although it was a lakefront house, it was set well off the water. It was his long pier that made it seem closer, I guess. Henry didn't like to disturb much of nature, so when he built the house, he took down as few trees as possible.

There was still no action at his house. "I'll bet Lucas is gone. I haven't seen a sign of life since Dan told him about Sandy," I said. "Martin is our main concern, I'm sure."

Maggie agreed. "It's unnerving that he's still here. Why stay? He knows we're here, but he doesn't come over to see if we're all right. Why is that?"

Looking through the glasses, I said slowly, "Because he's probably watching us right now. For some reason, he's gone all day. This is not a huge lake, guys. Where does he go?"

The green illumination of the glasses was giving me a headache. I took them away and blinked. I handed them to Maggie. "Here, you look for a while. I'm going cross-eyed."

Maggie held them up to her eyes and watched. I put my head back and closed my eyes. "I wonder..." I said, thinking aloud. "I wonder what connection we have with Sandy's death. I wonder what connection Martin, Lucas, and Phil had with Sandy. I wonder when I'll stop wondering and get some answers." I sighed.

I'd better come up with something, fast. I had a sinking feeling in the pit of my stomach. That Ouija board said "he was coming soon."

I wished to God I knew who he was and why is he coming for me.

Chapter Twenty-Three

The loons were very active calling back and forth, echoing over the lake throughout the night. Finally, at five, I slipped out from underneath Maggie and dragged myself into the shower.

As I stood under the hot water, I thought about that boat. I would have said it was my imagination had not Teri and Maggie both heard the same thing. Who would have been out on the lake in the fog? I saw no boat, but we all heard the motor…and we all heard the laughter. Now what, I thought.

While I was thinking about it, what in the world was chaskote? I thought a Native American name perhaps. Whoever or whatever it was said he was coming and had killed him and Sandy Meyers. I was at a loss, should I believe Scrabble letters? And what of Ireland and the treasure we found and what boat? My logical mind said no, get the facts and stay with them. However, in the past year, too much of the unknown had played a big part in solving the mysteries in which I had found myself.

So do I discount this now, when I hadn't in the past? Christ, I don't know. Teri, I believe, is the conduit for all of this. She has a psychic ability whether she wants it or not.

I stood there letting the hot water beat on my head, and although the water was hot, I started shivering uncontrollably. I instantly felt an urgency to solve this. Something was about to happen, and if I didn't get some handle on it, it would be out of my control. I suddenly worried for Maggie and Teri, again wishing they had gotten out with Hannah and Ben.

"Okay, chaskote whoever or whatever you are, if you can help, *now* is the time," I said to the ceiling.

As I made breakfast, I looked out my kitchen window. The

morning fog still lingered as the cool moist air hung over the warm lake. So much for meteorology. I wasn't sure if I wanted the fog or not. Although I couldn't see the woods, the lake, and whoever was still there, I felt safer; perhaps they could not see me. Maybe.

Maggie walked into the living room looking tired and worn. "Thanks," she mumbled as I put a cup of coffee in front of her. "What's going on here?" she asked, looking for an answer. I wish I had one.

"Maggie, I think Martin is deeply involved here. He's going by a different name, sitting in the dark, cleaning a gun. Good grief, those are not the actions of a normal person on vacation. Unless he's planning on shooting all the fish in this lake," I said flatly, and Maggie chuckled.

"Well, that's one way to get them into the boat." She laughed and I joined her.

"I feel like I'm going insane." I laughed. "First floor, ladies lingerie. Second floor, bedlam."

Maggie laughed and spit up her coffee.

We both looked up to see Teri standing there with her hands on her hips. "What in the hell are you two doing?" She gave us a worried look.

"Nothing. We were discussing what kind of bait I should use..." I said, and Maggie started laughing all over again.

After breakfast, we decided to check the rising creek. We didn't need to take the Jeep. We could see the water in the woods. It had to be at least knee deep. Maggie and Teri looked dejected. I, however, took this as a good sign. When I said that to them, they both looked at me as though I were insane.

"Think about it. If the water is this high, we can get the rowboat in it and float down the access road to the main highway. We can call Dan and tell them which direction we'll be going. It's only four miles. We can make that in a heartbeat," I said. "And if the water is that high, maybe we'll be able to maneuver around that tree that's blocking the road. It's worth a try."

Maggie looked out at the woods. "Maybe, but you've got that

trolling motor on it. I'm not sure that will be able to propel us enough," she said, looking worried.

"I have that little rebuilt motor in the shed," I said with renewed enthusiasm. "It's all ready to go, plenty of gas and oil. I checked it Saturday. We can put that on it. Let's see how the day progresses. We listen to the weather. If the creek rises any more, so much the better for us."

I wanted to figure out this mess. However, I wanted Maggie and Teri off this lake first.

"I agree. Let's go with this," Maggie said as we walked back to the cabin.

"Depending on how much it rises, we may find our cars in the lake," I said.

"Who cares? As long as we don't wind up in the lake," Teri said with equal sincerity.

We sat at the table in the living room, looking out at the lake—not that we could see much. The fog was getting thicker.

"Damn," Maggie said in frustration.

Teri put her hand on her arm. "Easy, Maggie."

"We take nothing with us. With the three of us in it, that little boat will be low enough," I said, and the phone rang.

Hannah's happy voice came through. "Good morning, Kate. I have somewhat good news. The creek has stopped. They tell us it may only get another foot, if that. Isn't that wonderful?"

"Great..." I said flatly and explained what we wanted to do.

"Oh. Well, according to Dan, they can start tomorrow to come and get you. The power lines should be fixed by morning. How are you holding up, dear?" She sounded worried and tired.

"We're fine. Look, I hate to rush you, but I'm waiting on a call." I explained about Bob and what was happening. Then I told her what to do in the event the power goes out here and I lose the phone.

"Don't worry. Ben and I will handle anything. The power will not go out and you will be here in thirty-six hours," she said confidently and I chuckled.

"Okay, Hannah, whatever you say." I gave her my love along with Maggie and Teri's. I could hear the worry in her voice as she rang off.

I watched Maggie and Teri's face as I explained about the creek. Maggie looked deflated, but Teri still looked confident. "At least they'll be able to come to us. If we can't get out, we'll wait for them. It's just one more day," she said hopefully.

I shuddered to think what could happen in twenty-four hours.

Standing still, he watched the cabin. They're trying to figure out how to leave, he thought, frowning. Why are they taking her away from me?

I know she doesn't want to go. Why are they doing this? He angrily pounded his fist on the tree. "Why, why, why?" he whispered aloud. He wanted to do it right then, but he knew he had to be patient. The fog would be to his advantage. He turned and ran back to make everything perfect...

Time was dragging; it was noon when we decided to take the speedboat out. I grabbed my phone and the binoculars and took off. The day had turned cooler, so the light fog still clung to the lake. The atmosphere was damp, and my neck was aching horribly. As I absently rubbed it, Maggie warned, "The human barometer is at it again. What—more rain?"

"God, I hope not. It's the damp."

We motored around the cove and behind Martin's cottage; that's when we saw it—a rowboat. It was pulled up on shore.

"That's just about where I docked mine yesterday morning," I said.

"Maybe it's Martin's," Teri said logically, and I shrugged.

"Maybe." I nervously looked around. "I've got the creeps," I said childishly, and Teri felt the same thing as she nodded and looked around.

"God, I hope there's no one else here."

"What are you talking about, Teri?" I asked, watching her. She was looking around the lake, as if she were waiting for someone to appear.

"Teri?" Maggie asked gently.

She looked at both of us and chuckled nervously. "Sorry, I have the feeling we're being watched. Ever since that incident on the shore the other night, I've had this feeling someone is constantly watching us."

I snorted. "I've thought that for the past week. C'mon, let's get out of here."

We motored around the lake, stopping at Henry's. Maybe Lucas was still there. Maggie gave me a worried glance. "What are you doing?" she asked as I hopped out of the boat and tied it off.

"I'm gonna say good morning," I said, smiling. Maggie started to get out of the boat.

"Whoa, Maggie. Stay with Teri. I'm going to the front door. Nothing will happen, promise." I started up the long pier. I looked at Henry's uncovered speedboat as I continued. Then I stopped and looked back at the boat.

"What?" Maggie called in a whisper.

"His boat's uncovered," I said thoughtfully.

"Kate, hurry up," Teri said.

"Oh, right."

I continued to the porch and opened the screen door and knocked a few times on the front door, then peered through the small pane. Did I see someone? My heart raced. *No jumping to conclusions, Ryan.* I knocked again and looked through the window. Nothing. However, the basement door was slightly ajar, which was no big deal.

No answer, so I walked on the deck and peered through the window. The blinds were closed, so I tried to look through the cracks in them. I saw no movement at all. Why wouldn't he answer the door? Maybe he did leave. I tried the windows; they were locked as was the front door. Then I walked off the porch and down the gravel driveway and squatted to see in the basement. The shades were drawn there also. I strained to see between the shades, but it was dark and there was no movement there, either. The place looked deserted.

I stood and looked up at the window above me. It was too high for me to see into; it must be a bedroom window. I looked back to see Maggie and Teri waving me to come back. I waved back and laughed as I put my fingers to my lips. Maggie glared at me and shook her fist.

I looked around and saw an empty crate by the garbage cans. I picked it up and smelled a putrid odor.

"Good grief. Take out the garbage, Lucas," I said.

Grimacing, I took the crate and placed it by the window. Standing on it, I could barely see into the window. Of course, the shade was drawn, but I could see under it. It was a bedroom. The bed was made and clothes were laid out on it. I couldn't make them out. It looked like... I strained to see, and with that, the crate fell out from under me. I went crashing to the ground with a grunt.

Scrambling to my feet, feeling every bit the klutz, I chuckled and looked at Maggie and Teri. Teri had her hands covering her eyes. Maggie was still glaring at me and now violently waving me over to them.

I nodded and waved. "Okay, okay," I whispered.

Putting the crate back where I found it next to the smelly garbage, I quickly went down the pier and into the boat.

"Are you all right?" Teri asked, and I laughed as I started the engine and backed away from the pier.

"I'm fine. I slipped."

Maggie was glaring at me the whole time. "You said you were going to the front door."

"Oh. I did?" I asked innocently.

"Did you see anything?" Teri asked anxiously. Maggie was sitting there watching Henry's house as I motored back to the cabin.

"No, it looks like he's gone. There's no car, no movement in the house. The shades and blinds are drawn and no lights on." I shrugged.

"Where were you looking when you fell off the crate?" Maggie asked.

I watched the dancing flames in the fireplace. "A bedroom. I couldn't see much, but there were clothes on the bed," I said, not knowing what that meant. However, my father's words were always with me. *Don't discount anything, everything means something.*

Staring at the fire, I thought of that bedroom and something else.

"Okay, look..." I sat forward in my chair.

Maggie and Teri turned to me with hopeful anticipation when the phone rang.

Once again, it was Bob.

"Bob, good news, I hope," I said as I sat by the fire.

"We'll, it's information, Kate. You've got to figure out if it's good." I could hear papers rustling and I sat forward.

"Martin Joseph Andrews, sergeant USMC for ten years. Hails from St. Louis. Parents did die in a car accident, together when he was eighteen. Had a sister, died eight months ago. Drowned, was found in a lake in a state park in Kirksville, Missouri. Presumed an accident since the body had been badly decomposed." He stopped, and once again, he was fidgeting with papers.

"Here it is. Irish, I went to the library, took me all day, but I found a clip from the time she was found. It appears another body was found at the same lake two months later. No connection was made with your Marine's sister. However, this guy had his head caved in. They're saying it was murder and no suspects yet. He's a John Doe." He took a deep breath.

"Bob, are you thinking what I'm thinking? Too coincidental that both Sandy Meyers and this guy have their heads bashed in. St. Louis is the connection," I said slowly, and Maggie and Teri sat wide-eyed. I wished I had a speakerphone.

"Where was Martin all this time? Was he ever a suspect?" I asked.

"According to Captain Halloran at Camp Pendleton, he was stationed in Japan, came back for the funeral, and took a furlough. He's, as you know, on leave now. I don't know what he's doing there."

"Were you able to find anything more on Thorn?" I asked as my mind raced.

"The only one I have left is a guy in Lakeview, Missouri. I

can't find much on him yet. But I will," he said confidently. "I've got Mike Kelly at the precinct finding out. Remember Mike? Big, ruddy Irishman? At the old precinct?"

I thought for a moment, then laughed. "You mean the one who used to play Santa Claus?"

"Yep. The bastard's a lieutenant now. Close to retiring. God I'm gettin' old," he said, chuckling.

"You and me both," I said, smiling.

"Not you, Irish, you'll be young forever."

"Thanks for all the information. I knew I could count on you."

"Not a problem. Kelly said he'd probably have an answer by early evening. I'll call you then," he promised and hung up.

As I told Maggie and Teri what Bob found out, I paced in front of the fire. "So Martin was in Japan when his sister was killed. Everything he told us was true. Why hide his name?" I asked, irritated. There was a connection here; I knew it.

I looked out at the afternoon sky. It was still cloudy and cool. The lake was still so high. We decided to check out the boat to make sure all was in order. I changed the trolling motor and put on the little five horsepower. I pulled the cord, and it took a couple of times, but it started.

Smoke came out the back of it for a second as Maggie and Teri gave me a skeptical look. "It'll be fine," I said with a laugh and checked the throttle and choke. It sputtered for a second, then settled down in a low hum.

"There, perfect," I said, waving off the gasoline smell.

Coughing, Teri said, "Great. At least it starts."

"Let me take it for a quick spin." I motored out to the middle of the lake, then circled back and docked it. I turned it off, waiting for a minute or two, then tried it again. After one good pull, it started right up.

"See, no problem. We can take the boat right up that flooded boat launch and out on the main road. I'm calling Hannah and telling her we'll be leaving by tomorrow morning. Whatta ya say?" I asked, smiling, and they both agreed as we walked back.

I really wanted to find out what was happening on my lake.

Too many things had happened that week. Too many things I couldn't explain, and that bothered me very much.

However, I wanted Maggie and Teri off this lake before, and now was our only chance.

Chapter Twenty-Four

I juggled the phone with one hand. "Just what are you doing in Hannah's room?" I asked Ben and winked at Maggie.

"Don't be a prude, Kate. Seriously, we were talking about all of you. So you still plan on leaving in the morning?" Ben asked with a chuckle.

"Yes, indeed. How's it going there? Did they fix the power lines?" I asked hopefully.

"They're working on it. They've been at it around the clock. Dan says by early morning. We should synchronize," he said firmly. "Dan figures by nine a.m."

"Okay, I put the five horsepower on the rowboat. It's small enough to get up through the boat launch area, then we'll head east on the access road. Can't go the other way, that downed tree is there. We'll leave here by eight tomorrow."

"Good idea with the smaller motor. So if the boat launch is flooded, it won't be too deep, but you have an easy time maneuvering that small rowboat through the launch, then just follow the floodwaters, Ryan. Now if anything should happen and we cannot get in touch with you, I don't care if the power lines are fixed or not, we're coming in. Tell the girls the Navy will once again save your ass," he said, laughing. "Hold on, Hannah wants to talk to Maggie."

I handed the phone to Maggie. For a couple of minutes, she talked, then she listened. "I will, Aunt Hannah. I love you, too. We'll see you tomorrow." She hung up the phone. I watched her as she chewed on her bottom lip.

She sat by the fire, gazing at the flames. Teri and I said nothing for minute or two. Finally Teri asked, "Maggie, what is it?"

She looked at us and chuckled. "Nothing really, Aunt Hannah said Ben wanted to make sure all bases were covered. He said he didn't want to fall asleep this time. I know he was talking about that incident on the aircraft carrier," she said sadly, then continued. "Ben has ordered us to call before we go to bed. At least by midnight. Then again before we leave in the morning. If we don't, the Navy will be here one way or the other," she said, smiling. I could tell there was a great deal of uncertainty behind that smile.

I stood with a confident air. "One way or another, we're off this lake by nine a.m. There's nothing to do now but eat!"

Over dinner, I tried to piece everything together. "It's weird that Martin is from St. Louis and Lucas Thorn is from Lakeview, Missouri. I find that curious," I said as I ate my salad.

"It might be a coincidence," Maggie said.

"I find it odd all the things that are missing," Teri said absently. "I mean the nightgown, the perfume, and your keys."

"There were two nights when I thought for sure someone was walking around the cabin. Naturally, I thought it was one of you using the bathroom," I said and put my fork down. "I don't know what it all means." I tossed my napkin on the table. "Damn it. I have this overwhelming feeling that everything is connected—from my getting knocked on the head right down to Sandy Meyers's death."

I put on the coffee and stared out my kitchen window into the twilight. "Who's out there? What the hell do you want?" I whispered to myself. I turned to both of them; they were watching me cautiously.

"Why would someone take certain things from my cabin?" I asked, then something struck me.

I started to speak as my mind took off. I looked at Teri and said calmly, "Everything that's missing has to do with you, Teri."

Her eyes flew open and she thought. "You're right."

"God, why didn't I see this? Your nightgown, your perfume, your favorite picture..."

"Martin says the resemblance between you and his sister is

remarkable," Maggie said, and I could tell her mind was racing, too.

"I feel we're close to something here," I said and rubbed my forehead. "I don't know what's going on, but since the rains, the only person we've seen is Martin. Everyone else has left..." My voice trailed off as I watched both of them.

My mind wandered back to the Ouija board because my mind had been wandering all week. "What in the hell is chaskote? It is a name or a place? It's truly beginning to bug the hell out of me," I said, and Teri got up and came back in the room with a pad of paper and a pen.

"When we did this, that glass was going all over the place," Teri said while she wrote. Maggie and I stood behind her to watch. She had written the alphabet down in the same manner, as they would be arranged on a Ouija board. I patted her shoulder in understanding.

"That glass might have been all over, but it was trying to spell something. I know it," Teri said firmly.

For the next twenty minutes, we scrambled the letters of chaskote, trying to come up with something that made more sense.

"Fine, so to top things off, we have a dyslexic spirit in the Ouija board," I said and stared at the letters. "This isn't right. We're doing something wrong here." Then it struck me. I stared at the word and the letters Teri had written down to assimilate the Ouija board. Then it jumped out at me and my blood ran cold.

"Geezus! Am I stupid!" I shook my head as Maggie and Teri looked at me, then back to the paper. "What a moron. We're going about this all wrong, ladies. Don't scramble the letters we already have. Geezus, Teri, Maggie, look—" I took the pen and circled each letter we knew.

"I don't get you," Maggie said.

"When that glass was all over, it knocked into several letters and moved them out of place. We assumed those were correct. What's next to the letter—S?" I circled the—R.

"Now what's next to—K?" I circled the—L.

I put the pen down and Teri picked it up and wrote down

something that now made sense.

"Charlotte," Teri whispered.

Maggie looked incredulous as she sat down. "Who's Charlotte?"

I grinned and picked up the phone. "I'll bet my log cabin," I said as I dialed Bob's number.

"What are you betting on?" Maggie asked and leaned forward.

I put my hand up as Bob answered. "Bob, Martin's sister—what was her name?"

"Hang on, Irish," he said, and I heard him leafing through papers. "Okay, sister, sister…ah, here we go—Charlotte."

I was still grinning as I nodded. "Thanks, Bob. I love it when I'm not a moron."

Bob chuckled. "Well, I do, too, kiddo. Call me if you need anything else."

I put the phone down. Maggie and Teri were watching. Maggie glared at me. "Martin's sister's name is Charlotte, isn't it?"

"Yep," I said, feeling very smug. "Charlotte. She was found in a lake, an accident."

"So Charlotte warned us he was coming, but who is coming? Martin?" Teri asked a little frightened.

"Can't be, he was in Japan," Maggie said, scratching her head, then looked at me. "Wasn't he?"

"Honestly, after this week, anything is possible." I let out a dejected sigh. "He lied about his name."

Teri grabbed Maggie's hand and mine. "Don't worry. We're out of here tomorrow morning," she said firmly.

"That can't come soon enough for me," I said.

After dinner, Teri lay on the couch. Maggie lounged in the big chair by the fire and soon both of them nodded off. I sat there staring at the fire, glancing at the clock on the mantel. The only sound was the crackling of the fire and the tick, tick, tick of the clock. It was driving me nuts.

Although I knew Martin was up to something, I had a nagging feeling he was not the real problem. I didn't know why. My instincts were working overtime as my mind wandered to Lucas

Thorn. Remembering earlier when I looked into that bedroom, there were clothes laid out. *Why?* I got irritated at myself for falling off that crate.

I sat forward in my chair looking to Maggie and Teri. They slept so peacefully. I couldn't wake them, so I continued talking to myself, grateful I was a good listener.

My mind was running the hundred-meter dash, then I remembered Henry's speedboat. The cover was off. If Lucas Thorn had left, why didn't he put the cover back on the speedboat? It was covered during the storm. I remembered seeing it as we motored by after finding Sandy's sandals.

Sandy—that too made me think. Her boat was not covered. There was at least six inches of water in her boat. To me, that meant she was not at home when the rains started. She wasn't out on the lake in her boat as Dan suggested. The poor woman was already dead by then, I bet. If she were home, the cover would have been on her boat. I rubbed my forehead. I had a colossal headache.

I was so tired as I tried to keep a straight thought. However, there were so many different scenarios flashing through my mind, it was driving me mad. Who killed Sandy and why? Who broke into my house and took various items important only to Teri? This coupled with the fact that, by Martin's own words, his sister bore a striking resemblance to Teri, made me shiver. Christ, I hope Martin Reese or Andrews really wasn't a Section Eight as Teri and I had joked about the other night.

There was one huge piece of this convoluted puzzle missing, and I knew it was staring me right in the face. Tiredly, I got up and poured myself another cup of coffee. *Just what I need, more caffeine.*

I walked past my sleeping beauties and out onto my porch, noticing how cool the early night had become. The crickets chirped, and every now and then, my loons called to me. The fog was gone, but the clouds remained, hiding the moon and the stars. Sadly, I thought of the first night when I arrived. The stars were like a million diamonds in the sky and the crescent moon as it rose hung low over the tree line. I thought about Maggie. How we watched the stars from the lake that night.

Now it was cool, cloudy, and ominous. A portent of how the next few hours would develop, I'm sure. I looked across at Henry's, then I gazed across at Martin's with the same result: There was no sign of life anywhere. At least, none that I could see.

As I walked back into the cabin, I threw another log on the fire. Maggie and Teri still slept. I covered them with an afghan and turned off the light. I then locked the doors and left them snoring peacefully.

"Good gracious, I thought you'd never call," Hannah's wonderful voice came through the phone.

"Sorry, we were talking. How's everything?" I asked and sat on the edge of my bed.

We talked for a few minutes. I assured her we'd call about seven the next morning. By then, come hell or high water, which I hoped would be the case, we were off the lake.

"I for one cannot wait to see all of you. How's Margaret?"

"She's fine. Though I wish she would have left with you, I-I'm glad she's here." I took a deep breath. "Is that selfish or what?"

"It is not. You care for her and naturally, you want her near you. So how are things between you?"

I knew my face was red hot.

"Kate, are you there?"

"Oh, um sure, yeah, I'm, um, I'm here," I said and winced at my stellar evasive tactics.

"Hmm. Things must be progressing nicely if Margaret has you stammering." I heard the laughter in her voice. "We'll see you in the morning. Get some sleep."

I lay there staring at the phone. I looked up to see Maggie standing in the doorway, giving me a curious look.

"You okay?"

"Yes, I'm fine. I just want us out of here and safe," I said, feeling my patience slipping away.

"We will. By tomorrow night, we'll be sitting at Sutter's having a nice cold beer." Maggie sat on the edge of the bed.

"I just wish you and Teri could have gotten out."

"I wish we all could have, but we didn't. So let's make the

best of this and get some sleep and get the hell out of here in the morning."

"Doctor's orders?" I asked and smiled.

The blue eyes smiled back. "Doctor's orders."

"Thank you, Maggie." I stifled a yawn.

All at once, my eyelids were getting heavy. "I desperately need to get a cohesive thought going," I said lazily. "I think I would only admit this to you. I'm scared. I don't know what's going to happen. I feel helpless not being able to get off this lake. Not knowing who's here..." I knew I sounded frazzled.

"Kate," Maggie said. "You need to sleep. Give your mind some rest. Tomorrow, we'll be out of here."

"God, I hope so," I mumbled. My eyes were burning, I was so tired.

"Now lie back and go to sleep," she whispered.

"'Kay," I whispered and fell back against the pillows. I fell sound asleep, feeling Maggie's soft hand on my brow.

It was the last peaceful sleep I would have that week.

Chapter Twenty-Five

I was dreaming when I heard Maggie yelling. I tried desperately to open my eyes. Then someone was shaking me and my eyes flew open.

"Kate, wake up! There's a fire at Ben's," Maggie said urgently as I leaped off the bed.

As we ran to the door, I stopped Teri. "Call Ben at the hotel and let him know." Teri nodded and ran to the phone.

Grabbing the small fire extinguisher off the kitchen wall, we raced out the back door. It was still the middle of the night, pitch black, and I had no idea what time it was. There was indeed a small fire on the porch. As we got to it, I activated the extinguisher. Within a few minutes, we put the fire out. For good measure, we doused the porch with buckets of water.

"I think that should do it," I said. "How in the hell did that start?" I looked around Ben's property and saw nothing out of the ordinary.

Maggie dumped the last bucket of water on the porch. "I have no idea, but this is too odd. I don't like this."

"Who did this?" I asked and shivered, looking around. "Let's get back, I've got the creeps."

In the darkness just before dawn, Maggie and I stood there watching the woods, knowing someone was out there, watching us.

We walked into my kitchen and I called to Teri. "All clear. Did you get a hold of Ben?"

Maggie looked in the living room. "Teri?" she called. We both looked at each other and immediately split up. I looked in my room and the spare room, then both bathrooms. Pulling down the staircase, I ran up in the loft and tried to flip the light. The light didn't work.

I raced down the small staircase, and Maggie was trying the lights. "Electricity's out. Where's Teri?" Maggie asked urgently.

"I don't know." I lit a lantern on the table in the living room. The front door was opened. Then I noticed the phone. It was on the floor, the cord ripped out of the wall. Maggie saw it and turned white.

"Oh, God," I exclaimed and ran into the kitchen with Maggie right behind me.

We each took a flashlight and combed the woods, calling out for Teri. As we got farther into the woods, the water was too deep, almost to my knees. Maggie was about sixty feet or so away as we searched. My heart was pounding as I fought back my tears.

"Please, God," I begged as I call her name. I heard Maggie's heart-wrenching pleas as she called her.

Finally, we found ourselves on my back porch. Maggie looked horrible as I shined my light toward her face.

"My God, Kate. Where is she?" she almost sobbed as I put my arms around her.

"Let's get in and regroup. She's got to be somewhere, we weren't gone that long."

He watched her as she tried to regain her senses. Putting a hand to her forehead, she felt the cold cloth on her brow that he had placed there. She was lying on a bed. She blinked, trying to focus, when his face came into view.

She let out a cry and his hand quickly covered her mouth. "Lottie... Shh," he said soothingly. "Sorry I had to hit you, dear. I thought you were going to scream." He put his other hand to her hair and smoothed it back. "There now," he whispered. "No screaming?" She only nodded as he took his hand away.

"Raymond, what are you doing? Where am I?"

"Home, dear. I tried to make it like home," he said, looking around. He pointed to the nightgown, lying at the foot of the bed. His robe was next to it. He watched as she looked over at the dresser. The cologne, the pictures of her, and her family. He

smiled...all for Lottie.

"Raymond, please..." she pleaded with him.

His face grew dark as he scowled at her. "I thought you'd be pleased. I lost you, and when I found you in Chicago, I couldn't believe you came back to me, Lottie. We were happy once."

He stood and glared down at her. "Until he came along. I see you've taken another lover, Lottie." He waved his index finger at her. "Shame on you."

He put his hand on the headboard and loomed over her. "You belong to me. Say it, Lottie," he warned.

"I-I belong to you, Raymond," she said. He knew she was scared; she looked frightened. He didn't want her to be frightened.

"Call me dearheart like you used to." His eyes held hers.

"D-dearheart."

He roughly grabbed under her chin, and she let out a small cry. "Well, that's not like you used to, but it'll do for now, Lottie. You'll be more affectionate later." He roughly let her go. "Or I'll kill them..." He laughed, genuinely amused by himself.

"Now I'll give you a little time to prepare yourself. Remember, Lottie my love, no screaming or trying to leave again. You know I'll kill them both." He bent down to kiss her and she turned her face. Laughing, he kissed her cheek. "I'll be back."

"We shouldn't have left her alone," I said angrily.

I lit yet another lantern when Maggie and I heard a noise in the front.

Maggie perked up. "She's in the front." She raced to the front door as I tried to stop her. I wasn't at all sure it was Teri.

Someone was on the porch as Maggie beat me to the door and flung it open. "Teri!" she called, then realized it wasn't Teri. I couldn't see much, but Maggie started to back up into the room so fast, she nearly knocked me over.

It was Martin Reese. *Why does this not surprise me?* I pulled Maggie behind me all the while I watched Martin. I took a step toward him and heard the familiar sound. Martin had pulled the hammer on his weapon and had it aimed right at my midsection.

Maggie gasped and held onto my arm.

"Goddamn it, you scared the shit out of me!" he said and leaned against the door. He looked at Maggie. "I almost fucking shot you!"

I watched him for a moment. He was shaking like a leaf. I stepped toward him again and Maggie held me back.

"What the hell is the matter with you?" Maggie yelled at him, but right in my ear. I winced at the decibel level.

"Me? Lady, you don't know how close I came…Fuck me!" he exclaimed helplessly.

"You could kill someone with that thing!" Maggie said, still quite loud.

"Both of you, calm down," I said, grappling with my patience and the sick feeling in my stomach at the thought of this Marine shooting Maggie. "Where is Teri, Martin?"

Martin stared at both of us. "I have no idea. I heard all the commotion…"

I believed him. I don't know why. "Martin, Teri is missing. There was a fire on Ben's porch. Maggie and I went to put it out and now Teri's gone."

"You don't believe this whack job?" Maggie asked me and gave me an incredulous look.

I put my hand on her arm to steady her. Martin looked at me and released the hammer on the gun and flipped it over and presented the butt of the gun to me.

"I have no idea where your sister is. However, I have an idea of what's happening, if you'll let me explain."

Incredibly quick, Maggie grabbed the gun and looked at it. I raised a scary eyebrow as she awkwardly held the gun. "You'd better be telling the truth. Believe me, I'm not afraid to use this," she threatened, holding the gun.

Martin Reese swallowed and gave me a pleading look as he raised his hands.

I rolled my eyes. "Gimme that," I said firmly and took the gun out of Maggie's hand. "Martin, what's going on? Quickly now," I said as we sat at the table. Maggie stood in the doorway like some sort of sentinel.

"My name is Martin Andrews," he said, and I waved at him impatiently.

"Yes, I know you're a Marine from St. Louis, parents dead, your sister Charlotte died eight months ago. You've been in Japan. Your sister drowned..." I repeated and he looked shocked. Then he recovered.

"She was murdered," he said flatly, and I raised my eyebrows and Maggie looked at him.

"Murdered?" I repeated stupidly. "Explain."

He rubbed his neck. "Lottie was married. I never even met him. She married him when I was in Japan. She sent me several letters while I was overseas. In all the letters, the same thing was said. She was worried about her husband. He had changed, he was moody, slapped her a few times. I wrote her letter after letter telling her to leave this guy.

"Finally, she sent me a letter telling me she couldn't take him anymore. She had met a nice guy and was going to leave Ray. That was the last letter I received. Two months later, I get the notice she was found in the lake. An accident, they said. I believed them until they found a man's body three months after that, same lake, a John Doe." He sighed and I sat back looking at him. Maggie still had not taken her eyes off Martin.

He took a deep breath and continued. "I went back for the funeral. He wasn't even there. It was as if he vanished. No one knew where he went. After the funeral, I went back to their place and I...broke in. I was sure something was screwy. In the bedroom on his dresser, I found some papers. A driver's license, passport. It was Lucas Thorn. So I hired a detective. He traced him to St. Louis to Chicago and here. I got a special leave for two weeks and came here hoping he'd slip up, hoping for, I don't know what. I watched him for a few days before you got here. Then at the barbecue when I saw your sister, I was shocked. She looks so much like Lottie I was amazed. It's uncanny..." His voice trailed off.

I stood up and paced my mind racing as the pieces were beginning to fit. "When I met Lucas Thorn at Sutter's, he said he'd got in and hadn't even been to Henry's. You say he was up here for three days prior," I said and looked at Martin. "Who's Ray?" I asked stupidly. "Why does that name sound familiar...?"

"Lottie's husband, Ray Hamilton," Martin said, and Maggie and I looked at each other in amazement.

"Oh, my God, Teri," Maggie said helplessly and stared out at Henry's house.

Martin gave both of us a confused looked. "What's wrong?" he asked nervously, and I explained who Raymond Hamilton was. The creepy guy from Teri's classes.

I paced furiously, trying to think. "Geezus...." I looked at Henry's house. "She's there. He's got her at Henry's," I said firmly and Martin stood up.

Maggie said urgently, "Let's go..." I grabbed her arm.

"Maggie, wait. This guy is nuts. My guess is he's associated Teri with Charlotte. We've got to be extremely careful," I warned. "We've got to get her out of there."

"We'll get her out," Martin said.

"Okay, look. It's still dark. We can use that to our advantage," I said and desperately tried to think of a plan all the while my stomach was churning.

"We can't get there through the woods. He'll expect that. Besides, the floodwaters are almost waist deep. It would take forever," Martin was saying as I looked out at my little rowboat and remembered the boat launch. I looked at my watch—five on the dot. It would be dawn in thirty minutes. We had to move quickly.

"Here's the plan. We take my rowboat using the trolling motor on the front, which is silent. We stay close to the shore and dock it near his house in the tall weeds. Then we get him out of the house, get in, and get Teri, although I haven't figured out how the hell we're gonna do that. We have to get to his house while it's still dark. If we can hold out till seven, the cavalry will be here, especially since we haven't called in as planned. I don't know what this crazy asshole is thinking."

"Could he really think that we wouldn't try and get Teri out of there?" Maggie asked in a quiet panic.

"He's not thinking, that's my guess. His only thought is to get

Teri, believing she's Martin's sister. Having her back is his only objective," I said. I took a deep breath and hoped I was right.

We all agreed. Maggie leaned over to blow out the lanterns and I stopped her.

"Leave them. If this Raymond is watching my cabin, it'll look as if we're still here."

Maggie agreed. I handed the gun back to Martin, who slipped it into his belt.

"Sorry, Martin," Maggie said seriously.

"I don't blame you," he said and followed us to the beach.

We trudged, as quietly as we could, in ankle-deep water as we made our way to my pier. I got in and started the trolling motor. No sound and it started right up. Maggie got in and Martin pushed us off and jumped in.

In total darkness, it was hard to see where we were going. I only hoped we didn't hit a stump or something else unforeseen in the floodwater. "Martin," I whispered, "pull up that motor so the propeller isn't hanging in the water." I watched as Martin turned and did as I instructed.

It took the better part of ten minutes to putter along the shore to Henry's property. Finally, I turned off the motor and tied us off to a felled tree stump. Quietly, we got out of the boat and waded through the water until we were under Henry's pier.

The house was completely dark. Maggie whispered in my ear, "Are you sure she's in there?"

I nodded. "When I was looking in the window the other day, remember I thought I saw clothes laid out on the bed? I know now Teri's missing nightgown was one of the items."

"God, Kate, he's really insane, isn't he?" Maggie asked.

"Unfortunately, yes. So we must be very careful," I whispered. Martin nodded in agreement.

"Now what?" Maggie whispered and Martin winked.

"We get him out and you get in. We need a diversion," he whispered and crawled up the muddy grassy incline to the house. I grabbed for his ankle, and he shrugged me off and continued.

"Damn it, he'll get himself killed," I hissed.

"He's right, though, we need to get in."

Maggie and I literally crawled up the muddy incline; we were kneeling in water as we hid behind the trees lining Henry's property. Where the hell was Henry? Did he go to Minnesota? All sorts of ugly scenarios were going through my head.

Maggie and I sat there soaked, cold and waiting for I don't know what. Then it happened. We heard glass breaking. Maggie and I looked at each other. We figured Martin was breaking windows in the back of the house.

"Christ, that's not going to work," Maggie was saying as the front door creaked open. I grabbed Maggie, not realizing I was digging my nails into her arm. We watched as the screen door was opened slightly. I felt Maggie's body tense and coil, so I held on to her arm and violently shook my head at her.

In the eerie pre-dawn darkness, the loons wailed behind us. My heartbeat was nonexistent as we watched a figure step out onto the porch. It was Thorn, I could tell. He looked in every direction, his head cocked. He held some contraption in his arms; I had no idea what it was. I gave a questioning glance to Maggie, and by her shrug, I assumed she had no clue, either.

I looked back at Thorn; he was just a black figure walking in the dark. He was about to go back in when another window broke. He stopped and silently walked off the porch and down the gravel drive, seemingly following the noise that Martin was making.

It was now or never, as Lucas Thorn disappeared behind the house. The decision to get into the house and get Teri out was already made.

Chapter Twenty-Six

"Quickly now," I whispered to Maggie as we scurried up the front yard. We made it to the porch and into the living room. "Maggie, close the door and bolt it," I said quickly. I looked at the fireplace and noticed the andirons. I ran over and picked one up, and as I turned, the small rug on the floor moved, as well. I nearly tripped over it. Maggie steadied me.

"Kate, look," she whispered.

I followed her gaze and looked down at the floor. There was a sizable patch of what looked like dried blood on the wood floor, hidden by that rug. I instantly remembered the other day when I saw that rug, thinking it looked out of place.

"That's blood," Maggie said.

I was already down the hall. "Teri?" I whispered and tried the door; naturally, it was locked.

"Kate? He's locked the door," Teri said urgently from the other side.

"Teri, we'll get you out," Maggie said.

Teri was crying. "No. Go. He'll kill you both."

We both tried the door. I rammed my shoulder against it, but it wouldn't budge. I tried the andiron—it wouldn't fit and I didn't want to start banging on the door. I handed the andiron to Maggie as I turned and opened the cellar door. "I'll find something else."

Maggie continued to beat the hell out of the door as I ran down the cellar steps. Noticing the musty smell of a cellar, I was reminded of how I hated cellars and basements. Shivering, I looked around in the darkness, straining to find a crowbar or something. Then I saw a large chest. In the dark, I couldn't really tell, I hoped it was a tool chest. I pulled it open and cold air came out. *Ryan, you idiot.* It was a freezer. I looked down and stared into it, blinking.

I closed my eyes and shook my head. As I looked back, the light came on and suddenly I heard a grunting noise, and Maggie's cry, "Kate! I got her—"

With that, the cellar door opened, and I heard a terrible crashing noise. Someone cried out, and I saw Maggie tumble down the stairs, grabbing for the railing as she fell. She cracked her head painfully on the last couple of stairs and lay in a heap at the foot of the steps.

"Maggie!" I cried out to her and took a step, and when I looked up at the top of the stairs, I saw Lucas Thorn standing there, wild-eyed and breathing heavily.

He took each step slowly, almost zombie-like. He came down the stairs, staring at me the whole time. I backed up and glanced around. Maggie was struggling to get to her feet as Thorn stood in front of her. He nonchalantly stepped over Maggie as she groaned.

He looked at the freezer, then gave me a harsh look and shook his head. "Hey! You're thawing out Henry," he said flatly.

He was holding a crossbow at his side, which is what he was holding when we first saw him. Now there were no arrows, just the bow. He watched my glance and smiled. "Sorry, we can't play. None left. Martin took the last one." He laughed childishly, and my heart sank. He tossed the crossbow down.

I looked at Maggie. She was breathing steadily and trying to focus. I slowly looked back at the freezer. There was Henry, blue with a layer of frost all over him. My stomach lurched as I took a deep breath.

"You see, Kate, everything had to be perfect for Lottie. She's come back and there's nothing you can do," he said and looked down at Maggie. His face grew dark as he gave out an ugly laugh. Then he looked back at me.

"You know, Kate, I am now wishing I hit you harder last Saturday, really I should have," he said, shaking his head, then he looked at me and cocked his crazy head. "But I did it for Lottie. I couldn't kill you. She seems to like you so."

He looked down at Maggie who was not sitting and shaking her head. "However, I can't say as I know this woman. So I can kill her." He pulled his foot back.

"Lucas!" I said quickly and took a step forward.

He stopped and frowned. "Lucas?" he asked curiously, looking at the ceiling. "Nope, I don't know a Lucas."

My heart pounded in my ears and my mouth was bone dry. "Raymond," I started.

He put his hand to his forehead. "Will you make up your mind?" he hissed and closed his eyes.

"Why?" I asked stupidly, trying to buy myself some time.

He opened his eyes and looked at me. "Why what?" He seemed totally confused, and that scared the hell out of me. "Why kill Henry? Well, for obvious reasons, Kate dear. I don't think he would have let me stay. Do you?" He gave me a curious look. "I think not."

"Why did you kill Sandy?" I asked. "What did she do to you?"

Then I thought for an instant, and it dawned on me. I looked at Lucas, Raymond, whoever. "She saw you that day before I arrived. You were the one who was trying to get into my cabin. You stacked the wood." I thought and realized why. "To see in the bedroom window. You stood on the wood, didn't you? I must have just pulled up. You didn't have time to put the wood back. I knew I felt someone watching me. You were in the woods. You've been in the woods ever since."

Everything became clear. "You took my extra set of keys. It was you in the cabin at night. You took Teri's nightgown, her perfume, and the pictures." I began trembling, thinking about having the crazed man in my cabin even while we slept. "I'm right, aren't I?"

"Teri? No, Lottie," he whined impatiently, trying to make me understand. He shook his head and rubbed his temples.

"So you killed Sandy. You crushed her skull and put her body behind Henry's property. That's where we found her shoes..." My voice trailed off.

"She saw me at your cabin. It was only a matter of time before she remembered. I knew that at the barbecue, which was fun by the way, don't you think? So, yes, to answer your question, you're right.

"Sandy expected sex, I'm afraid, but hell, I'm a married man. Lottie would never allow that. You know women. Not knowing *what* else to do," he said, "I killed her. If it wasn't for the lousy weather, she would have stayed put, but the lake gave her up," he said sadly and shrugged. "*So* much trouble."

"As it gave up Lottie and her lover," I said.

His face grew dark and menacing then, and as he took a step toward me, he stopped. He sighed heavily and took a deep breath, ignoring my remark. "Now behave yourself and come over here. You and I need to talk." He crooked his index finger beckoning me to him. "C'mon now. There's no way out of here."

Then out of the blue, he shut his eyes and bit at his bottom lip. He winced painfully as he rubbed his temples and whimpered. Oddly, he reminded me of Jimmy Cagney in *White Heat* and how he stood at the top of that oil tower and yelled, "*Top of the world, Ma!*" just before he blew up. Raymond was holding his head now and rocking back and forth.

"You were out that night on my pier, as well, weren't you?" I quickly looked around and saw a piece of pipe on the table next to me.

Raymond looked up in pain. "On your dock? No. It was a torrential downpour. Why would I stand on your dock in gale force winds?"

I had to admit that was a good point. That wouldn't make much sense, even for a nutcase. *Who was on my pier then?*

"I tried so hard, so very hard, to make her happy," Raymond continued, his face now etched in pain. "I couldn't let her go, but she's come back as I knew she would."

Watching him, I slowly reached for the pipe. I took my eyes off him for a split second, and I grabbed for it. I heard him growl, and all at once, he was on me. His hands encircled my throat, his eyes blazing with anger as he shook and squeezed. I clawed at his face but couldn't reach. I felt myself losing consciousness as I desperately grabbed for the lead pipe.

My senses were leaving me as I heard a voice from the top of the stairs...

"Raymond, dearheart," Teri's voice called to him.

He loosened his grip on my throat as he looked at me. I stood perfectly still. He cocked his head and unmercifully threw me across the room. I slid against the freezer.

The light bulb that hung from the ceiling swung back and forth. The shadows in the cellar danced wickedly as Raymond turned to watch Teri as she took a step down the stairs.

She had put on the nightgown. I was terrified, and I thought she'd get herself killed. I quickly looked around for something, anything...

"Lottie," he said almost pathetically and stood there.

"Raymond, what have you done?" Teri asked shamefully and looked at me.

I nodded and saw the piece of pipe. It was on the floor a few feet away. I looked over at Maggie. I motioned for her to stay still.

Raymond hunched his shoulders like a dog being scolded. "I didn't do anything," he sniveled.

"Why did you kill me?" Teri asked and now she gave me the creeps.

"But...but...you're not...you've come back," he cried like a small child. "You've come back!" he insisted. Then his hands flew to this head and he whimpered again.

I quickly picked up the pipe, and as I reared back to hit him, he turned to me. I got him with a glancing blow that staggered him. Blood seeped down the side of his face as he snarled and leapt for me. I quickly hit him again and winced at the sickening sound as he folded to the floor.

He lay there, not moving. Teri flew down the staircase. We both rushed to Maggie.

"I'm okay, okay," she said and rapidly shook her head. I put my arm around her to steady her as Teri and I got her to her feet.

Maggie looked at Raymond's body. "Is he dead?"

I steered her to the stairs. "I don't know and we're not sticking around to find out," I said as pain shot through my throat. Together,

Teri and I got Maggie up the stairs.

Maggie was more alert as we got to the top of the stairs. I ran and grabbed Teri's shirt off the bed and threw it around her shoulders. "God, Teri, are you all right?"

"I am now. Let's get out of here."

We quickly walked down the hall. I turned to the cellar door, and as I reached for it, Raymond staggered up the stairs, his face a bloody mess.

He was growling and yelling, "Lottie, *no!*"

We all froze for just a moment. I pushed Teri out of the way, and as Raymond crawled to the top of the stairs, I kicked him dead in the face. He fell backward, tumbling down the stairs as I slammed the door.

As we ran out of the house and into the cold dawn, Martin came staggering down the driveway holding his right arm. The broken end of an arrow stuck out of his chest below his collarbone. His chest was covered with blood. Maggie quickly examined him. "I can't do anything with this now. If I take it out, you'll bleed all over." We grabbed him and headed for the pier.

I thought of taking Henry's boat but no key. "Stay here, I'll get our boat."

Jumping into the cool water, I swam to the boat. Once in, I tried the motor. It wouldn't start. "You stinking sonofabitch!" I pulled the cord and nothing. Cursing everything I could think of, I turned on the trolling motor and puttered over to the dock.

We quickly got Martin in the boat; he was groaning and losing consciousness. Maggie put a life jacket behind his head and made him as comfortable as possible.

Teri cried and put her face in her hands, and Maggie reached over and grabbed her hands. "It's over, Teri," she said. Teri nodded quickly and took a deep breath.

"We're not stopping until we see the town," I said.

As we slowly neared the boat launch, we all heard him. He ran out to the end of the pier.

"Lottie!" He let out a bloodcurdling scream.

"Hurry, Kate," Teri almost pleaded. "Hurry."

I pulled the cord again and again. Nothing. Frantically, I

looked back. Raymond had gotten in the speedboat and started it. The engine roared as he took off after us.

"Damn it!" My voice sounded like gravel.

In a panicked frenzy, I yanked the cord again as Raymond gained ground. We were still headed for the boat launch, and all at once, the little motor started. I pulled on the throttle, and through the smoke, the little engine sprang to life.

God, get me out of this deep water, I prayed as I let out the throttle. We had too many people in the small rowboat; we were going as fast as we were going to go.

Raymond was screaming behind us. He was standing up in the speedboat calling, *"Lottie, wait!"* We barely heard him over the roar of his motor.

Teri put her hands over her ears as Maggie held onto her. Martin was unconscious; he would never know how lucky he was.

I looked back to see Raymond shortening the distance between us. Soon his powerful boat would be right on us. "C'mon, just a bit farther," I begged every saint in the heavens as I looked to the boat launch area.

I knew we were close to shore. "Hold on!" I cried to everyone as we finally motored through the shallow water.

Then it happened just as I hoped it would. Raymond's boat was too big, too deep and going hopelessly too fast for the shallow water of the boat launch. With the floodwater, you couldn't tell where the boat launch started and the lake began.

He had no idea he was in such shallow water. The horrid noise of metal scraping the concrete bottom echoed as the speedboat hit the inclined launch, and launch was an appropriate word indeed.

It looked like a dream, all in slow motion. The boat screeched along at high speed and flew out of the water as it hit the concrete incline of the launch at full speed.

Raymond flew with it and let out a high-pitched almost animal-like scream as his body went flying through the air helplessly following the boat. The smell of gasoline permeated the air as the boat flew into a grove of trees on shore and exploded.

As quick as that, it was finished. All of us sat there, staring at the blaze; the speedboat was unrecognizable.

"God help him," Maggie said and hugged Teri.

I was shaking. I noticed my poor little motor had given up. In the confusion, we had drifted and found ourselves about fifty yards away from the boat launch.

"Maggie, start the trolling motor," I said when I recovered from being stunned.

Maggie leaned forward and tried not to move Martin too much. She started the trolling motor and steered us toward the shore.

Off in the distance, we heard boat motors. Maggie looked back at me. "The cavalry."

I leaned forward and put my hand on Teri's shoulder. "It's over, Ter."

She half turned and put her hand on mine. "Thank God."

I cannot believe what happened next. Something came out of the water behind me and grabbed at my shoulder. I let out a yelp and got a glimpse of Raymond, his face blackened and bloodied and contorted in pain. He was whining as he pulled me overboard.

Beneath the surface, he clawed at me. I heard the muffled noises of Maggie and Teri's screams as I once again was grabbed by the throat. I desperately tried to hold my breath. Kicking out at him, I heard a groan and was momentarily free. I kicked and swam, trying to reach the surface. As my eyes opened, I could see the morning sky through the water as I swam upward.

In an instant, I remembered what happened last spring, how I struggled with Bridget Donnelly the same way…the boat off shore…the treasure…Ireland.

Breaking through, I let out a cry as my lungs filled with air. The boat was almost to the shore. Maggie looked like she was going to jump in after me.

I waved her off. "Go!" I yelled.

I started swimming and my lungs felt like they might burst as I swam as fast as I could.

Maggie leaned over the side of the rowboat. "Kate! Swim faster," she yelled.

Faster? Never looking back, I swam as fast as I could to shore. Then I felt him grab at my ankles, and letting out an angry sob, I kicked out again. I could feel my feet touch the concrete incline of the boat launch. I was half swimming half running up the launch, slipping on the slimy surface.

It was then I saw two or three small boats on what was my access road. Gasping for air, I pulled myself through the water. Maggie was yelling for me to get down. Totally disoriented, I couldn't move. Then I was grabbed and thrown and landed painfully, hitting my head on the shallow concrete bottom.

I heard several gunshots, then nothing.

Chapter Twenty-Seven

"Kate," Dan said as he helped me out of the water. "Geezus, are you all right?" He looked scared to death.

I was completely dazed as I clung to him and nodded. As we waded through the shallow floodwater, I noticed Maggie giving orders to the state police and laughed quietly. She watched as they gently put Martin in one of the boats. She then sent them on their way down. She turned to me and I gave her a short wave. She shook her head as she waded over to us.

"Are you all right?" she asked as she now stood in front of me. I nodded and she jumped into my arms. I wrapped my arms around her and nearly lifted her out of the shallow water.

"I'm fine, really," I said while she had a stranglehold around my neck. "Sweetie," I wheezed.

She let go slightly. "Oh, sorry," she said and examined my neck. "Damn it, Kate, you're not all right. Wait until we get back to the hotel."

Out in the shallow water, two deputies were pulling Raymond's lifeless partially charred body out of the water. Ben was with Teri. He had wrapped a blanket around her. She looked terrified, as she sat in the boat, but she was safe; Maggie was safe. Nothing else mattered.

I put my arm around Maggie as we waded through the shallow water up to the shore. I glanced over at the wreckage. They had extinguished the flames and all that was left was a charred heap of twisted metal.

"Christ, what a mess," I said tiredly.

Maggie made a huge fuss over me, which I truly loved, and wrapped a blanket around my shoulders. As Ben helped us into one of the boats, he put his hand on my shoulder. "Ryan, what the hell happened?"

"We'll tell you everything back at the hotel, Ben," Maggie said and pulled the blanket around me. I could tell she was gonna start bawling any minute. "Enough for now," she finished and ran her fingers through my hair.

We said very little as we followed the state police along the flooded access road.

Back at the hotel, Hannah was waiting, crying, and laughing all at the same time. She hugged the life out of all of us as we walked into the lobby.

"Good heavens, what happened to your neck?"

I waved her off but kissed her cheek. "I'm fine."

Maggie was looking after Martin and once again ordering the state police around. "He needs a hospital right away," she said and gently did as much as she could just as the ambulance arrived. I went over to him and knelt beside him.

He smiled and whispered, "You got him?"

I nodded and held his hand. "Yes, Martin. They got him."

"Tell them all of it." He gave me a pleading look. Then tears sprang into his eyes. "She can be at peace now, right?"

Teri came up behind me, and we explained about the Ouija board. He looked amazed, then he smiled and nodded. "Unbelievable...thank you."

I bent down and kissed his cheek. "You take care. We'll come and see you at the hospital."

The paramedics quickly took him out of the lobby as Dan walked in.

"Unbelievable, that's an understatement," I said, and Teri put her arm around me.

Dan looked like he might faint when he joined us in the lobby of the small hotel. "Thanks for showing up," I offered.

"When you didn't call, Ben told me what you planned. Your friend Bob called also. He was worried about you when he couldn't get through. It appears he had some information about the real Lucas Thorn. Apparently, he found out that Lucas Thorn was

Charlotte's boyfriend. I guess you've got a friend in the Chicago Police Department, Kate. In any event, we got in the boats, and that was that. I couldn't believe the sight when we arrived. We heard the explosion. God Almighty," he said, shaking his head.

The state police had taken Teri off to the side. Teri looked exhausted as she answered their questions.

I turned to see Maggie standing there looking up at me. "Hey," I said. My heart lurched when I saw tears well in her blue eyes. Her bottom lip quivered and I instinctively opened my arms.

"I was so worried," Maggie whispered as she wrapped her arms around my waist.

"We're all right," I said and held her close. She pulled back and sniffed loudly.

"I knew you couldn't go for any length of time without getting hurt."

I immediately frowned with the change of her voice. "Like I could help it."

"Well, I'm not letting you out of my sight." She wrapped her arms around me once again.

Hannah was grinning as she watched. "Well, it appears you two have come to your senses."

Maggie pulled back and nodded happily. I put my arm around her and kissed her head. I glanced at Hannah who looked back and forth from me to her niece, then back to me. My face once again was red hot.

Hannah's eyes flew open and the grin spread across her face. "You did more than grunt!"

Maggie laughed and glanced up at me. "Yes, Aunt Hannah, she did more than grunt."

"And I missed it!" she said, completely dejected.

"There'll be a repeat performance," Maggie said with a wicked grin.

"Which you will *also* miss." I felt the need to interject this quickly as Hannah and Maggie laughed. "You crazy woman."

I left the laughing Winfields and joined Teri and the police.

"We found Henry Jorgenson in the freezer and fifty pounds of rotting venison in the garbage," the officer said. *So that was the horrible smell.*

"Raymond Hamilton killed him to use his house to get to Teri," I said sadly.

"How did he know to come to Deer Lake?" one of the troopers asked.

I looked at Teri who explained how and why she knew Raymond. "All of us in the study group talked about our families. I'm sure I mentioned the lake several times. I had no idea..." Her voice trailed off as I held her hand.

"I agree that this is all connected, Miss Ryan. We've got a call to the Missouri State Police. I imagine that John Doe is Lucas Thorn, Charlotte Hamilton's boyfriend. This is quite a story. When Sergeant Andrews is up to it, we'll talk to him, as well. It appears Lucas Thorn was killed in the same manner as Sandy Meyers. Raymond Hamilton left a horrible trail behind him. He was one sick bastard." The trooper stood, and after getting a few addresses, he and the other state troopers left.

For a moment, we sat there staring at nothing in particular. Ben was the first to speak. "What a tragedy. Four lives lost."

"Insane bastard," Maggie said with contempt, then looked around the table. "Well, I think this is sufficient for the day. Why don't we all go back to our rooms and rest? No offense, but we all look like hell."

"Tomorrow, I want to see if I can get back to the cabin. The creek is receding. I'm sure we can get in," I said seriously.

Ben agreed. "Well, Ryan, once again it took the Navy to—" He let out a groan as Hannah slapped his midsection.

"Thank you, Hannah," I said and glared at Captain Harper.

I had no sooner gotten to my room than I heard a knock at my door. Teri poked her head in. "Can I come in?"

"Of course," I said as she closed the door. She came over to me and we hugged each other, not saying anything. She let me go and I looked at her.

"Did you call Mac?"

"Yes, he's flying home as we speak."

"He'll never let you out of his sight again."

"That would be fine with me." She was still trembling and I couldn't blame her one bit.

"Pretty scary," I said, and she nodded.

"Very." She sat on the bed and sighed. "I can't believe he followed me here and did all this. I feel numb. Geezus, he was insane."

There was not much more to add to that. "Teri, in time, we'll get this behind us. This was a very bizarre situation. How about tomorrow, if we can, we go back to the cabin? I think that would be a good idea. I love my lake. I don't want to be afraid of being there. Raymond was mentally unstable, but he's dead. I won't let what happened keep me from what I love," I said positively, and Teri stood up.

"You have great strength. I admire you for that. However, as I said before, you can't hide in your cabin. I think you've found something to love other than your lake," she said and hugged me again. "Thanks for coming to the rescue."

I hugged her back. "All in a day's work, sister," I whispered affectionately. "But I think you should thank Maggie. Remind me never to give her an andiron."

"So what do you think that was with the Ouija board and Ireland?" she asked.

I shrugged. "I have no idea. I'm at a disadvantage with that stuff mainly because it scares the crap out of me."

We both laughed, but Teri went on, as I knew she would. "It's probably nothing."

I gaped at her. "Oh, you big liar!"

Teri laughed once again. "Let's let it lie for now. I'm exhausted. I'm going to lie down for a while."

As she opened the door, there stood Maggie. "Am I interrupting?"

"Nope. I think you're right on time," Teri said and glanced at me. "I'm going to take a long hot bath." She kissed Maggie on the cheek as she walked out.

Maggie stood with her hands behind her back, leaning against the door. "How do you feel?"

I was standing on the other side of the room, leaning against the small desk. "I'm fine. I was so scared when I saw you tumbling down those steps," I said and ran my fingers through my hair. "This has been one crazy week."

"Yes, it has."

Again, we stood there in silence. We both looked at each other, then like maniacal moths drawn to a flame, we were in each other's arms. "God, Maggie you scared me so badly."

Maggie hugged the life out of me. "I was, too, Kate."

I wanted to say, "I love you." *God, why couldn't I?* That vulnerable feeling crept back. That sick feeling when one begins to let go. I fought the wave of anxiety as I looked into Maggie's eyes.

"I understand, Kate," she said in a quiet reassuring voice. "We take it slow and see how this goes." She smiled and opened the door.

I quickly pulled her back into my arms. "Maggie," I whispered desperately.

"I know," she said. "I know. I won't leave you."

"I don't know what I'd do without you now," I said and damned the tears that flooded my eyes.

I heard her sniff and tighten her arms around my neck. I reluctantly let go as she pulled back. She smiled then and wiped the tears off my face. "This is much too much emotion for you all at once, Miss Ryan."

I nodded furiously in agreement, not daring to speak. I'd be blubbering like a fool.

"I'll check on Aunt Hannah. Get some rest, sweetie."

Then when she made a move to leave, something came over me that I could not explain. I grabbed her by the arm and pulled her back, hearing her gasp. "Maggie," I said in a coarse voice. My body was shaking as I kissed her so deeply I thought I'd knock a tooth loose.

Oh, boy....

All at once, we were fumbling with each other's clothes. "I need to feel you," I said raggedly. My hands shook, but I persevered. I tried to unbutton her blouse. "Damn it," I cursed under my breath, and God help me, I ripped her blouse open.

Buttons went flying, and I flinched as several hit me square in the face with projectile force.

"Yes, Kate," Maggie gasped and pulled my shirt out of my jeans. It was still damp, so getting it off was a chore.

"Damn it," I hissed and tried to strip it over my head. *Good Lord, should it be this much trouble to get undressed?* I virtually danced around trying to get the damp shirt over my head. When I felt Maggie's hands on my breasts, I nearly had a heart attack. I thought of forgetting about the shirt, but now, with it over my head, I was on a mission.

"Oh, for godsakes." I heard the exasperation in Maggie's voice as she helped.

Suddenly, we were groping each other, kissing, and trying to make our way to the bed. Flopping down on it, I was amazed how quickly we got rid of the rest of our clothes. Jeans flew in one direction, bras and panties in another.

I never held on to someone so tight. "Maggie," I whispered as I kissed her furiously. I needed to feel every inch of her.

It would appear that Maggie felt the same way. Her hands roamed freely over my body. Passion quickly took over as I engulfed her small breast. My heart raced as I heard her gasp. I rolled her onto her back, all the while hungrily suckling her breast.

"I need you so badly," Maggie said in a desperate voice.

I pulled back slightly. "So do I, Maggie, so bad," I whispered and arched my back as I felt her fingers slip inside. She pushed me onto my side and mirrored my position.

"Together, Kate, please," she pleaded, and I nodded furiously. My desire, my want for her was overwhelming. She drew up her knee and pulled my hand down. It was immediately engulfed in her arousal.

We were both moaning and gasping as we loved each other. I couldn't believe the feeling. My head was spinning as I felt my orgasm start. In the back of my mind, I was thinking of the time when we would make love slowly and not this stroke-level frenzy. "Maggie," I called out my warning and arched into her touch.

Maggie cried out as I thrust deeper, feeling her inner walls tighten around my fingers. "Kate!" she cried out again.

I swear I heard her heart pounding against me. When Maggie came, I was in heaven, and I followed her right over the edge. Bodies shaking, lips trembling, we came together with such force I nearly knocked her off the bed.

Maggie was calling out my name. I was doing the same, amazed that I didn't have a stroke. However, I *was* having some sort of seizure—my body was in overdrive.

I don't remember how in the hell it happened, but suddenly we were in each other's arms. Legs entwined, bodies shaking and sweating. I wrapped my arms around her as we tried to calm our racing hearts. In a moment or two, there was silence. I was breathing like a bull; so was Maggie.

"Good God," I said, gasping for air. I flopped onto my back and stared at the ceiling. Maggie loomed over me and grinned.

"That was incredible!" she said, and I saw the gleam in her eyes.

I gave her a horrified look. "Don't even think about it, young lady. I think I ruptured something of great importance."

Maggie let out a laugh and kissed me. I groaned happily, as her tongue lightly flicked across my lips. She then pulled back and kissed the tip of my nose. "Good thing I'm a doctor," she said in a sultry voice and nestled close to my side.

I laughed and wrapped my arm around her as she flung her leg across my body. She snuggled and moved until she let out a contented sigh. "This is going to be a ritual with you, isn't it?" I asked and kissed her damp hair.

"If you're lucky," she whispered and kissed the top of my breast.

"They say that relationships that are borne out of an extreme emotional situation don't work," I said as she swirled her fingers around my breast. *Damn this woman's touch.*

Maggie looked up. The smile on her face nearly broke my heart. "The hell with 'em, Kate Ryan. Let's prove them wrong. Besides, you're not getting away that easy—you owe me a blouse."

I laughed and held her close. *Maybe we could prove them*

wrong.

The floodwaters receded. It took a few days, which most of the time Maggie and I spent in our room, trying to keep Chance off the bed. Hannah was gracious enough to take the little darling canine to her room. By that time, everything that had happened seemed like a dream. Teri's van was salvageable, and she was anxious to get on the road as Mac would be home later in the evening. Hannah was to leave with Maggie, who had to get back to the clinic.

They all wanted me to come back with them. However, I needed to go back to my lake. Something inside me told me if I didn't, I'd regret it.

Teri knew I needed to do this alone. She kissed my cheek and quickly got into the van. "Call me the minute you get back. And get that phone fixed today," she threatened.

"Call me, as well, Kate," Hannah said and kissed my cheek.

"I will," I said and stepped back and turned to Maggie. She was standing by the opened car door.

"I don't want to leave you," she said and took my hand.

"I know, but I'll be home in a few days. I-I have to do this, Maggie. I don't know how to explain it…"

Maggie put her fingertips against my lips. "I do understand. I know you need to do things alone, you always will. I'll wait for you," she said and pulled me down for a long loving kiss. "Call me, and do *not* run off to parts unknown in the meantime. Deal?" she asked firmly and stuck out her hand.

I laughed openly. "Deal," I agreed and took her small hand in mine. "God bless you, Maggie." I raised her hand and gently kissed her palm. "Thank you."

She ran her fingers through my hair and kissed me once more. "See ya, Kate."

"See ya, sweetie."

She got into the van and slammed the door. I stepped back and watched as they pulled down the road and out of sight.

How many times will I let this woman go?

Epilogue

I pulled into my driveway and drove up the hundred feet or so of woods. As usual, I saw the lake, and as usual, I was filled with anticipation as I parked my Jeep behind my cabin. Chance jumped out and made a mad dash around the cabin.

I watched a few clouds as they drifted by in the late summer sky, then turned my attention to my property. My beach was back—all of it. Everything looked normal, everything felt normal, subdued, and it still look like a bomb hit it, but normal.

Then I noticed poor Henry's house was up for sale. I looked down at Sandy's, and that too would be for sale, I was sure. Sadly, I looked around the quiet lake. I seemed to be the only one there, and I felt lonely.

As I walked into the cabin, I realized how much I missed Maggie. I missed the blue eyes and my mild stroke when those dimples started.

I didn't want to be alone anymore, but as I said, old fears still had a tight hold on me.

Just then, I heard a car door slam. "Maggie!" I said and ran to the door.

It was Ben. "Good, you're back. Here, this is for you."

"Thanks." He handed me a small package. It was wrapped in plain brown paper. No return address, no stamp, and no name. I laughed openly. "A gift from you, Ben? You shouldn't have."

"Not from me, Ryan. When I came back, I saw this lying on your back doorstep. I didn't want it to be left outside."

"What the hell is this?"

"Well, open it, ya dope."

I cautiously tore the paper away and inside was a small book.

I looked at the title with Ben peering over my shoulder. "Oscar Wilde, eh?" he asked. "Didn't know you read that kinda stuff, Ryan."

I couldn't imagine who would give me a book by the Irish poet. "I don't really."

A plain white bookmark was placed halfway through, and I opened the book to that section and read the title of the poem. "The Ballad of the Reading Gaol," I whispered. *Why does this sound familiar to me?*

"Well, enjoy. Come on over for dinner later," Ben said and walked out.

"S-sure," I called after him and closed the door as I looked at the book. I turned the book over, then placed it on the countertop. "I have no idea."

Forgetting the book, my mind went back to Maggie, as it always will from now on—the idea was as scary as it was wonderful. I looked around the cabin and fought the pang of loneliness and the urge to jump in my Jeep and head to Cedar Lake.

I stood there staring at my keys on the counter and grinned. "The hell with this," I said and grabbed them and ran to the back door.

As I threw it open, I stopped abruptly and looked down into the sparkling blue eyes and grinned.

The dimples started…So did my life.

-The End-

About the author

Kate Sweeney was the 2007 recipient of the Golden Crown Literary Society award for Debut Author for *She Waits*, the first in the *Kate Ryan Mystery* series, which was also nominated for the Lambda Literary Society award for Lesbian Mystery. The second in the series, *A Nice Clean Murder* was released in December 2006 to great reviews.

Her novel *Away from the Dawn* was released in August 2007. She is also a contributing author for the anthology *Wild Nights: (Mostly) True Stories of Women Loving Women*, published by Bella Books.

Born in Chicago, Kate resides in Villa Park, Illinois, where she works as an office manager—no glamour here, folks; it pays the bills. Humor is deeply embedded in Kate's DNA. She sincerely hopes you will see this when you read her novels, short stories, and other works by visiting her Web site at www.katesweeneyonline.com. E-mail Kate at ksweeney22@aol.com.

Other Titles from
Intaglio Publications
www.intagliopub.com

Accidental Love by B.L. Miller	ISBN: 978-1-933113-11-1	$18.50
Assignment Sunrise by I Christie	ISBN: 978-1-933113-55-5	$16.95
Away From the Dawn by Kate Sweeney	ISBN: 978-1-933113-81-4	$16.95
Bloodlust by Fran Heckrotte	ISBN: 978-1-933113-50-0	$16.95
Chosen, The by Verda Foster	ISBN: 978-1-933113-25-8	$15.25
Code Blue by KatLyn	ISBN: 978-1-933113-09-8	$16.95
Cost of Commitment, The by Lynn Ames	ISBN: 978-1-933113-02-9	$16.95
Compensation by S. Anne Gardner	ISBN: 978-1-933113-57-9	$16.95
Crystal's Heart by B.L. Miller & Verda Foster	ISBN: 978-1-933113-29-6	$18.50
Define Destiny by J.M. Dragon	ISBN: 978-1-933113-56-2	$16.95
Flipside of Desire, The by Lynn Ames	ISBN: 978-1-933113-60-9	$15.95
Gift, The by Verda Foster	ISBN: 978-1-933113-03-6	$15.35
Gift of Time by Robin Alexander	ISBN: 978-1-933113-82-1	$16.95
Gloria's Inn by Robin Alexander	ISBN: 978-1-933113-01-2	$14.95
Graceful Waters by B.L. Miller & Verda Foster	ISBN: 978-1-933113-08-1	$17.25
Halls of Temptation by Katie P. Moore	ISBN: 978-1-933113-42-5	$15.50
Heartsong by Lynn Ames	ISBN: 978-1-933113-74-6	$16.95
Hidden Desires by TJ Vertigo	ISBN: 978-1-933113-83-8	$18.95
Illusionist, The by Fran Heckrotte	ISBN: 978-1-933113-31-9	$16.95
Journey's of Discoveries by Ellis Paris Ramsay	ISBN: 978-1-933113-43-2	$16.95
Josie & Rebecca: The Western Chronicles by Vada Foster & B. L. Miller	ISBN: 978-1-933113-38-3	$18.99
Murky Waters by Robin Alexander	ISBN: 978-1-933113-33-3	$15.25
New Beginnings by J M Dragon and Erin O'Reilly	ISBN: 978-1-933113-76-0	$16.95
Nice Clean Murder, A by Kate Sweeney	ISBN: 978-1-933113-78-4	$16.95
None So Blind by LJ Maas	ISBN: 978-1-933113-44-9	$16.95
Picking Up the Pace by Kimberly LaFontaine	ISBN: 978-1-933113-41-8	$15.50
Preying on Generosity by Kimberly LaFontaine	ISBN 978-1-933113-79-1	$16.95
Price of Fame, The by Lynn Ames	ISBN: 978-1-933113-04-3	$16.75

Private Dancer by T.J. Vertigo	ISBN: 978-1-933113-58-6	$16.95
Revelations by Erin O'Reilly	ISBN: 978-1-933113-75-3	$16.95
Romance For Life by Lori L Lake (editor) and Tara Young (editor)	ISBN: 978-1933113-59-3	$16.95
She Waits by Kate Sweeney	ISBN: 978-1-933113-40-1	$15.95
She's the One by Verda Foster and B.L. Miller	ISBN: 978-1-933113-80-7	$16.95
Southern Hearts by Katie P. Moore	ISBN: 978-1-933113-28-9	$14.95
Storm Surge by KatLyn	ISBN: 978-1-933113-06-7	$16.95
Taking of Eden, The by Robin Alexander	ISBN: 978-1-933113-53-1	$15.95
These Dreams by Verda Foster	ISBN: 978-1-933113-12-8	$15.75
Traffic Stop by Tara Wentz	ISBN: 978-1-933113-73-9	$16.95
Trouble with Murder, The by Kate Sweeney	ISBN: 978-1-933113-85-2	$16.95
Value of Valor, The by Lynn Ames	ISBN: 978-1-933113-46-3	$16.95
War Between the Hearts, The by Nann Dunne	ISBN: 978-1-933113-27-2	$16.95
With Every Breath by Alex Alexander	ISBN: 978-1-933113-39-5	$15.25

You can purchase other Intaglio
Publications books online at
www.bellabooks.com, www.scp-inc.biz, or at
your local book store.

Published by
Intaglio Publications
Walker, LA

Visit us on the web
www.intagliopub.com